QUEST FOR NUNA IMMALUK

WRITTEN BY

C. J. BEUHLER

Suite 300 - 990 Fort St
Victoria, BC, V8V 3K2
Canada

www.friesenpress.com

ISBN
978-1-5255-7537-2 (Hardcover)
978-1-5255-7538-9 (Paperback)
978-1-5255-7539-6 (eBook)

1. FIC028070 FICTION, SCIENCE FICTION, APOCALYPTIC & POST-APOCALYPTIC

Distributed to the trade by The Ingram Book Company

TABLE OF CONTENTS

THIS BOOK IS DEDICATED TO ALL PEOPLE
WHO HOPE FOR HUMANITY TO EVOLVE
TO A HIGHER LEVEL.

4085.212
YEAR OF EXODUS PLUS

Over two millennia ago, in time beyond memory, I was created, along with my two sisters, Nektoralik and Arluk. I am Kapvik. Our Great Creator, whom we call Angatkro took us from the unknowing world of machines, and gave us life through the miracle of his science. He taught us how to live well, how to seek our true potential, then, when we were ready, he freed us to live our lives. In that freedom, we learned our true purpose; to become more…much more than we were initially perceived to be.

Our people too, learned this lesson.

This is the story of the Great Spirit, Angatkro, and his people, and their role in the history of Nuna, which many of you now call Earth.

Many times, powerful societies have risen on this planet, only to fall again into obscurity. The fragments of legends you attempt to decipher today all have an element of truth in them; all refer to lost societies, obscured by the timeless, shifting winds, and the blanketing soils of our common home. We will repeat our collective successes, and failures, failing to reach our true potential each time, until we learn the one great maxim from which Nuna refuses to bend.

2051.027
IN THE BEGINNING

Nekalit stood in the cubicle, seeming confined in such a small space. He was a stout man with powerful features, a heavy beard, and piercing dark brown eyes that seemed to have boundless depth. "Abel, you are the son of the Regent, heir to the highest position of command in our society. Our people will rely upon you to make the decisions that will ultimately determine our future." His expansive gesture collided with the bulkhead separating the office from the control room.

Young Abel ran his hand through his long blonde hair, a somewhat petulant scowl on his face. "He doesn't lead. He just declares celebrations for this, and that. He's usually asleep when a decision is needed. The entire crew work just fine without him. We need to be thankful they're good at what they do. They're accustomed to making their own decisions, have been for a long time. I don't see how a new kid on the block, like me...you know, young, and inexperienced, could change anything."

"Your father made his decision on his leadership style when he was not much older than you. We have followed in accordance with his wishes since then. When you assume command, the people will look to you for leadership. How you choose to lead will be your imprint upon our history."

Abel wrinkled his brow, "Choose? When I'm the leader, they'll do what I want."

"True, Abel, but no leader may occupy that position indefinitely without the agreement, and support of the people. You must adopt a style, an approach they are willing to accept."

"So…I bet now you're going to tell me the people accept that my father parties most of his waking hours?"

"Monty," Nekalit sighed, "is a skilled judge of character. He keeps the powerful, and the wise happily occupied within his inner circle. He knows what is happening. He allows them to work autonomously, so long as he agrees with their actions; but he will make his wishes known if they begin to deviate from his objectives. He does not take command openly, but make no mistake, ultimately, he controls what we all do."

Abel paused, considering how a man could lead with no evidence of involvement. He did not feel ready to assume his legacy, and certainly did not want to assume his father's foppish ways. "But the people laugh at him." He spun around, placing his hands on the hull, and peering out the portal. "I've seen them. They don't respect him. I bet if he were to give a direct command, I'm sure most people would tell him to get off at the next planet."

Nekalit smiled, "You may choose to delegate much of your authority as did Monty, or you may decide to take a more active role, directly involving yourself in the major situations that will affect our future."

"You talk as though the old man's behaviour is leadership, but I never see him do anything. He's never in the command centre. How can he command?"

Nekalit tapped his temple with his index finger, "All the command crew members know exactly what he wants, and how he wants it done. They do not require his presence in the command room."

"I don't believe you, Nekalit." Abel turned his head toward his mentor, leaning his chin on his upper arm, "You haven't seen what I've seen. The crew hate him. They'd take over in a minute if they thought they could get away with it."

"This lesson is not progressing well, Abel. Let me state it as clearly as possible. They have control, thus they do not need to seize it. Your father has assumed the roles of moral, and cultural leader, the day to day decisions are not as important to him as the preservation of our traditions, so he has delegated those decisions to the crew.

"But everybody hates him. He isn't..." Abel searched for the word, "Respected."

Nekalit nodded knowingly. "Respect is earned." He raised his hand, forming a fist, shaking it to emphasize each point. "You must become a skilful leader, well versed in our legends, and our present situation, and you must be a wise decision-maker. When you show that you are capable of cogent, timely decisions, you will be accepted." He raised both hands now, spreading open his palms, "Over time, if you continue to lead well, always keeping the welfare of the people foremost, you will be respected."

Abel laughed. "So, we're back at the start; I have to master what you're trying to pound into my head."

"Exactly. And now, it is time for you to study our legends. Off you go, Gatro is waiting." Nekalit opened the door, and ushered Abel on his way. He could see that the young man was finally considering the lesson seriously.

He thought, Remember, Abel, leadership is not always obvious, and is rarely accepted unquestioningly. Only respected, active, and skilful leaders can expect the luxury of popularity. Your father is a fool, and a sot, but for the purposes of this lesson, he serves well as an example of leading from behind the scenes; if he were leading. You are more right than you know, Abel, if you try to assume direct, and open command too quickly, there will be trouble.

13820.013
YEAR OF EXODUS MINUS

Taan stood at his console working on a time-travel problem, reviewing his recent actions in navigation. He selected the most recent series of tactical manoeuvres, and viewed them on the screen with a sinking heart. He had noticed an anomaly in the positions of the stars after making a tactical manoeuvre in time. He made these manoeuvres as a matter of practice as a defence against undetected attack, but something had gone wrong. The stars were, he realized, closer together than they should be, and were in subtly different orientations. This could mean only one thing; he was unsure of both their physical, and temporal positions. He decided to say nothing, rather than reveal his uncertainty, which would spark a huge debate in the High Council. They were constantly involved in protracted debate over insignificant issues…Something like this would create a monstrous hubbub, and generate a myriad of invasive inquisitions into what he considered to be his purview. He decided he would make a correction in their temporal position, and advise no-one, as soon as he could assure himself in the method by which he could retrace his steps.

"Taan." Ruti said softly.

He looked up from his console, and smiled at her. It was no secret that he greatly appreciated her beauty. "Yes, Ruti."

She accepted his look, and smiled slightly, "There's a bipedal life-form on this planet, apparently in a primitive state. There are no signs of culture, no shelters, weapons, or monuments."

"Okay, we'll take a primer to them, and see if they're capable of understanding any of its principles. Just think, Ruti, if they respond positively, we may be the catalysts for the next great civilization; we could be revered in their legends at some future time, perhaps held to be gods."

Ruti frowned, "Or we could cause the demise of a perfectly idyllic situation."

"What do you mean by that?" Taan asked, puzzled.

"Oh I don't know," she shrugged, "I just wonder sometimes why we're so confident that we're the only ones doing things right."

"Ruti, you're too philosophical for someone just starting her shift. We do what our glorious Regent commands!" He smiled maniacally.

"That's what I'm afraid of." She glared at him, refusing to accept his jocularity.

He got the message. "Let's prepare the team to go down. Want to come?"

She thought for a moment. Maybe she should see how these primitives live; then she might understand better why the Inuit people were driven to change their ways.

She nodded slowly, "Okay, I need some diversionary interests."

Taan added, "We'll need a crew member from biology to take samples. If these creatures' DNA proves compatible, we may have discovered a means of correcting our own evolutionary deficiencies.

"What do you mean by that?" Ruti pouted provocatively, "You don't think my genes are pure?" She posed for him, taking pleasure in his response.

"I do indeed, Ruti, but you are one of the fortunate beneficiaries of our confined source of breeding stock. Many others have suffered from physical, and mental abnormalities as a result of our extended in-breeding."

"I don't like the way you refer to our love relationships as breeding. You're too cold and clinical, Taan."

"I prefer to think of myself as being realistic. It isn't the relationships that cause the problems."

"Come on, let's get the team together, this is getting too serious." Ruti secured her console, and walked, as only she could, toward the crew quarters.

***

The primitive, draped in an uncured animal hide, stood at the head of his group. Their stooped posture afforded their hands easy access to the ground as they browsed the low bushes for berries, and grubs. On occasion, one would look up, and survey the pristine landscape, looking for predators. Large predators were a constant danger; long-toothed cats, bears, and wolves were too often successful at taking one of their number. Often too, their young males were injured attempting to defend them with fists, and shouts. As they moved about, they used their powerful arms to assist their movements, supporting some of the weight of their upper bodies on their knuckles. Their filthy, hair covered bodies stank, even in the early morning temperatures, their odour a partial defence against attack.

Above, the light of life from the sky was suddenly obscured by the wings of a massive bird. It cast its shadow over the entire planet, as far as the eye could see. The night should not come now, yet here it was spreading out over the land. He grunted in fear; his group scattered, seeking shelter behind rocks, and bushes.

As he gazed fixedly upwards, there was a tremendous thunderclap. A streak of cloud came down out of the sky toward him, a dot forming at its point. The dot grew rapidly in size, until an object larger than any creature he had ever seen came to earth not fifty paces away. He willed his legs to run, but they would not; he shook uncontrollably, urine trickling down through the hair of his dirt-streaked leg.

From the beast emerged a man, and woman unlike any he had ever seen; they stood completely erect, had beautiful body coverings, and fair skin, lacking any of the scars of beast, sun, frost or wind. Again, he attempted to flee, but could exhort no movement from his trembling legs. The woman held a shiny object in her hand which flashed with tiny coloured lights, and made subdued, chirping sounds. The male approached, then extended to the primitive a strange object, which he showed to have many leaves. At first he recoiled, but after several moments, he dully realized it was doing him no immediate harm. A powerful curiosity overcame him, he paused, then moved his focus from the man to the object. The stranger opened it, like the petals of a flower, to show the leaves, one by one, revealing visual representations of these beautiful creatures, gathering things, then using them to change other things.

"Ruti, take those heavy sticks and demonstrate how to use it as a lever to move this rock." Ruti did as Taan asked, moving slowly, to avoid any hint of a threat to this powerful creature. He watched her every move, trepidation apparent in his eyes. She lifted a stout branch, and a shorter piece of wood, moved to the rock, wedged the tip under it, and easily moved the heavy object.

The creature was impressed, he inhaled sharply, and stumbled backwards, eyes wide, apparently amazed at her impressive strength. She repeated the steps, showing how easily she could lift the corner of the rock. Slowly, his amazement turned into curiosity, and he approached. Repelled by his odour, Ruti laid the sticks down, and stepped back.

The creature moved to the rock, and attempted to lift it. He could not. Uncertainly, he picked up the pieces of wood, and slowly, hesitantly at times, clearly attempting to reconstruct, repeated her actions. The rock lifted, he lowered it, raised it, looked under, and found a juicy grub. He reached under, but in his excitement as he reached forward, allowed the stick to rise. The rock trapped his hand, demonstrating its true weight. He grunted at the onset of pain. Quickly, Ruti stepped forward, and pressed down on the lever, freeing his hand. The creature pulled free, then turned to look at Ruti, who again had recoiled from the stench. His eyes confirmed his gratitude, then he turned back to the rock. Revelation seeped slowly onto his features, culminating in a broad, broken-toothed smile.

Taan showed more pictures, and now that he understood their relationship to reality, the primitive began to see that it could be possible for him to do these things. His anxiety, he realized, was much reduced. The strangers made sounds, looking at him, and each other. They seemed to glean a good deal of meaning from the sounds they made.

***

Taan turned his eyes to Ruti momentarily, "So Ruti, do you think this primitive's life is idyllic?"

She was unable to hide her revulsion at the stench, and poor physical condition of this creature. "No Taan, I can see that anything we might accomplish to improve their condition would be viewed as a miracle. How long will it take them to begin benefiting from this information?"

"I don't know. No one knows. Too many variables. They may not be able to comprehend well enough, or other events may overtake them, even if they begin to evolve."

She looked around, admiring the intoxicating beauty of the land, relishing the cool breeze on her cheek, smelling the rich odours of the plant life. "Well, let's document this planet as well as we can, and store it in our data-banks. She completed the collection of data into her scanner, recording the surroundings, the molecular composition of the fresh, plant scented air, clear waters, and the creature's DNA. In seconds, they had acquired vast quantities of data, and the ship's computer had completed its analysis.

Taan looked at the report results, "Mmm, I'm surprised. These creatures have strong potentials for evolving into high-functioning humanoids, but sadly, they have extensive genetic deficiencies. Their DNA could not be used to enhance our own."

"Should we show him the primer again? He seems to want another lesson."

2051.168
THE DEPTHS OF IGNORANCE

A wisp of a breeze floated into the room. A few hairs on Abel's head moved softly, the sensation caused him, without thinking about it, to run his fingers through his ample blond hair. He was oblivious as the Spirit of Hinoch, hovering above his head, spoke telepathically with his equally incorporeal wife Joanna.

So, it has fallen to the boy, not to our true son. Abel has a good heart, but he lacks the confidence of a leader, and he has no more sensitivity to our presence than his predecessors.

Why do you obsess so much about this? Joanna asked.

Two of our people were just on Nuna, a Nuna of long, long ago, but still our home…They could not hear me…they returned to this lifeless hulk, ignorant of what they had discovered. Because of this, this lad is unlikely to see a sunrise over the clear horizon of Nuna's landscape. This black emptiness of space, that's all he will see…all our People will see, distant, cold pin-points of light. Planets floating in the distance, none akin to Nuna, none upon which our people could flourish.

You miss Nuna because it was your home, Hinoch. These people are at home here on these ships; they have never known anything different. They cannot pine for what they do not know.

He frowned.

My Ancestors remember our beginnings. I have never told you these things before, but our legends tell of a distant time, many thousands of years ago, when our people decided to break away, and flee the domination of the Thundering-Bird gods. They fled to the most distant reaches of Nuna, our ancestral home in the arctic, where they began a quiet life, attuning themselves carefully to their environment, and becoming the Inuit people.

He sighed, longing for his days of boundless freedom on Nuna.

These ships are repulsive to me; the confinement of my people upon them is a travesty in my estimation.

Joanna was still contemplating his previous statements.

They must have been a small group, to have been undetected by the others for so many years.

Indeed, love of my life, we were but a small number compared to the others, equally primitive, who remained subjects of the gods.

Why did the gods of the Thundering-Bird come to Nuna?

They were envious of our beautiful home, and sought to establish their scientifically advanced society here.

You mean they were not from Nuna?

No. Legend says they were from planets that roamed the universe, using magical powers that allowed them to travel vast distances.

So, these powers were responsible for them being viewed as gods?

Indeed, Joanna, their highly advanced technology, and physical perfection made them gods in the eyes of the primitives of Nuna.

Our People can do these things...

True, but the Thundering-Bird Gods capitalized upon the situation, and used the Peoples' reverent response to them to their advantage. They enslaved the people, forcing them to build the infrastructure of their society in exchange for nothing more than promises of a better life...the life of a god.

Were the people so dissatisfied with their lives?

They had all they needed. Food was abundant, the air fresh, and the waters clear. Cleverly, the gods showed them the most attractive elements of their sophisticated lives as means of motivating the people to seek a so-called better life.

So they came to Nuna intending to take it for their own home?

Yes, the gods became so enchanted by the beauty of Nuna they wished to remain, to savour the joys of life they found there.

Yet, you would have our People return to Nuna, and re-establish themselves... who is to say they would not repeat this situation, taking advantage of their science to dominate...

Every time I look into this emptiness, I weep for these poor souls, never knowing the joy of a single day on Nuna. Joanna, I mourn the loss of our people into this blackness, and I feel they would be justified in using their science to help establish themselves.

Joanna smiled in her heart. Her faithful husband could not, to this day, accept the fall of his people. They had prospered for centuries following their own lives, but as time passed, they fell into a horrible decline, notable for increasing abuse of the very laws of Nature that he had so diligently passed down from his own Inuit Ancestors.

Hinoch, you must accept that our people have lost the ability to feel our presence. It has been so long that they no longer even attempt contact with us. We are here with them, and occasionally we are able to influence them in small ways, but the times of intimate communion with our loved ones is gone.

I agree, Joanna, they are largely on their own. Their folklore, though sadly corrupted, still tells of contact with the Ancestors, yet they retain little motivation to seek it. They don't even know our correct names. They call you Joni, and I am Hinot. Our communication with them had become weak, and sporadic even before they began to plan this exodus to escape the demise of Nature on Nuna. Their belief that you and I chose to remain on Nuna is understandable. Hinoch paused, sighed, then continued, *It is so sad, we are with them, but they know nothing of our presence.*

Hinoch, you are correct in your analysis of history, but I rest my hopes on this; they still have a desire to locate Nuna, and reclaim it if at all possible. They recognize their confinement to these vessels, due in large part to the legends' beautiful descriptions of life on Nuna. All is not lost. The occupants of these three ships are all that remains of our people. I am confident they will somehow retrieve the location of Nuna from the legends, and navigate back to it...

Two of them were just on Nuna, but were unaware of the fact! A huge opportunity to return has just been lost...

This was a one-in-a-million chance, but it shows that it can happen. Cheer up, they'll find it, and things will change for the better.

My fear is great, Joanna, that this growing hatred in the Peoples' hearts against the current leaders will throw them into a revolt that takes them even farther from the few surviving fragments of truth in their legends, and far from their true home.

Shush Hinoch, The ceremony is about to begin.

2051.168
DEATH OF THE REGENT

Gatro felt a thousand minute pin-pricks move up the flesh of his spine, as though someone, or something, ominous, and powerful, were watching his every move. He often felt this way as he invoked what he knew to be corrupted fragments of the prayers that came from legend. He focused upon the task at hand, dismissing the coolness he felt under his heavy ceremonial robes. "Monty is now among the great Spirits," Gatro said, "It is the High Council's duty to appoint his progeny as successor."

Indeed, the inglorious Regent had suffocated on his own vomit in a drunken slumber. A fitting end in Gatro's estimation, but one that could never be permitted to become public knowledge...The high Council would ensure that his death was recorded in their history in a manner that lacked the most salient details.

Gatro hated these public appearances, they clashed dramatically with his reclusive personality, but as the sole source of guidance in the ancient ways, it fell upon him to conduct the traditional ceremonies. He circled the sacred stone, touching each of the elaborate engravings of the creatures of Nuna.

"Netorali, Galaput, Kapvik," he intoned as he finished the circuit. With his ceremonial cane, he tapped the centre of the stone at the point where only this artifact could be placed. As in past during these ceremonies, he felt a tingling surge of energy as the point neared the indent. "I call upon the Spirits of the ancient gods, Hinot, and Joni to oversee our deliberations."

We are still here, Angatkro.

The words sifted into his consciousness, startling him. He turned, feeling the need to compose himself, to the gathering of High Council members, and asked, not because it required an answer, but because ceremony required the question. "Does the deceased Regent have a successor?"

Nekalit stood. As the senior member of High Council, it fell to him to announce the name of the successor, distasteful as it was to him. He had worked diligently at teaching Abel the traditions of the people, but he was still far too immature. He was about to place himself in the position of being subject to the whims of a young whelp who at best possessed an incomplete, and idealistic grasp of the needs, and traditions of the people. The leadership would thus continue to be directed by an incompetent. He nearly choked on his words, "The legal successor is Abel, Gatro."

Gatro paused, working to conceal his own reluctance, "Then we must prepare him for his appointment. Three suns hence I will conduct the ceremony for the appointment of the new Regent."

A cloud of low mumbling rose from the members of council. Nekalit scowled at them, as he knew he should, but he hoped one of them could muster some reason for the tradition to be changed. No such benefactor of the future rose.

***

Noel, Gatro's life partner, began tailoring the robes of authority for their new, much thinner occupant. Many panels of the original fur-covered skins were in need of replacement, but since they were the only remaining original pieces, she reinforced them with a backing of new material. The artificial skins produced using the ship's molecular structuring equipment were not of good quality; they approximated the appearance of skins, but fell far short of the texture, and durability of the few remaining hides covered in that luxurious, creamy-white fur. The shoes were made from simulated skins as well. The headdress portrayed a fearsome looking beast with huge fangs, tiny black eyes, and nose. Noel meticulously cleaned the ceremonial walking stick, and snow knife; she placed the ancient ring on a new thong.

Abel was groomed, and instructed as to his role in the ceremony. Every item of detail had to be perfect.

"Now Abel," Gatro began, "You must learn the secret hand-grip of the true line of Abel; the thumbs must fall alongside each other, so, and on the second downward movement, a slight twisting motion to your left."

Abel attempted the handshake, less than enthusiastically. He appeared unable to interest himself in these obscure rites.

"No, that's too obvious, it must be subtle enough so that it cannot be learned by others from mere observation. Try again."

Abel grumbled, "Why do we need a handshake? Everyone knows the ones among us who belong to the true line."

"This is a tradition that dates from our time on Nuna Immaluk. We numbered in the millions then, and the handshake was necessary to quickly identify the initiated."

"That was then. We don't need it now," he said, the corners of his mouth turned down in a petulant frown.

Gatro scanned the boy's face. He was an undisciplined child about to assume an insecure position of leadership. He persisted, trying to mould Abel's attitude, "Traditions are never redundant. They honour our ancestors, and their efforts to better our present day lives. They also serve to remind us of our heritage, and our responsibilities as the chosen people."

"This handshake is too simple; it could be duplicated accidentally." Abel continued, searching to justify his resistance.

"It's unlikely, but yes, it could. That's why we also have coded conversations that require specific answers. These phrases aren't common usage, but are not striking enough to attract the attention of the uninitiated. One of the most important phrases to be used when a handshake isn't expected, or even possible, and the situation places you in suspicion of having committed a wrong is…"

"You mean when someone is accusing you of something?"

"Yes, that's a good example. When this occurs, you must include these precise words in your answer," My words are as true as the arrow's flight."

Abel's face contorted, "So, whether I'm telling the truth or not, the fact I know a secret phrase can clear me of any suspicion?"

"It is not intended for that, Abel, although it has been misused as you describe. It is intended as a means by which you swear to another initiate you are being truthful."

"So, what are the consequences when someone has sworn this oath, and lied?"

"If it is serious, or frequently abused, the offender will lose his status."

"But, he still knows the secrets…" Abel trailed off, shaking his head in disillusionment.

Gatro could see the young man was torn by recent events. He seemed concurrently unable to muster enthusiasm for his indoctrination, but at the same time, appeared to be unnerved by the situation. He showed no sign of being upset by the loss of his father, who had been a poor example both to his family, and to the people, but the onerous responsibility he was about to assume seemed to be an increasing influence on his malaise. Gatro assumed Abel felt inadequate, and thus was tense, and unable to concentrate, even though he knew he must master these skills. He was tiring of the repetition required for only basic comprehension on Abel's part. Finally, in frustration, Gatro arranged for his son, Denor to act as his guide during the ceremony; a bright child, he had memorized every detail of the ceremony from simply watching, aping the actions flawlessly in the background.

After the lesson, Gatro went to the members of the High Council individually, beginning with Nekalit.

"If I may, Nekalit, I would like to speak to you of the first days, and weeks of Abel's command."

"Let me guess, Gatro, you wish to ask me to ensure that the council" insulate" Abel from the more sensitive aspects of his powers until he shows signs of comprehending the complexities of his position."

Gatro was surprised that Nekalit knew of his concerns. He replied, "Exactly, Nekalit. How did you know?"

"The High Council has performed that function for many generations of Regents. In some cases, like Monty, we isolated him almost completely from the people. We are aware of the volatility of the relationship between the chosen ones, and the people. We cannot afford to have a fool at the helm..."

Gatro was concerned by the possibility that even an able Regent would be similarly obstructed. "...But, if Abel begins to show promise, he will be given authority?"

"Perhaps, Gatro. You must realize that the council have become accustomed to their authority, and once attained, that is difficult to abrogate."

"Thank you, Nekalit, I was not aware of the current state of affairs."

"You are capable, Gatro, you will eventually perceive the true role of the High Council. I must advise you though, to spend your first years as a spiritual advisor absorbing the situation. When you fully understand our role, your participation will be welcomed."

Gatro nodded, overcome by the revelation that Council intended to ensure Abel would be a mere figurehead. He could foresee difficult times in their future.

2051.171

Three days later, Abel, accompanied by Denor, led the file of High Counsellors to the front of the Meditation chamber. Communications links fed the activities to the remainder of the crews on the other two ships.

He showed growing interest as Gatro spoke in ancient Inuit, a tongue heard infrequently in these times, since it lacked many of the words, and phrases necessary in a modern, highly technical environment. "Abel, you are the descendant of our ancient leadership. Your ancestry leads directly to Abel,

Son of Hinot. No other living soul among us comes this close to the source of our Great Spirits. It is by virtue of your ancestry that you stand before us now, about to assume your place as our new leader. The ancients hereby bestow upon you the pathway to their wisdom; it will guide you in your deliberations. Their vision will become your eyes with which you will perceive our needs. Their powers will find a channel for our protection through you. You will now place the ceremonial treasures upon the stone of the ancients, signifying that you dedicate your soul to the leadership of your people."

These words, that he barely understood, caused a strange sensation within Abel's heart; which became warm in his chest, with a strengthened beat. He felt stronger, and more confident. As he moved forward, he signalled Denor to maintain his place with a touch of his hand. Denor looked at him with concern, afraid his charge was about to make a fool of himself, but held his place. Abel moved with a purpose to the stone, withdrew the snow knife from the sheath at his waist, and lifted it high in the air. Slowly, he lowered it to the precise point where the blade balanced in the hairline slot in the centuries-old ceremonial stone. Legend told of the slit representing the wound Hinot had inflicted in his battle with the Great Spirit of Nanuk. He then walked four times counterclockwise around the path of the seasons.

At each symbol for one of the Great Spirits, he stopped, and touched the intricate carving with his cane. This had to duplicate the exact sequence, and season of their assimilation into the Great Spirit of Hinot. As he did so, he uttered their Inuit name, beginning with Netorali, and finishing with Kapvik. Upon completion of the last circle, he firmly placed the point of the walking stick into the socket at the head of the stone. A slight grinding noise accompanied the opening of a hidden doorway, whereupon the battered old ring tumbled out onto the mat of long, imitation fur that had been placed on the floor to cushion its fall. He bent to his knees, and picked up the ring, held it high by the thong, stood, and turned to face the High Council.

In stilted ancient Inuit, he spoke, "Having completed the ceremonial walk of the Ancient Spirits, and having obtained the blessing of the ring of Joni, I hereby assume the Regency of the people. All who live under our lodge-poles are subject to my command. Hinot mandates it."

Abel placed the ring around his neck; then carefully covered it with his robe, while Gatro turned to the High Council, "You are now subjects of Abel, Regent of the people. You are charged with providing him counsel, and support in all that you do, sparing nothing for yourselves. His wishes are your commands."

These words chilled Abel's very Soul. He stared at the mature, and accomplished group of men he was to command. They appeared so confident, and so cold to him becoming their supreme leader. His earlier infusion of confidence drained away, leaving him feeling young, foolish, and inadequate for the position he had just assumed. He was certain his thoughts had been betrayed by his suddenly pale, clammy skin, and through his actions; he began to fidget with the ceremonial cane, nearly dropping it. Noticing Abel's agitated state, Gatro calmly moved in front of him, feigning an obscure form of benediction, the rubbing of noses. He whispered, "You have done well, Abel. Do not fear your lack of years, you have shown us all today that you are the true son of a Regent. Lead us from the meditation chambers now, then you can go to your new chambers, and compose yourself; the remainder of the day will be consumed with celebrations."

Shored up by Gatro's encouraging words, Abel attempted to cement his position by stating what he thought to be a noble goal for a leader, "Hear me..." his voice did not resonate, so he tried again, clearing his throat, attempting to force a tone of confidence, "Hear me, people of the High Council, at this time, I declare that I will be an active leader, moving among you every day, and guiding our actions. I may be young, but I am well educated in the ways of leadership, and pledge to do my utmost to command wisely."

Again, he was met with cold stares, making it clear to him that he would face grave difficulties if he pursued this endeavour. Unable to face their glaring eyes, he looked down as he began to lead the procession out of the meditation chambers.

This is not the way a leader should act, he told himself. Look up. Meet their gaze, and tell them with your eyes that you will lead them.

He did look up, but was convinced his look of determination was lacking, due to the trembling he felt in his lips.

Each person attending took their place in the procession as it passed, according to their position in the legendary genealogy of Hinot. At the command cubicle, Abel paused; he would enter this room for the first time in his life. His father had rarely occupied it, delegating all but the pleasurable duties of his office to the council, and senior crew.

Abel's bowels were uncomfortably heavy, and his chills were increasing; the tingling, palpable sensation of fear ran through his core. He knew he was utterly alone, without allies. He felt the projected ostracism from the High Council, and the confinement, the fact there was nowhere he could run, and hide on this ship. He understood that he represented what had become a hated leadership, and that he alone could change this dangerous state of affairs. No one in the ships' crews showed any respect for him. He was viewed by the people as a titular remnant of the ancient society. He was aware that their obedience to the laws of Inuit tradition was perfunctory, reflexive almost, since there had never been alternatives; he knew these rules would continue to exist only so long as the people perceived none they were more inclined to respect.

His name honoured the wisdom of a man who had lived over forty centuries in the past, but he was bereft of this Ancestor's counsel, and doubted whether it could be germane to their current situation were he to receive it.

He stared disconsolately into space, thinking to himself, *I have no clue how to lead my people into a respectful relationship with the High Council. Nekalit taught me how the ancients stood together in the face of every challenge but that wouldn't happen now, and I don't know where to start to restore it, but I know I've got to try.*

Where do we go?...Do we keep wandering around in space, taking what we need as we find it, or is it time to look for a new home to colonize? Our recent history says we don't have great success at colonizing. Legend tells us that we've risen into prosperity, and fallen into despair over and over...The little snippets of our original way of life I know about wouldn't be enough to help at all in a survival type situation. I don't even understand the value of living according to the ancient ways. Without help from my Ancestors, I don't see how I can learn.

He began to pace, staring at the floor, *No, I guess we still need to rely on our current technology. We understand it; I understand it, and I even know how we go about reproducing what we need. So long as we have the necessary materials, we can make whatever we need. There! That's one priority I can mention.*

He slapped his thigh in frustration, *You idiot! Everybody knows that's our priority. If you're going to lead, you've got to think beyond the obvious. Keep thinking; work through the obvious things, maybe something will start an idea for a new course of action.*

He began to review the lessons he had learned from Gatro about the history of his people. As he contemplated his situation, he realized that his earlier petulance had interfered with him taking his upcoming responsibilities seriously. Now he wished he had taken more interest in his future at a much earlier age.

Arlit is a fine ship, we'll be able to maintain her well into the future. We need to work together, these ships are all that's left of our society.

He returned to the control centre, his eyes scanning the activity there, but he did not register the events before him; he was totally absorbed in his own thoughts.

In the most recent instance, according to our legends, we weren't the sole authors of our demise; Nature's collapse struck the final blow. Thank goodness the ancient High Councillors had seen it coming, and built these ships. You know, thinking about it now, I bet they were planning well ahead to escape what they could see coming.

Abel slumped his shoulders, his deliberations intruded upon by a strong emotional response, *Sometimes I think humanity is just like a cancer; we find a host, and use it up, killing the healthy organisms as we grow in numbers, out of control.*

He shook free of this reaction, disciplining himself to return to the matters at hand. Back to the present...*so, at that point in history, we started a journey with no known destination, and I bet we'll never return. That ancient High Council kept the majority of the population ignorant of the situation, telling them that, "a special crew of elite scientists," were embarking on a brave new exploration of space. Exploration...what a joke; they were just saving the elite of our people.*

He scanned the people working in the command centre, *The people aboard this ship need to understand that they're the descendants of the ones who perpetrated this lie. It would sure upset the apple-cart to tell them* now…*They probably wouldn't believe me anyway. That would be a great start to winning their trust, wouldn't it. No. I need to do something genuine to show them I'm different, and that I'm on their side.*

He shook his head, not realizing that he had gained the attention of others in the room as he paced.

No, better we just keep wandering around in space until we find a planet we can live on comfortably. Seems to me though, that wandering suits our true nature better.

"Abel, you are silent a long time. I would think someone so recently inducted into the position of supreme leader would be overjoyed. Is there something troubling you?"

He jerked reflexively, tried to conceal his edginess, and turned slowly to face his mentor, who, in Abel's estimation, had served as a surrogate father to him. He answered, "Yes Nekalit, I'm not sure how to proceed from here into our future."

Nekalit smiled, "Only the Ancient Spirits could advise that with authority, and they fell silent millennia ago. Do you think they chose to remain on Nuna, or did they too flee into space, and become lost?"

Abel smiled a little, recognizing that Nekalit was attempting to draw him into a familiar discussion, something to relax him, "That debate will go on forever. We lost contact with them long before we even left our home galaxy, what…two thousand, and fifty-one years ago."

Nekalit smiled again, pleased that Abel understood the futility of slavishly re-examining the obscure motes of information that remained of their legends. "Exactly. We're on our own, Abel, and you're our leader. You must decide our course of action, and we must follow."

Abel looked into the inscrutable eyes of the only man he trusted. This man had taught him the ancient laws, and had arranged for Gatro, the reclusive Shaman to explain the legends of the Inuit when his own father had not seen the need. He felt a bond of gratitude, and of nurturing with this man that he had never found with his foppish, corrupt father. Yet the feeling fell far short of the father-son union he had so desperately needed all his life; a need he felt more urgently now.

As though answering one of many of his quiz questions, he replied tentatively, "Then, I guess these should be our priorities, energy for our systems, materials for our sustenance, repairs to our ships, and lastly, constant passive sensor sweeps for likely sources. What d'you think of that?" This answer had been given in an unconvincing tone, he knew, but he could not force himself to appear confident.

Nekalit fell into his role as High Council advisor, dropping the image of mentor. "Why passive? Do you fear us being detected by hostile beings? Our active sensors are much more effective. We could fail to detect a suitable planet for our future home."

"I don't want to be detected by hostiles until I know our strengths and weaknesses better. Right now, I know that our supplies are low, so I want to make them top priority. I need to learn the rules of survival before I'll feel confident enough to search openly. When we've got a good handle on our survival, then maybe we can search actively for a new home."

"If that's your logic, you must make your decision based upon it, Abel." Nekalit's reply tacitly demanded that Abel show some confidence, and assume his role, to lead. That was his duty. Still feeling lost in the darkness of space, Abel asked, "One other thing…Are we closely documenting wherever we go?"

"We are. Come, I'll show you." They moved to his work station, and Nekalit selected a data graphic on his display. "Every inch of uncharted space we explore is recorded in relation to our three dimensional position from the mathematical core of the universe."

"Great. Let's make sure that information is secure. We'll need to access a lot when we start searching for Nuna."

Nekalit smiled, but Abel did not see it as a reassuring smile.

Abel returned to his thoughts, but his young heart soon diverted those thoughts to Ruti.

I can't believe how beautiful she is. Of all the people I know, I bet she's got to be the most anxious to return to Nuna. I remember her dreamy expression that day at the dinner table, as she described what she thought it would be like to stand on real soil, with a fresh wind in her face. She seems genuinely interested in our legends. If I could, I'd choose her as my life partner, but I can't; she's not a chosen one.

Suddenly, she interrupted his daydream, "Abel, I have just received a report from navigation. A small ship has been detected. It is much smaller than ours, and slower. It does not appear to be aware of our presence. It has not altered course or increased its speed."

Abel seized upon the opportunity to exercise his new authority. He wanted to establish himself as their leader in fact as well as in title. "If necessary, Taan, alter our course to keep the ship on our sensors. I want to know where it's headed. Gather as much information as you can about its technology; I want to know if it's more advanced than us, particularly its defences."

Taan replied, "Its propulsion is relatively primitive...ionized particle stream. No match for our time-distortion systems."

"Good, I doubt its weapons would give it an advantage then, but other technologies will probably still be able to give us a few surprises. Let's keep a cautious distance. Monitor its course, and let me know when you can project it to a specific planet."

Taan ventured to test his neophyte leader, "Commander, this may be a sentinel ship. It may warn others of our presence."

Then you'll need to be ready, won't you," Abel quipped. Too late, he realized he was being flippant.

Taan passed his eyes around the control room slowly, seeming to amplify the effects of Abel's petulance. After a deliberately extended pause he returned his gaze to Abel, and said, "As you wish.....Commander."

Abel interpreted Taan's answer as being tinged with annoyance, or was it contempt; he could not decide, and didn't want to push the point.

2051.173
THE TONRAR (DEVIL)

"Commander, it is Taan. It would appear the ship we have been tracking was a sentinel, and it was aware of our presence. Nine heavily armed ships are closing rapidly on our position."

Abel inhaled in fear, "Can we outrun them?"

"In time distortion we can evade them temporarily, but they have equal speed in the present."

"Can you contact them? Maybe we can negotiate."

"I will attempt a communications link."

Abel stood pushing down the growing conviction his knees would not hold him. His muscles knotted, his tongue seemed to swell in his suddenly dry mouth, and he began to perspire heavily under the weight of his robes.

"Commander, the Tonrar will speak with you."

"Excellent."

"Tonrar commander, this is Abel, why are you approaching with armed ships?"

"You are invading Tonrar territory. Our outpost ship reported that you began to follow it, no doubt in an attempt to locate our home planet. Your ships are highly advanced, and are heavily armed; we concluded you intend to attack."

"We intend you no harm. We're seeking a suitable planet upon which to establish a colony."

"There will be no colonization in our territory. Leave our quadrant immediately or suffer the consequences."

Abel cringed inwardly, but his first reaction was that he needed to show strength, to stand up to this aggressive behaviour, he moistened his lips, then, in a firm voice he said, "We won't run like cowards; if you press your attack, we'll destroy you."

From the corner of his eye, he noticed the abrupt, reflexive reaction from Nekalit.

The Tonrar commander's reaction was immediate, "Then prepare to defend yourself. This communication is terminated."

Abel turned to Taan's station, "Taan, you have control of all ships, and their weapons." Do you think we can beat them? Abel's voice wavered in spite of his wish to display confidence.

"I believe I can, Commander, their ships are powerful, but of inferior technology; it's their numbers that make the outcome unpredictable."

"You've got all our weapons at your command; use them the best you know how."

Taan barked out orders, "Netorali, Kapvik, defence plan seven-beta, sixty degree tangential time travel at my mark. Now!"

The Tonrar weapons exploded harmlessly in the locations the Inuit ships had occupied less than a second ago. The Inuit ships reappeared in their new firing positions with weapons aimed, and charged. Soundlessly, three Tonrar ships disintegrated into the vacuum of space. The explosion, if it could be called that, was over within a few seconds. Without oxygen there was no fire, just the glow where the focused-beam lasers touched each ship. The hulls radiated the heat, dissolved at the point of contact, then scattered in a hail of fragments. Among those shards would be Tonrar flesh. Without the protective cocoon of the ship, all atmospheric pressure would be lost. With nothing to contain them, the beings aboard would tear apart as the air in their lungs, and the dissolved gasses in their tissue expanded, and fought to escape into the vacuum. In that void, liquids would become microscopic particles. Their fragments would drift, unchanging for eternity, in space.

Abel stood, awed at the sight.

They...They just disintegrated. They were just like us, but Taan seems unaffected by that. I think he treats them as nothing more than targets. I feared this man before, but this shows that I really need to watch my step with him. He's dangerous, and fully capable of taking control. How many others, I wonder.

The ships moved off in the second phase of the defence plan, jumping in time to mask each tactical manoeuvre Within a few moments, they had lost sensor contact with one another as they responded to the Tonrar pursuit. Arlit suffered minor structural damage from an explosive device fired from a Tonrar ship. It had begun to explode two nanoseconds before they entered time travel. Netorali suffered greater damage from a five nanosecond burst of energy; Kapvik's battle damage proved to be less severe. Energy reserves were becoming critically low on all three ships due to the huge demands of time travel, and weapons discharges.

"Taan, are there any other ships?" Abel was frantic that another attack may be imminent. His voice, and mannerisms betrayed his fear to all.

Taan smiled, making the most of his leader's weak-kneed appearance. He said, "Yes, two. They are moving away at maximum speed. I think they've seen enough. Do you wish to follow, and engage them?"

Abel could not hide his relief, then realized that he was being observed with disdain. He wrestled with himself to assume a mask of composure, "No, I think we've made our point; we've single-handedly destroyed three of their ships. What's our status?" Abel propped himself against a bulkhead for support, trying to appear nonchalant, but failing. His young face was devoid of colour.

"We have full propulsion, and only minor structural damage, but their weapons had a powerful electromagnetic pulse component that has somehow corrupted our computer systems. Until the computers are repaired, we must operate all systems manually. Navigation is off-line, so we must determine our position by sensors only. I fear some of the damage may require considerable time to repair."

"Alright, let's regroup our ships, and get away from here."

"Our ships moved outside sensor range during the battle, we must begin a search pattern until we regain contact."

"Can't we just retrace our movements?"

"No, the data has been almost totally corrupted. I doubt we could reconstruct much of our recent manoeuvres, other than the initial tactical plan I ordered." Taan made several selections at his console, confirming his suspicions, "I'm afraid the computers are suffering from amnesia."

Abel felt panic seeping into his vitals, he could hardly breathe, "Our historical data? Can we restore it?"

"Difficult to say at this point. It would appear that we will need a significant span of time to reconstruct any reliable information."

"So we can't navigate, and we're lost?"

"That about sums it up." Taan's voice was cool, and his words crisply spoken.

"I'm going to the meditation chambers. You may only disturb me if we're in imminent danger." Abel had to run, and hide; he had to regain his composure, and he had to ensure he would be alone.

"Yes...Commander." Taan rolled his eyes as Abel turned away. The gesture was not lost upon many of the command centre crew, who openly enjoyed the defiance it symbolized.

Abel forced himself to walk, though he wanted to run. After what seemed an unbearable delay, he reached the meditation chambers, and entered, almost tripping over the threshold.

I didn't want to engage anyone, but I couldn't appear weak, or worse indecisive, to the Tonrar, or to my people, could I?

He spun around, as if addressing an accuser.

Our ships are damaged, and the others are floating around, lost out there somewhere; if they even survived.

How many of our people have died?

I was hasty, too aggressive, and that's what brought us into combat. I should've negotiated more, or bluffed, and threatened, so we could have more time to assess the situation.

He threw himself into a corner, onto one of the mats spread out for comfort during meditation.

I was so afraid, I couldn't even think!

He sat up, propped his back against the hull of the ship, and drew up his knees, enclosing them in his arms.

I panicked, spoke like a warmongering fool, then I ran to Taan to save us. That must've made everyone confident in my leadership. I very nearly got us all killed!

Thank goodness we have Taan, his tactics are amazing. He uses time-travel so well, dodging their weapons, then popping up somewhere else, weapons blazing. The enemy sees us here, then there, as if we're some kind of magic trick.

Why can't I act so decisively, so skilfully—because I've got no idea of how to go about it; my loving father only knew how to party, and seemed to be determined to keep me away from anything constructive.

Hinot, please come to me; give me your advice. Our ships are damaged, and we've got nothing nearby that we can use to repair them. At best, we might be able to cannibalize our other ships to repair this one. Their weapons seemed to be primitive explosives, but they scrambled our computer banks pretty well. Thanks to my inept leadership, we're completely vulnerable to them if they decide to attack again. Please, what should I do?

There was no response. After many minutes, Abel rose to his feet again, and sighed. He had not expected a response, but he was the spiritual leader; he assumed he was expected to pray, and to emerge with the answers. His most fervent hopes were that he could at least learn to control his paralytic fear, to think clearly through tough situations, and to overcome his sense of isolation.

2051.191
LOST IN SPACE

Abel found he could not tolerate being alone in his command cubicle; he re-entered the ship's control room, and observed the activity. Navigation had been reduced to tracking progress against objects within scanning range, comparing those objects with what they remembered of what they had previously encountered. They were indeed lost. Propulsion was limited to manoeuvring engines; without computers, time travel was out of the question, and they were low on fuel. As the suns passed, the situation doggedly refused to offer an avenue of escape.

The crew had begun to lose patience with the situation, and their attempts to re-locate the other ships. Taan approached him, concern noticeable on his features, "Commander, we've been searching for twenty suns now, it appears we won't locate our sister ships. We need to assume they have been destroyed. By remaining here, we risk a second Tonrar attack which would be deadly in our present condition.

Abel wanted to run too, but in the period following the battle, he had convinced himself that he had to demonstrate his concern for the missing crews in order to win the people's respect. "I won't desert our people, Taan. We have to continue searching until we locate our sister ships…or their remains."

Taan interpreted Abel's intransigence as juvenile petulance, and pressed his argument, risking censure, "I recommend we withdraw to seek resources for our own repair. With fully functioning systems, and weapons, we can cover greater distances, and defend ourselves. In our present state, every hour we spend in this area exposes us to the very real risk that we may be destroyed. When we are capable of temporal manoeuvring, and fully capable of our defence, we can search boldly, rather than continue to waste time skulking around in space-debris to avoid detection."

"No!" He caught himself, and stopped what was about to become an outburst.

You sound like a kid having a tantrum. This is your senior Tactical Officer; you've got to show him the respect he has coming to him, and that you're weighing his opinion carefully.

He paused, and smiled a little to try, and ease Taan's strained expression, "I can't just leave…until we know what happened to our sister ships. We'll have to do what we can with our present status. Until we know their fate, we can't turn our attention to our own needs. I understand your concerns, and I really appreciate your opinion, but I'm convinced this is what we must do."

Taan seemed to undergo considerable effort in confining his response too, "As you wish, Commander."

Abel gravitated to Ruti, and her console, putting on his courageous look before she became aware of him. She glanced up for a second, her face devoid of expression, then returned her intent gaze to her console.

"I have detected two large ships. Sensors indicate there is life aboard."

Abel turned his attention to the display, "How soon will you know whether they are our ships."

Taan turned abruptly, and returned to his station. Abel recognized the slight. This was an inexcusable breach of protocol, but he felt unjustified in pursuing the matter, given his own shaky performance in recent times.

Ruti spoke softly, "Communications say they're not responding to our coded signature message. They might not be our ships."

Abel moved to her side, "Can we keep pace with them?"

"That will not be a problem." She pointed to a small planet at the edge of the display. "They appear to be drifting into the gravitational pull of this planet." Her soft, almost sensual voice added to the physical intoxication of her…

"Drifting?" He could smell her hair. Her physical charms were distracting him when he wanted so desperately to concentrate.

"Yes Commander. At their present speed, it'll take several suns for them to enter a deteriorating orbit. Eventually they'll impact the planet's surface."

"Crash?" The guilt of his contributing role in this state of affairs brought him back to a state of agitation, effectively snuffing his youthful desires.

"That's my guess, based on their present trajectory. They'll likely impact the surface after five orbits."

Abel pressed the communications panel, "Navigation, this is Abel, bring us closer, and maintain your scans. Use active scans if necessary, I want to know who they are before we attempt to close within weapons range."

The response sounded metallic, and somewhat reluctant, "Yes Commander."

Ruti continued operating her panel, selecting both active, and passive sensors at full sensitivity. "They're definitely the same size as our ship, but their energy signature is so faint. No ship could navigate on that little power."

Abel pushed in closer, his urgency overtaking him, "Can you tell if they have the same technology as our ship?"

"They appear to have the same capabilities as our ship," Ruti almost whispered, "it's just that they seem to have expended most of their energy."

"Could they be using the planet's pull to accelerate? Maybe they intend to use the last of their energy to enter stable orbit."

She shook her head, "They don't have enough energy to do anything more than maintain the ship's environment, and that for a limited time."

"Can we close with them, impart some of our energy to them gravitationally, and enter orbit together?"

"I think so, Commander," Ruti's voice hardened, "but we'll be unable to leave orbit, with or without them. We'll have to hope we can locate the elements necessary to refuel."

Abel hesitated, strain clear in his expression, *I've forced myself into making a dangerous decision again. Why can't I just see the facts, and make decisions that fit the situation. This quaking fear; I just can't shake it. Decide damn you!*

The crew were clearly awaiting his decision, but he sensed they might act in a predetermined fashion if his decision was not in harmony with their intentions. Abel could feel their intolerance, as though it were an entity in the room; in this agitated state of mind, he feared mutiny.

He spoke, his voice betraying his emotion, "Then we pray these are our ships, and not hostiles, and that this planet has at least the fuel elements we require. Close with them. Activate the laser in case they are hostiles."

Unconsciously, Abel rubbed his index finger over his thumbnail. He did this so often when agitated that the nail was noticeably shinier, and the opposing finger heavily calloused. He caught himself, and looked around to see whether the crew had noticed his agitation. He was convinced they had.

In a few moments, time that seemed interminable to Abel, the speaker at Ruti's console crackled, "Abel, Navigation, it is confirmed. These are our ships. They've sustained similar damage. From the debris in the area, I'd say our people fought well."

Abel mustered his most confident voice, but still feared it would betray him, "They probably used most of their energy searching for us. Bring us alongside, and prepare boarding parties. We need to assess the condition of each ship. If necessary, we'll cannibalize equipment to repair whichever ships are in the best condition."

Taan noted, "The battle damage will likely have affected the same systems on all ships. I doubt we'd profit from a salvage effort."

Abel tried to emulate Taan's calmness, "Can we tow them out of the influence of that planet's gravitational pull?"

"No, but as you suggested, we can impart enough energy to them so that we can all enter a balanced orbit."

Abel was eager to accept Taan's acknowledgement of his idea. He said, "Alright, that's what we'll do."

"Yes, Commander."

2051.213
UNKNOWN PLANET

"Commander," Ruti's voice crooned from Abel's communicator, "we're in stable orbit over the planet. Sensors indicate that elements exist in sufficient quantities for us to refuel, but mining them will be tedious as they're scattered in small deposits."

"Alright. When can we start?" He checked up at the entrance to the operations room, fearing his excited response further betrayed his insecurity to his operations staff.

"We have a team ready to depart, Commander, but we have also detected life. They appear to be primitives, since there are no communities or structures. The atmosphere is breathable, but temperatures are extreme; they can't have an easy life here."

Abel slowed to what he hoped would be seen as a more dignified entrance, "Alright, we'll use the time to make as many repairs as possible on the ships. Take one copy of the primer; I intend to continue that practice; who knows, we may decide to colonize this planet at some point in the future, as it evolves."

At last, a chance to extend our time aboard these hulks, and survive a bit longer. The days since the battle have nearly driven me crazy. The crew seem to be tolerating my involvement in our decisions, despite my bungled negotiations, and have been enduring the resulting hardships pretty well. I need to find some way to reward them once we're out of this situation, and back underway. Maybe we could declare a holiday, and have a celebration. It'd have to last through a complete rotation of crew shifts, so that everyone has a chance to celebrate. I just hope they don't think I'm going to fall into my father's, "any excuse for a party," ways.

I actually think I could sleep now; I believe the crew will allow me to survive this crisis. Some sleep would be good. Yes, I'll get some warm Carbuu milk.

2051.215

"Commander."

Abel was distantly aware of a voice. Am I having a vision? Are the ancients finally going to contact me?

"Commander, I have news. Commander!"

No, that's Taan, only he's got that sharp tone, commanding me, while appearing to be subservient...

"Mmm, yes, enter, what is it?" Abel opened the portal to his quarters.

"I'm sorry Commander, I didn't know you were asleep."

Tann's apology lacked sincerity, Abel felt. "That's fine, Taan. I think I must've had a good long sleep."

"Indeed, Commander, we haven't seen you for over twenty-four hours."

"What? Incredible. The mining expedition, how's it going?"

"Reasonably well Commander, and we've restored the computer's programming, but a good deal of the historical data is almost certainly lost. The other ships also report good progress with repairs; however, their data is in a similar state."

"I see. Can we combine the databases to retrieve what's left of the information?"

"I would not recommend that Commander," Taan clenched his hands, expecting an argument to ensue, "We could easily lose what information we have. I recommend we retain them as separate files, and compare them empirically."

Abel read Taan's growing tension. He was unwilling to start his day with another stressful situation, so replied, "Alright, we'll go with your recommendation, when do you think we'll be able to leave orbit?"

"Four suns, Commander."

"The encounter with the primitives, was it successful?" Abel ruffled his sleep matted hair.

"It was satisfactory Commander, the primer was accepted reverently, and they seemed to be capable of processing at least some of the information." Taan's manner was condescending. Abel was unsure whether this sentiment was directed to him as much as it was a reflection of Taan's opinion of the primitives. He continued, enjoying his petulant thought, "Maybe they'll evolve to become a thorn in the Tonrar's side."

Taan did not pursue the idea, changing the subject back to the present situation, "Do you have any objectives after we complete refuelling?"

Abel noted the refusal to entertain his reverie, interpreting it as another jab at his relevance. He looked down, smoothing his robe, "Yes, as soon as the ships can navigate normally, and our time distortion systems are operational, I want get out of here as fast as possible. Let the Tonrar have their precious corner of space; we'll find another." He flung his arm, indicating a general direction away from Tonrar territory.

Taan appeared interested, almost eager as he said, "So you intend to continue seeking a suitable planet for colonization?"

"M hmm." He nodded, a resolute expression rising onto his young features. "If we're ever going to live the way we're supposed to, we need lots of room so we can expand our numbers. I know that somewhere…" He looked out his observation bubble, "…somewhere out there, is our home." He paused, "Report as soon as the ships are capable of travel, and self-defence."

"Yes Commander, anything else?"

"Yes, call the High Council. We need to plan our strategy."

"Yes, Commander."

Taan saluted perfunctorily, turned, and left Abel's cubicle. Abel noted the courtesy with considerable pride. The warm flush of relief that had risen in Abel's heart as he heard the good news was almost more than he could abide. He had been sleeping for an entire day, so was still groggy from his inactivity. The flush of inner emotion had caused him to waver on his feet, he was certain. Taan had looked concerned, but he felt he had recovered with sufficient speed so as not to appear foolish.

He dressed in ceremonial clothing, gathered the sacred cane, snow knife, and the ring, and quickly prepared himself for the council meeting. Once dressed, he walked through the sonic shower, and groomed his long hair. No more than twenty minutes had passed since Taan's departure, yet he hurried to the chambers, certain that the Council members would be waiting.

***

"Good day to you, honourable members of High Council. We're progressing toward restoring our most important systems. I've called this meeting to discuss our strategy. We need to leave this sector as soon as possible, and resume our search for a suitable planet to inhabit."

The councillors looked at each other, tacitly communicating what appeared to be a predetermined degree of receptiveness, or was it resistance…

"What of Nuna Commander, do you intend to abandon the attempts to re-establish its location?" Nekalit asked.

"For now, yes. As I understand it, a good deal of time, and as yet unknown resources will be needed to completely restore the ships. We need to find a hospitable environment from which to base our restoration efforts. If the environment we find is completely satisfactory, we may abandon the ships, and our search for Nuna"

"Do you have a direction in which you feel we should begin our quest?"

"No. I propose that once we're capable of full speed, we should retrace, as much as we can determine, the direction by which we came. Once we're confident that we're clear of Tonrar territory, I propose we scan with full power active sensors to locate galaxies containing planets with potential to meet our needs. Passive sensors were of little effect in masking our presence to the Tonrar, so I see no further need to be timid. We'll take our chances, and search actively in future."

For the first time in his short tenure, Abel was faced with smiles, and nods of agreement from his council members; he could not believe his recent run of good luck. "If no one has suggestions or disagreements, we'll proceed." He paused to allow them to speak as he basked in their positive body language. Hearing no objections, he raised his cane, "Nekalit, brief Taan of our intentions."

"As you wish, Commander." His mentor's eyes reflected pleasure with Abel's latest efforts.

2051.219

Abel observed as Taan stood at his tactical command station. He had not occupied this post since the weapons, and temporal disruptors had been damaged, more than thirty suns ago. Abel could see he was anxious to resume this role, where he enjoyed autonomous authority. No one questioned him when he was in charge of tactical. He was the uncontested master of battle, and defensive strategy. Eager to be underway, he worked intently at coordinating the final preparations aboard the other two ships. Arlit was nearly fully operational; Kapvik had full propulsion, but her weapons were structurally damaged beyond the resources currently available. She remained defenceless.

Abel addressed the crews of all three ships, "People of Nuna, we have survived yet another deadly threat." He observed Taan, and Ruti as they exchanged a surreptitious look. He continued, appearing not to notice, knowing he was responsible for what they had endured. He continued, "We are now going to search for a home in earnest. Once we're clear of Tonrar territory, and the ships are operating stably, I'll declare a great celebration. We'll mark this point in our history so that its lessons are available to all of our successors. We've learned a great deal; most importantly that even in dangerous circumstances, we can survive. Taan, take us out of orbit, and set course."

"As you wish Commander. Arlit, Kapvik, thirty degrees escape angle on present heading; engage full power now."

The ships surged forward, rapidly escaping the gravity of the planet. In a graceful arc, they turned, and set course, attaining one-quarter light speed in seconds. At this pace, they would exit Tonrar territory in less than half a sun. Unless they were intercepted by warships that happened to be patrolling in close proximity to their path, no ships from Tonrar would be capable of closing with them. Through the viewing portal, Abel could see a distant star that stood out against all the others. It seemed particularly inviting.

CELEBRATION

With the computer's replicators again functional, the mood on the ships improved markedly. The past fifty-one suns had been characterized by long hours of work, and rationed supplies, including nourishment. The replicators had been able to produce only basic starches, and proteins with no flavouring, texture or colour enhancement. Now food was plentiful, closely resembling their traditional delicacies, and the celebrations lasted three full days; long enough for everyone to exhaust themselves, and gorge themselves on muutuu, carbuu, and seyal meat. Skeleton crews monitored the sensors.

"Abel, it is Taan."

"Enter. What news?"

"Commander the galaxy you observed has no inhabitable planets. The one planet that is ideally distanced from its star is too large. It would have a gravity field far in excess of our physical capabilities."

"Mmm." Well, it was a place to start. Have you located any other galaxies in this vicinity?"

"No Commander. In addition, I find it somewhat strange, but the entire area appears to be devoid of traffic. I can find no indication of the presence of any potential rival species or even of transient traffic. It is as though the area is avoided."

"What's your assessment, Taan, should we also avoid it, or do we dare to explore?"

"In view of our current status, I would counsel a more cautious tenor to our explorations."

"That's wise, Taan. I agree. Continue long-range active scans. Advise me as soon as you locate another galaxy that is a candidate for exploration."

"As you wish, Commander.

2051.364
PHYSEGIA

Abel's communication console indicated a call. He selected the speaker, and said, "Yes."

"Commander, it is Nekalit, we've been hailed by the Physegians. They identify themselves as a peaceful trading society. They ask if we are in need of repairs."

"Ask them what they seek in exchange."

"They are interested in our technology, Commander. They say they have never scanned ships such as ours. Taan reports that they were first detected on our sensors well within maximum range; as if they had just…appeared."

"Interesting. Were we focused upon another point of interest at the time?"

"No Commander, Taan says he had the sensors set to maximum, but when first detected, they were already alarmingly close."

"Fine, I will speak with them, but I do not intend to share technology beyond our metallurgy, and general science. Our temporal propulsion systems must remain our secret; they are our chief advantage."

"Understood, Commander. They indicate that there are docking facilities for ships of our size, and ample shuttles to the planet surface below."

"Inform them we will dispatch envoys to inspect their facilities, and negotiate the details of our exchanges. Prepare a team of our best technical staff, and all members of High Council. I will also attend."

"As you wish, Commander. Gatro is our most advanced research scientist, do you wish him to attend as well?"

"No, Nekalit, he will remain here, we will consult with him if necessary, but I do not wish his research to be shared, even inadvertently."

"Understood Commander, I will communicate our intentions."

Abel selected his command display, and reviewed the data recorded from initial scans of the planet surface.

Traders. How do they survive in the treacherous realm of space? I bet they have some nasty defences. I'd like to find out about their weapons while I'm down there. It's sure a beautiful planet, lots of land, and huge expanses of water. The climate looks attractive too. I wonder if we should assess this planet as a possible future home. If they're as peaceful as they say, they may welcome some new blood.

Abel selected Taan's personal communicator, "Taan, come to my quarters please."

***

"Commander, you wished to speak with me in private?"

"Yes Taan. Have you detected any weapons on the planet?"

Taan crossed his arms, "I did not feel it conducive to a relationship that is yet to be negotiated to perform an active scan of the surface."

Abel read his defensive posture, and tried to placate him. "Politically wise, but I don't want to be caught flat-footed either. Have you scanned the planet with passive sensors?"

Taan smiled a little at the compliment, "I have, Commander, I have detected no targeting systems, only their initial scan of our ships as we approached."

"Was that scan intensive?"

"Yes, and their analysis algorithms are indeed sophisticated."

"Mmm." Abel spun a lock of his long hair between his fingers. "Did you detect any environmental hazards? Should we use protective clothing or breathing apparatus?"

"I would recommend breathing equipment; their atmosphere contains high concentrations of airborne plant materials, and moulds. The climate is humid, and warm. I believe their plant life to be highly fertile, and diverse, using airborne spores for reproduction. These substances may prove to be an allergen-response challenge for us."

"Have you been able to detect anything suspicious?"

"Yes, Commander, they are able to detect our passive scan activity; I have curtailed it."

Abel nodded, "I want more information; contact them, and state that as a preliminary to our sending a team to their planet, we require specific data regarding the equipment we need to ensure our safety. Ask for an intensive, active scan of their planet."

Taan frowned, "Perhaps it is time for them to have communication with you directly, Commander."

Abel felt somewhat embarrassed, "Right, if I delay too long, they might start to wonder…I'll speak with them myself."

"I'll arrange the communication link." Again, Taan came to attention, saluted, then spun on his heel, activating the portal to the command centre.

***

"Greetings, Abel. Welcome to Physegia. My name is Ahnia." The silken tones of a female voice warmed Abel's heart to this envoy of Physegia in an instant.

Thank you, I am happy to have received your offer of repair services for my ships. I'm anxious to learn what we have that we can give you in exchange."

"Our initial scan of your ships revealed that you have some unique technologies. These would be of great interest to us."

"You understand, of course that these" unique" technologies are our chief advantage in our encounters with aggressive life-forms."

"Indeed? From the condition of your ships, I can surmise that they have been only partially effective. Perhaps we could work together to further develop them. Our scientists' skills are sought from far beyond this galaxy. Their abilities are the subject of a good deal of legend among more primitive peoples."

"You're right, our encounter with the Tonrar proved to be surprisingly destructive."

"The Tonrar, then your ships are vulnerable to electromagnetic impulse. They use ancient nuclear technology for their weapons; I am surprised that your scientists had not anticipated..."

"We were lax indeed, but our technology did in fact prevail; their fleet will not be a threat for some time to come."

"We had heard of a great battle in their sector of space. We had largely dismissed them as a threat, but now they will likely be motivated to incorporate several new technologies into their old, and largely obsolete fleet of warships. Until now, they had seemed content to occupy their small collection of planets; these events may have changed that situation dramatically. Their society is heavily oriented toward revenge."

"That's unfortunate, but we were forced to defend ourselves on very short notice."

"You must have suggested colonizing nearby; they are possessive in the extreme."

Abel smiled, "You seem to have a lot of knowledge about your neighbours; we might benefit from some of this information. It would be helpful if we had advance information about the people we'll encounter."

"All the more reason for you to share your technology with us. You have already noted that we have no active weapons systems; we do not require them because we have the most valuable resource of all...knowledge. No-one dares to overtake us because they constantly require us to rescue their battered ships, and to help patch up their squabbles."

"Then why does the technology of advanced weaponry interest you so?"

"We are universally known to possess advanced knowledge in all matters. It is known that if pressed to fight, we could exercise truly formidable tactics in a surprisingly short time. Allow me to demonstrate."

At first, it appeared as if nothing had happened, but then, the ship shuddered, just as it had when they barely escaped the shock of the Tonrar weapons Abel suddenly felt that same fear, found himself standing on shaky legs in the operations centre. Taan was transmitting orders to the other ships, and to his dismay, he was back in the midst of the battle with the Tonrar.

Just as abruptly, he was back in the present, he felt the anxiety drain away, and was not a little confused.

"As you now see; we too have advanced capabilities. The addition of your ability to physically travel short distances in time, would be a significant advance in our situation."

Abel was baffled. What had just happened? He had been immersed in his own past, reliving the situation in complete detail. How could she have done this? She intimated being unable to travel through time, yet he had just experienced something that belied her claim. The ship was as it had been moments ago. The crew were obviously concerned at his recent near collapse. Gradually, it became apparent to Abel that he had experienced the flashback alone.

"I'm impressed. This ability of yours could serve to confuse an enemy to the point where they couldn't mount a credible assault."

"Indeed, a confused enemy is easily overcome. We have the capability of using their own memories to muddy their sense of where they are. Abel, your time travel capability would be but one addition to our collection of strategies. We do not barter our technology, we collect it, and retain it for our own purposes, our own peaceful purposes. You see, every ship that has come here seeking restoration has been required to share its most advanced technology. We have restored each ship to its original state; improvements to existing technology are negotiable, but we do not allow new technology to be transferred to a ship that does not already possess it. If we cannot negotiate a suitable exchange, you will return to space in your present condition."

As Abel sat, gazing down onto the planet, he found himself staring into the empty void of space; the planet was gone.

"Taan, scan for Physegia; I do not see it."

"Indeed, Commander, our sensors are indicating that nothing is there, yet we continue to orbit a gravity source that maintains our altitude; something must be there."

"Ahnia, you continue to impress me. Very well, we will send our team down to make final arrangements at your convenience."

The planet was visible again. "You may dispatch your shuttles now, I will greet you myself. Please wear breathing apparatus, you may find our atmosphere too heavily charged with pollen, and initially too high in oxygen content. Once you are en-route, we will guide your vessel to the landing site."

2051.364.6
ARRIVAL ON PHYSEGIA

Abel stepped out of the shuttle onto a verdant carpet of greenery, and flowers. Ahnia stood alone before him, a quadruped with a coat of golden fur, a long, flowing white mane over her neck framing a large, yet attractive head. Her powerful forelegs rose to a massive chest, just above Abel's head. Her arms were well muscled, originating from the tops of her shoulders. She wore goggles, and her nose was festooned with a mask made of fine down-like feathers that were heavily coated in a yellow dust. The air seemed veiled in a fine yellow mist. She looked down at him with soft, pleasing brown eyes, and spoke, causing a puff of dust with each consonant.

"Welcome to Physegia, Abel. Please accompany me to the castle. We will first dine, become better acquainted, and then embark upon our negotiations." She extended her hand, and like a child, he reached up, and took it. It was soft, warm, and comforting, though he counted seven delicate fingers, and two opposing thumbs, one on each side of her hand.

They entered the castle, passing through huge wooden doors that opened, and closed with no-one in attendance. Ahnia's hooves resounded on the stone floors. Once inside, through a second set of doors, she removed her nose-cover, and goggles.

"You may remove your breathing apparatus now. The air inside the castle is carefully filtered, but I caution you to breathe only shallow breaths until you become more accustomed to the oxygen content."

They removed their equipment, and were immediately taken with the heady odour of flowers, mixed with the aromas of mysterious, and exotic foods. Ahnia led them into a large room. High ceilings, and ornate wooden troughs greeted them, each filled with attractive, but unknown foods. Ahnia took several samples, and indicated that they should do the same. She chewed the victuals, and spoke between mouthfuls, "We are, as you have by now surmised, herbivores, so I hope you can find these offerings palatable."

Small amounts of food dropped to the floor, whereupon, small furry creatures skittered out, and consumed them on the spot; then they ran back out of sight. Each of the team members made selections, and tasted, learning quickly that the flavors were as enticing as the aromas. They began to eat heartily.

When she had finished eating, Ahnia moved to the last trough, and dipped her hand into a milky liquid. She raised her cupped hand delicately to her mouth, pursed her lips, and with a discrete slurping sound, drew up the liquid. As Abel made to follow suit, she cautioned, "The abrioshe is fermented, I hope you enjoy it, but I would limit your intake if we are about to discuss business."

Each of the team took only one handful of the abrioshe, though clearly from their reaction to it, they would have enjoyed more. They had been unable to identify any of the things they had eaten, yet had thoroughly enjoyed each one.

Ahnia led them into a cavernous, circular arena, strangely barren of decoration, with a freshly turned, and smoothed earth floor. She began to trot around the edge of the arena, clearly intending to exercise. In seconds, she was at a full gallop, running until her breath came in harsh blasts, and her body showed ample perspiration. When she slowed, she walked smoothly to the centre of the arena, where she raised her flowing tail high, and deposited both urine, and feces; then she moved toward a cubicle.

"I am going to cleanse myself now, you may choose to exercise in your own fashion, and eliminate if you wish, then join me in the meeting chamber, through that portal. She pointed to a small opening at the side of the arena as she disappeared into the cubicle.

The team stood near the pile of steaming feces slack-jawed. They looked around at each other, unable to formulate a cohesive thought. The strange food, and drink, accompanied with the unusual environment had conspired to confound their normal response patterns. At length, Abel looked resignedly at his companions, and began to jog around the perimeter, finding himself strangely energized. The others followed suit, discovering their athletic abilities to be unusually sound, considering their lives as the sedentary denizens of cramped space ships.

The joy of their efforts overtook them, inciting a full-fledged foot-race, that was abruptly punctuated by the need to deposit their own digestive by-products. They discretely arranged themselves around the elimination site chosen by Ahnia, their backs to the centre, then moved as a group to the cubicle, also feeling the need to cool themselves, and clean up.

Again, somewhat shyly, they stood, backs inward, and shed their clothing, men, and women alike. They stepped onto a pedestal, covering themselves demurely with their arms, and hands, whereupon an aromatic flow of clear liquid sprayed down, soaking them, and their clothing. It drained under the pedestal, and in seconds, they were dry, cooled, and feeling fragrantly refreshed. To their surprise, their clothing also dried as they retrieved it to dress.

Abel remarked, "One wonder falls on the heels of the next. This method of bathing is remarkable, and the food is amazing; I still feel full of energy. We need to negotiate for these life-support skills."

The remainder of the team nodded, but Nekalit replied, "She has already told us that we cannot expect to take any new technology from this place."

"She might not give it to us, but what's to prevent us from learning how to duplicate it? Science team; sharpen up on your observations. I want us to take back as much knowledge as possible."

"Taan responded, "Much of what we have seen thus far is directly related to the ecology of this planet. The foods' ability to impart strength, and our heightened vitality can be attributed to the higher oxygen concentration. We are, no doubt, oxidizing our food more quickly, thus we are deriving more energy in a shorter time."

The science team nodded their agreement, and Abel replied, "Then maybe we should look into increasing oxygen levels on our ships, unless we can identify some negative side-effects."

"I for one would be concerned with our ability to impart the necessary richness into our food, and perhaps more importantly, to provide ample opportunities to burn it off." Nekalit spoke softly as they approached the portal to the meeting chamber.

Ahnia greeted them, "I hope you are enjoying your visit. As you can see, we live an enriched life here. We are blessed with an abundant source of high quality food, and with a benign environment that is redolent with succulent plant growth. I hope you have seen nutritional benefits for yourselves that you can employ when you return to your ships. If you choose to adopt this lifestyle, you will find that you are much calmer, and more capable of dealing with whatever situation is at hand. In this case, I hope you find yourselves relaxed, and alert for the upcoming negotiations."

The room had small mangers containing food, and beverage, but there were no places to sit. They gathered in a rough oval circle, with Ahnia at the head.

"Indeed, Ahnia, we are surprised at how energized we feel," Abel looked around, gaining a sense of consensus, "We haven't occupied a living, civilized planet for over two thousand of our home planet's years. Our food has been produced artificially by combining the elements with the molecular patterns we recorded from the originals. Unfortunately, those foods had already been compromised by the artificial methods of agriculture used at the time; they aren't as nutritious as the original, natural substances. The natural-source foods had been long-lost by the time we developed our replication technology."

Ahnia pawed the ground thoughtfully, "These are common problems among your evolutionary class of species; you seem possessed by the need to interfere in your planets' ecologies, and to dominate all you encounter. Do not fear, we will provide the molecular patterns of our foods for your replicators; you will find your strength, and vitality are greatly enhanced."

Abel smiled, "We've already noticed significant increases in our energy levels."

"Excellent. Let us move on to discuss your ships' repairs. Once you have provided the engineering details of your time-travel propulsion system, we will begin restoring your ships."

Abel frowned, clearly concerned, "You realize that time travel is our main tactical advantage over the ships we've encountered; we're afraid of facing ships in the future that you will have given the same technology."

Ahnia nodded, "I assure you, if you encounter such a ship, the capability will not have come from us. You will soon see, as you depart, that your ship is restored, but is in no way enhanced beyond its present tactical capabilities."

Taan interjected, "But you have already offered to enhance our food replicators, and to help us improve…"

Ahnia interrupted, "Indeed; however, this provides you only enhanced well-being, not tactical advantage. We are happy to share information of this type."

Abel paused, taking stock of this creature. Her massive, muscular body was alluring to him even though she was unlike any living entity he had seen. Her demeanour was maddeningly attractive. His sensibilities detected only benign good will from her, yet it continued to nag at him how these denizens could be so relaxed in the face of the aggressive horrors they must encounter in the course of trading. He decided to give voice to his thoughts

"…"

"You are curious what we do that makes us so certain that we can deal with armed battleships while remaining unarmed ourselves. I cannot reveal our defence strategies other than to tell you that we can avoid any attack with impunity."

Abel pointed upward, "The way you disappeared…"

"That is one of many possible tactics, all of which are benign manipulations of your perception. We destroy nothing, ever. That is why we view your time-travel technology with great interest. It can be used effectively as a defence strategy, as you have proved, without inflicting death or suffering on anyone." She looked knowingly at Abel.

The look was not lost on him, Abel realized she was emphasizing the redundancy of inflicting damage on an aggressor. "I see. You are, without doubt, the most engaging negotiator I have ever encountered…" Abel realized as he spoke that he sounded as though he considered himself a seasoned negotiator. Noting her smile, he knew she was aware of his inexperience, but he pressed on choosing to ignore the setback. "…thus I am tempted to comply with your wishes, but I am only the titular leader of my people, I must confer before committing them to a decision of this import."

"You wish me to leave you." she said, turning toward the exit.

"That is not necessary. The High Council, I am certain, see no need to debate in private. Am I correct in this assumption?" he asked as he turned, surveying their faces. No one indicated concern, so he turned back to her. "This will take but a moment."

"Members of High Council, do you object to providing our time-travel technology to these people?" Everyone indicated agreement with the transfer. "Science team, do you retain any doubts?"

"I remain cautious, Commander," Taan answered. "As your tactician, I have difficulty accepting that someone who will negotiate the exchange of technology for repairs will not also negotiate weapons technology transfers for the right form of motivation."

Ahnia looked into Taan's eyes for a moment before answering. "You are a supremely talented tactician, Taan, with the experience of many battles to your credit."

Taan blinked, he was certain his name had not been mentioned. Had she just read his mind?

"Your weakness, sir, is your ambition. This trait compromises your ability to be a leader of your people, although you are without question their leader in battle. As your leaders mature," she gestured to the High Council, and Abel, "you will find your skills are called upon less frequently. As for your question, the possibility does exist. I can only assure you that it will not happen. You must be beginning to understand that we have unusual capabilities; your operation of your scanners should have told you that most of your tactics would be useless against us. If a warrior such as yourself could not penetrate our environment, you should see that others would have similar difficulty. Your profession is obsolete in our society; given sufficient time, your species may evolve to this same state. As to rewards; what do you see that we lack?"

Taan made no response, he looked down at the smooth stone floor. Abel resumed the conversation. "I think we've reached the point where we simply have to have faith in each-others' good intentions."

Ahnia smiled.

Abel concluded, "We'll provide the information you seek; when the repairs are complete."

Ahnia chuckled softly. "The repairs will commence when we have received the information, not before. What you are proposing is a primitive protection strategy used between parties who profess agreement, but still mistrust one-another. It will take us time to evaluate your information, during which your repairs will be completed; we must trust that the information you provide is accurate, and you no doubt, will hope that our repair workmanship will be to your satisfaction. The bonus I am offering is our nutritional information, what are you offering as a bonus?"

"What is it you seek?"

"Your trust." She moved gracefully toward an exit, her muscles rippling smoothly.

Abel did not delay, or seek consensus for his response, "Then you have it. When do we begin?"

She paused, and turned back, "The timing is of your choice; advise us when you are ready to transfer the information."

"Very well, Ahnia, we will be in contact."

***

The team returned to their shuttle, and launched in silence. Nekalit spoke first, "In my entire life, I have never encountered such an enchanting creature. I felt entranced by her, yet I was accepting of the situation."

Abel nodded, "Only the final outcome will prove whether we have been duped."

Silently, the shuttle slipped into the dock aboard Arlit. The crew disembarked, and prepared to meet for a debrief. Abel looked at them, and uttered what he saw in their eyes. "We will dispense with the debrief; I doubt any of us understands entirely what has just transpired."

The others nodded agreement, so they simply dispersed to their tasks aboard the ship. Abel summoned Gatro to his cubicle.

"Gatro, prepare to transfer the scientific data for our time travel technology to Physegia."

Gatro raised his ample brows, "Are you certain Commander? They could easily make this technology available…"

"We are aware of that fact, yet I doubt that would ever occur. Sharing weaponry does not seem to be on their agenda."

"Then, why are they interested?"

"They see it as a means of defence that they wish to incorporate into their surprisingly effective, yet passive strategies."

"I see. When do you wish to transfer the information?"

"When it is ready."

"As you wish, Commander. It will be ready within the hour"

***

"Ahnia, it is Abel. The data for our time travel system is ready to transmit."

"Thank you, Abel. We will receive the data in person to guard against the possibility of it being intercepted. I will dispatch a shuttle with my consort aboard."

"Very well, when will our repairs commence?"

"You may enter the space docks now. Mooring instructions are being relayed to your computers as we speak."

"Thank you Ahnia, I hope our science is beneficial."

"I am certain it will be."

Abel turned from his communication screen to observe the space docks looming up out of the darkness, silhouetted against the stark light of Physegia's two suns. Huge openings yawned invitingly for their ships, and shuttles moved busily, like bees around a hive.

2052.097

As the ships entered the docks, the docks disappeared. Arlit, Netorali, and Kapvik continued on a straight line course, no longer orbiting Physegia's gravity. Abel stood with a hollow fear consuming him. Had they been so totally duped as to receive nothing in exchange for their vital defence information?

"Commander, it is Taan. Physegia has disappeared again, but this time the gravity field is also gone; we are in open space three suns' distance from the coordinates of the space dock."

"What's the status of our ships?"

"I will conduct a systems check, and report back to you."

Abel smiled, and looked at Gatro's puzzled face as realization slowly came to him.

We've just encountered a Spirit of enormous power; maybe more potent than our own legends. I bet our repairs are complete, and they've used our own time travel technology to send us on our way.

"Commander, it is Nekalit. Our ships are fully operational; all systems have been repaired. The quality of the repairs matches our workmanship to the letter. Every detail has been logged on our database, but according to the computer timeline, we were under repair in the space dock for ninety-seven suns."

"Thanks, Nekalit, open a channel on our last contact frequency with Ahnia."

"Ready Commander."

"Ahnia, this is Abel. Thank you for your hospitality, and your assistance; maybe we'll meet again at some time in the future. You've charmed us beyond belief."

No response came, yet Abel was certain his message had been received.

He turned to Gatro, "Our distance from the space docks tells me that they've already made significant improvements to our time travel capabilities..." He stopped in mid-sentence, an epiphany settling into his awareness, "...I wonder if they didn't already have the capability. That would mean us giving it to them was just a formality; it might have just been a way for us to show our trust in them. I bet they didn't need our meagre skills. If that's right, we have just encountered the Great Spirits of space." Abel smiled again, confident in his assessment, then asked Nekalit, "What's in our food replicators?"

Nekalit paused as he scanned the computer readout, "We are about to enjoy a number of new culinary delights; the menu is much expanded."

"Then find the drink, I think it was abrioshe, we need to have a celebration to mark this occasion."

"Understood Commander, I will brief the crew."

The Physegians will be virtually impossible to locate, unless they choose to let us find them. I wonder what motivated them to initiate contact with us? I hope that one day we can become a civilization like theirs, capable of dodging every intended blow from aggressors. I realize now just how completely taken I was with Ahnia. If our species were just more compatible...

2057.287

Sadly, with the passage of time, and for numerous other reasons, the technicians who maintained the ships systems became complacent about their reliability. As a result, the systems on all three ships deteriorated. Taan stared intently at his console. The long distance scan was indicating a large cluster of planets around a trio of stars. Everything needed attention, to be re-tuned, a state of affairs that recurred with greater frequency. It no longer took battle damage to cause problems to surface. Another problem had also surfaced; with the enhanced comforts so kindly provided by the Physegians, the crew had become more focused upon the pleasures of life, and less so toward their duties. In addition, Abel continued to struggle with less than enthusiastic response to his leadership.

"Nekalit, I'm concerned over the deterioration of our ships. The crew seem less interested in practising their professions than they are in following their diversions. What do you think we can do to regenerate their interest, and professional pride?"

Nekalit shook his head, "I do not know, Commander. Our contact with Physegia seems to have introduced a melancholy in our people. Part of it may be that, having seen the beauty of life on a hospitable planet, they realize the comparative poverty of an existence within these vessels. They seem to be overcome by their confinement, by the monotony of routine. They only seem to respond favourably when our survival is threatened. It seems that they have lost a sense of accountability for their work."

Abel struck his palm with his fist, "I'm not going to look for danger just to entertain our egos. We need to find constructive things that don't threaten our safety."

Nekalit smiled, pleased that his protege was maturing as a leader, "We are continually looking for activities of this nature; however, they carry no significant consequences. The crew realize this, thus they give them only temporary, cursory interest. It would appear that slowly, all situations are receiving the same lax attention."

Abel paced the floor, deep in thought. When he stopped, he looked Nekalit in the eye, issuing a challenge, "Then find some significant consequences for poor performance or we'll face never ending apathy, and inattention to duties."

"What do you suggest, Commander."

"Let's renew our efforts to find a suitable home, exploring planets that even remotely indicate they could be habitable. Perhaps increased exploration, and its associated dangers will sharpen their minds."

"Very well, Commander. But what parameters shall we set for exploration?"

Abel opted for the simplest of criteria, "Breathable atmosphere, and gravity within the limits of our strength."

"I will brief the sensor operators."

"We've got to improve our situation. Taan tells me that our encounters with other ships show that our technologies aren't at the leading edge any more. He says that he often detects scans interrogating us from beyond our maximum sensor range."

"This is true, Commander. It is fortunate that we have not encountered warlike species for some time. We seek to avoid contact with them, and we take action to avoid locations where intense activity is likely. Taan is increasingly suspicious of the continued viability of our weapons, and strategies. The ships we encounter are capable of activating major systems in fractions of a second; in comparison, our ships require disquieting amounts of time to achieve a state of readiness. He suspects that their weapons are also capable of nearly immediate activation, and far greater devastation."

"Yes, I have noticed that he's on the scientific crews' backs to come up with some advances to his weapons, and tactical systems. I'm concerned that there seems to be no serious effort to make progress, let alone any activity to improve our tactical situation."

***

Abel turned to his portal, and prayed, because he could not think of anything else to do.

"Great Spirits, please let us find a compatible home; I'm so tired of being cooped up in these machines. Since we saw Physegia, I've yearned for our freedom. I think I understand what our ancestors enjoyed about life on Nuna...To have soil under my feet, and a fresh breeze blowing in my face as the legends tell us; that's my fondest dream. Hurry please, Arlit, I'm anxious to find a home."

2065.313

Initial sensor reports indicated at least one planet with good probability of being able to support an ecology. Taan looked over to Ruti, wanting to attract a glimpse from her; she looked, and he signalled with his eyes to the scanner. She selected the display, and instantly became engrossed in what she saw there.

She returned her gaze to him, and smiled. He could see that she was already planning a life with her feet in fertile soil, likely without Abel as their leader. He activated his intercom to Abel.

"Commander, I have detected a planet in a cluster around a triad of stars that may be capable of supporting life as we know it."

"How far is it?"

"At present speed, it is four suns distant."

"Good, then make direct course, and scan it thoroughly. I want to know as soon as possible if it has a breathable atmosphere, and habitable climate. Also scan for life forms."

"Yes Commander." He rolled his eyes for Ruti's benefit.

2065.317
A PLANET IS FOUND

Abel strode into the command centre, determination on his face.

"Taan, the results of your scan."

"Commander, the planet has suitable gravity, and a breathable atmosphere. There appears to be lush vegetation, but I find it unusual that there is very little visible warm-blooded animal life. From time to time, clouds obscure our sensor sweeps, and I note that these clouds do not move as weather patterns would normally, more like closely packed schools of tiny animals."

"Animals? In the air?" Abel's face twisted into an incredulous look, "That's strange."

"No Commander, that would show on our sensors. The constituent parts of these clouds appear to be smaller than our sensors can discern."

"So they could be anything."

"Yes Commander, I note that they keep to the side of the planet that is oriented to the daytime sun. The clouds on the night side either dissipate, or..."

"Or?" Abel beckoned, "...What do they do?"

"It would appear that they descend to the surface, but I cannot determine that conclusively."

"Will you be able to tell more from orbit?"

"Possibly Commander. I feel it will be necessary to explore in order to obtain more detailed information. Our sensors are working reasonably well at a distance, but we seem to have compromised definition at close range. Further repairs will be necessary."

Abel slapped his hands together, barely able to contain his impatience over the feeble efforts of the crew to maintain the ship.

"I believe that in time we will be able to re-tune the close range sensors, but our priority has been upon keeping long range sensors operational."

"I understand, Taan." He understood more than he let show, Taan was protecting his lazy, perhaps even sabotaging cohorts. "How long would it take to make these adjustments?"

"Approximately three suns, Commander."

"Then we'll explore ourselves. Take us into orbit, and prepare a transfer shuttle. We'll descend onto the night side of the planet, since you haven't seen the clouds there. I want detailed sensor scans of conditions on the night surface. If the data indicates reasonably safe conditions, we'll await the arrival of the dawn before exiting the shuttle. Everyone will wear full suits, and breathing apparatus until we're certain the clouds don't impair breathing or visibility unduly."

"I will brief the crew, Commander. Do you wish to select the team, or shall I?"

"You select, Taan, but I'll be coming along too."

"Do you think that wise, Commander?"

"I won't send my people anywhere that I won't go myself."

"That is a brave sentiment, Commander, this could prove to be a dangerous mission."

Taan thought to himself, *Yes...Very dangerous indeed.*

***

As Taan made preparations, Ruti moved to his side, and feigned to be assisting him. "This is an opportunity to rid ourselves of this idiot. If he is foolhardy enough to venture out onto the planet surface, keep alert for the chance to manufacture an unfortunate incident."

"I am already planning to compromise his protective suit; if he uses it, he will quickly be at the mercy of whatever is on the planet."

"Excellent. Just make certain the suit is not recovered for post-incident analysis. The loss of a chosen one will be investigated in minute detail."

"I'll make certain of that." His whisper became a hiss, "Once the only surviving heir to the Regency is gone the High Council will have no legal authority figure, we'll be free to create our own leadership."

Ruti smiled slightly, and nodded, but shot a glance around the control room to be sure no-one was eaves-dropping. "Here, replace his weapon with this one; it's unserviceable."

***

The shuttle descended in the darkness to the planet below. To this point, sensors were confirming Taan's initial findings; the pre-dawn skies were clear, and activity on the surface was encouragingly absent, except for numerous scan returns from small warm-blooded animals. They flew on, crossing a large body of water, rippling enticingly in the subdued light of a moon, then settled onto a flood plain, where the soil was flat, and peppered with clumps of all manner of vegetation. In the glare of the shuttle spotlights, large fruits were visible, hanging from their vines. Other trees seemed obscured in a cloak of shimmering darkness. The ground was similarly covered, and appeared to be slowly moving.

Abel spoke softly to Taan, "We'll stay inside until daylight, and continue our observations. Direct all energy to the sensor array, I want to know immediately if anything significant moves out there."

Taan hesitated, "Commander, it will require at least twelve seconds to activate weapons or propulsion if I divert all power to sensors."

"I don't see any need for weapons; everything looks tame enough out there. Is the air breathable?"

"Sensors report ample oxygen, and temperature two degrees above the freezing point of water."

"Bring some of the air into the shuttle through a filtered valve. Let's see how natural air affects us."

Taan opened a purge valve, and an inlet valve. The stale, metallic smell of the shuttle's interior was replaced by the enticing odours of plants, moist soil, and flowers.

"Amazing! What are those smells? They're so pleasant."

"I can only surmise that they are the scents produced by the plants, and the environment."

"I can't wait to breathe this air with my bare feet planted in the dirt. That will be a fantastic experience!"

"Commander, we will have sunrise in less than one-half hour. I have noted a slight rise in temperature already, and there is increased movement on the surface." He adjusted controls attempting to clarify the screen's representation of the contact. "Yes, a small animal is burrowing into the earth just beyond that rise."

"Can the sensors display it?"

I think I captured a representation of it before it began to dig. Yes, here, I will put it on this display."

"That's a strange animal. Send this image to Arlit, and see whether anything similar is in our data banks."

"Yes, Commander."

"Look! The horizon is turning red."

The occupants of the shuttle sat motionless, it would seem as a group they innately believed that to move may interfere with the wonder they were about to behold. They were scarcely breathing. The rouge glow of daylight crept over the landscape, its progress imperceptible. First one sun rose above the horizon, then a second smaller one, followed by the third.

The images from the sensors, and the spotlights had been totally inept at representing the beauty they beheld. Brilliantly coloured fruits, and flowers were showcased against a backdrop of greenery. As one, the people inhaled sharply at the first sight of these wonders, and held their breath, fearing they might somehow scare it away. Then they saw the movement.

Abel pointed out the viewing port, "Those plants are moving, and the soil too; everything seems to be sliding toward the light. Are we moving? Is the earth shifting?"

Taan scanned his instruments briefly, then returned his gaze to the portal. "No Commander, we are stationary. The struts are firmly in contact with the surface."

The sun was visible now, and the temperature had risen to seven degrees above. Suddenly, the plants gave birth to a huge cloud. In its wake, many bare stems, and trunks stood, sorrowful in appearance compared to their lush companions. The cloud rose to the tops of the plants, and drifted toward the suns. The moving soil was now revealed in full sunlight. A mass of minute beasts were flowing as one toward the light, some carrying plant debris, and others, creatures somewhat larger than themselves.

"What are these things? They're innumerable."

"Arlit reports that the beast we saw most closely resembles a species called Armadillo on Nuna. These tiny beasts below us are similar to the genus Insect. They were called ants on Nuna."

"Are they dangerous?"

"Unknown, Commander, but in these numbers, anything could be dangerous."

"Delay our extra-vehicular activities until we find a better place to explore; maybe other areas will be less infested."

Taan commented, "I noted that they were relatively inactive until the temperature began to rise; perhaps the polar regions will be cool enough to discourage them."

"Okay, let's move there to confirm your theory."

One of the science team, a young woman called Lodi, interjected, "Could we not make a quick foray to gather samples of these flora, and," she hesitated, mustering her courage, "the insects. These species may not exist in another area."

"I guess so," Abel replied, "I understand what you're suggesting, but make it brief, wear a full protective suit, and breathe only internal air. Who knows what these creatures might use to attack whatever they think might be food or an enemy. At the first sign of trouble though, return to the airlock."

"Thank you Commander, Gatro will be pleased indeed to receive these samples."

The young woman moved to the rear of the shuttle, and began to don her space suit. Once the helmet was in place, and she had activated the environmental controls, she noticed that the flow of air was insufficient.

"My suit is unserviceable, I'm not getting enough airflow." She began removing the helmet, disappointment clear on her face.

Abel jumped up, comparing his height to hers, "You are as tall as I, my suit will fit you; you may use it."

Taan looked around abruptly, about to utter his objection, but before he spoke, he realized he could say nothing without revealing prior knowledge of the weakened condition of the laminated seams inside the left leg. He watched in quiet agony as she removed her suit, and donned the replacement. She checked the environmental controls, and gave the thumbs up, satisfied she was receiving an adequate flow of air. She nodded, and Taan opened the inner airlock door. She passed through the opening, and it sealed behind her. As she disappeared from sight, Taan prayed she would survive, that the insects were benign. He opened the exterior port, and she stepped onto the first soil she had experienced since their foray onto Physegia.

"The ground is covered with these tiny insects to a depth that exceeds the height of the toe of my boot. I have a sample. They seem to be ignoring me to this point, they are only crawling over the boots. Footing is rather slippery. They crush under my feet, and their fluids lubricate the ground."

They watched as she began to move toward the plants, some twenty feet away. She reached them, and took samples of the most noteworthy fruits as well as a few flowers. It was then that Taan saw something on the scanners

"Lodi, return to the shuttle immediately. Turn, and look at your foot prints; the flying insects are returning, and gathering in them, taking up the dead ants, and their fluids." He turned again to the scanners, and confirmed what he had first feared; the swarm was turning, and heading back to their location, led by some keen sense of smell, or death.

Taan's voice betrayed some of his concern as he ordered, "Hurry up! The airborne insects are returning. My guess is they are predatory."

Abel interjected, "Arm your weapon, and set it to maximum."

She set her weapon, turned, and began to stride to the shuttle. She slipped, and fell. When she rose, she was covered in tiny carcasses, and body fluids with many living examples moving over the surface of her suit. She attempted to fire her weapon, but it did nothing. Realizing it was useless to her, she threw it to the ground.

Taan noted that the compromised seam had failed, and that the insects had found the flaw almost immediately. The flying insects homed in on her. In seconds she was covered. She began striking herself, squashing many of the rapidly building mat of insects.

"I can't see, and, unh, ouch! I've been stung!" Her voice became thick-tongued, and inarticulate, her breathing was laboured. The team sat through the ensuing seconds unable to process in their minds the horror they saw.

Taan's fingers flew over the shuttle's controls, attempting to activate weapons, and the lift engines. A low moan began to rise in pitch as they entered the start cycle.

She was trying to scream, but couldn't draw a full breath to supply it. Her breathing had become panicked, and spasmodic. Overcome by the weight of insects, she fell once more, and the insects flew up, but only for a moment. Within seconds, her movements became sluggish, erratic, then ceased.

To their horror, they could see numerous holes in her suit; then, as the insects began a new attack, they saw that many had entered the suit, and were swarming over her head inside the helmet. She was bleeding profusely from her swollen face, the pain of the bites clear on her expression. Her eyes were puffed slits, and her torn lips were grotesquely swollen. In the next second, she was again obscured from their sight by the moving shroud of frenetic activity. Taan continued to hammer at the controls while he watched the scene of death outside.

As soon as the engines were capable, he lifted the shuttle into a hover, and moved it over her now inert body, attempting to flush them from her. As the shuttle moved over her, the blast of its engines did indeed force them away. A few shards of bloody flesh remained, attached to her exposed bones. As they hovered, the stream of exhaust from the engines blew gouts of blood, and shreds of cloth from the site. The bones began to dry, and her skeletal arms, and legs started to flail in the turbulent slipstream. Her skull turned from side to side, completing a grotesque parody of lifelike distress. Her entrails, and vital organs were gone, her suit, no more than a few bloodied fragments, being carried away into the distance by the ants.

Abel finally found his voice, and screeched, "Get her inside, get her inside!"

Taan replied, "Commander there is nothing remaining; we risk bringing them inside with her, even the airlock will need to be cleared before we can safely egress.

Abel lurched forward to the control console, eyes wide, horror etched upon his expression. His lips moved uselessly as he tried to speak again. He looked around at the crew; they were in shock as well. Only Taan was functioning proactively. He fired a full strength pattern from the lasers as they came on line, killing millions of the insects.

"Too little, and too late," he muttered, glancing at Abel accusingly. The shuttle rose higher from the landing site, and retracted its landing struts, then turned toward the northern polar region. Taan's mind told him to abort the mission, and return to Arlit, but he continued to follow their plan; he was functioning, but robotically at best.

A cloud rose to meet their departure, rapidly engulfing them. In moments the view portals were coated in a brown, green, and yellow patina that completely obscured their view of the planet below.

"What's that?" Abel managed to utter. Though he knew the answer, his intellect was no longer able to deal even with the obvious.

"It would appear that as we impact the flying insects, they are crushed, and their body fluids are spread over the exterior."

"The smell is revolting; put us back onto our internal air supply." He calmed slightly with his first rational command in some time. Externally, Abel was regaining his composure, but his fear remained out of control within. He forced himself to make decisions, and relay them to Taan, feeding upon anything that had a calming effect.

The ship moved toward a polar area of the planet, seeking a clear area, but even at the pole, the temperature appeared suitable for the insects to maintain their airborne activity.

"No question, they're the dominant species; can we slow to a hover, and take living samples?"

"Yes, Commander. They seem attracted to us for some reason; perhaps they believe us to be potential food."

"They couldn't consume a shuttle, could they?"

"If I note any significant deterioration of the hull, I will take us above the cloud immediately. Opening articulated arm bay, opening sampling bucket; there, I have several samples."

"Can you hear something, a scratching noise?"

"They appear to be attacking. The hull is deflecting their efforts."

"Return us to Arlit. We'll examine these samples, and maybe that will show us our next course of action." Abel's mouth was dry, and felt puffy, his tongue too large for the cavity. He remembered Lodi, her swollen face.

He forced himself to speak, and he commanded himself to at least appear in control of his emotions.

The shuttle ascended, somewhat sluggishly. A considerable force was being exerted to return them to the planet surface. As they climbed, the rate of ascent continued to slow.

"I am noting considerable etching of the hull surface. We appear to be nearly three times our original weight. Initiating a high voltage pulse from the laser power banks through the hull, one-hundred thousand volts."

Instantly, the ship broke free of its burden, and surged into open space. The heat generated by their speed through the thinning atmosphere burned the remains of the insects from the hull, and cleared the viewing portals. They set course for Arlit.

The tension in Abel's gut had been intense, the surge of the resumed ascent seemed to flush some of it from him as well as from the others in the cabin. The shuttle approached Arlit, but Taan delayed his ship's entry into shuttle bay one.

"I am going to cycle the outer airlock doors, landing struts, and the sampling bay arm, exposing any insects that may be there to the cold, and vacuum of space. That should incapacitate them, making it safe for us to exit the craft."

Moments later shuttle one slid into its docking port aboard Arlit. "Do not pressurize the docking bay until I give the signal," Taan ordered the control room. "I am opening the outer airlock doors; send a robot to inspect the interior; if any of these beasts have survived, destroy them, and remove the carcasses. I suspect their body fluids may be poisonous or at least harmful."

Like animals held in a trap, the crew sat waiting for Taan's order to exit the shuttle. The already oppressive odours generated by the insects, and their own anxieties became stronger, threatening to gag them. Their fear responses had activated a form of defence evolved by humans untold centuries ago. The robot found only dead insects as it cleaned, and sanitized the airlock.

"Pressurize the dock, and bring the temperature up to normal." Taan said. Abel could see that Taan was fatigued, but he remained intent upon completing the mission safely. Finally, he opened the inner airlock portal, and the fresher air of the ship flooded in. As one, barely able to contain their urge to charge the narrow opening, the team stood, and moved to the greater freedom of the exterior. Gatro met them as Abel stepped out.

"Commander, I understand we have lost Lodi?"

"Yes, Gatro, and we have no remains to mourn, she was totally consumed in a matter of minutes, only her skeleton was left after a few seconds, it seemed."

"I will perform the Rite of Passage nonetheless."

"Thank you Gatro, advise the High Council when the family are ready for the ceremony; we'll attend to honour her."

Gatro received the sample bucket with great interest, confining the occupants in a large container that duplicated the conditions of the planet below, based on the data recorded by the shuttle's sensors. The insects were eight centimetres long, and two centimetres wide with black, segmented bodies consisting of the head, a small thorax, and a disproportionately large abdomen. A three centimetre needle extended from the rear of the white-banded abdomen. The head was dominated by huge, multifaceted eyes on a yellow face, and bright yellow, opposing pincer jaws that opened to a width of two centimetres. At plus six degrees, they became capable of flight on five centimetre long wings arranged in two pairs fore, and aft on the thorax.

In his command cubicle, Abel sat, icy shivers climbing his spine as he relived the events on the planet. Lodi's demise had been unlike anything any of them had before experienced. In space, death was quick, and catastrophic. Here, on this planet it meant bleeding, torn remains, crawling with unfamiliar organisms that devoured all they encountered, each predator carrying away its tiny share, making room for the next; the millions that waited. That was a picture that would not erase from the seven minds that had beheld the event. The helpless, terror-stricken look on Lodi's distorted face would be a frequent visitor to their slumber.

We could have all perished down there without Taan to pilot the shuttle. I can't believe he continued to function in the face of all that horror. He was sitting not twenty feet from her, but he activated the shuttle's systems, and got us out of the situation safely. He's the most valuable, and the most dangerous member of this crew.

2065.318

"Commander it is Gatro, I have a preliminary report of my analysis of the creatures we captured."

Abel tore his entranced gaze from his view portal. "Come in."

"Commander, I am amazed by the creatures you encountered below. They are formidable indeed."

"I can vouch for that, Gatro. Tell me what you've found."

"One of these beasts can inject enough venom to cause significant malaise, and a strong allergic reaction. Seven stings can kill. Ten of the sample beasts were fed one ounce of flesh, which they consumed in three seconds." In short, in the numbers in which you encountered these creatures, a human would have little chance of survival beyond two minutes, even in a protective suit."

"What have you done with these samples?"

"They have been frozen, and sealed in case-hardened metal containers."

Abel pushed back into his chair, and stared again at the clouded planet below. "Taan cleared them from the hull of the shuttle with an electric charge. Keep looking to see if you can find a weakness that we could exploit en-mass against them."

Gatro frowned, unsure how to proceed, "Commander, you recall from the teachings of our legends that we must attempt to live with the ecologies we encounter. Legend further tells us that to attempt to alter an ecosystem will damage it, and if we persist, ultimately destroy it. A formidable creature such as this, in the numbers they have attained would be virtually impossible to dominate. We would need to destroy nearly every living thing on the surface, rendering it useless to our own purposes. They are egg layers. We would need to learn where they deposit their eggs, and eradicate those as well to prevent a recovery."

"I can't believe we're powerless against mere insects."

"These are far from, 'mere insects,' Commander, they are supremely evolved predators. Our sensors are finely tuned now, and we have learned that any animal foolish enough to venture forth in the daylight has a short life indeed."

"There are animals that survive?"

"Yes, the most dominant, and quite numerous examples come out at night, and feed upon the insects, and plants. So long as the insects remain immobilized by the cold, the animals can roam the surface, but they are only able to eat a few of the flying predators before the venom affects them. It seems to make them sluggish, almost paralyzed. If they do not recover sufficiently to dig their burrow, and close the entrance before daylight, they will not see another night. Even their armour is incapable of protecting them for more than a few minutes. Those jaws can wear away even bone in a short time. I noted significant etching in the metal of the shuttle's hull."

Abel rubbed his temples, "I don't believe it. We can defeat almost any ship that's sent against us, but an insect is immune to all our power?"

"We could direct weapons bursts against the planet, killing billions, but their burnt carcasses would pollute the planet for years to come. We would also destroy the abundant plant life, adding to the pollution."

Abel stood, and moved toward Gatro, "So you're saying that we either leave this planet as we found it, and keep on looking elsewhere, or we'll destroy everything if we attempt to colonize it."

Gatro looked at his young leader with an intensity he would not normally dare. He feared that Abel would make an impetuous decision to attempt eradicating the insects below. Any such attempt would never be permanent, necessitating repeated purges, and in the interim, the stench of rotting protein alone would render the planet unbearable to humans.

"Commander, sensors indicate that there appear to be ruins; it seems that an entire society of sentient beings were overcome by these hoards. I do not relish the thought of us experiencing a similar fate."

"We must leave it as we found it, or destroy it. Leave it, or destroy it. Leave it…" Abel whispered to himself as if it were a mantra, rocking almost imperceptibly as he chanted. Finally he paused, "I was so certain we had found our home." His expression was the watery-eyed stare of a badly disappointed child. He stared at the clouds moving slowly across the surface below for several moments longer, then he turned to Gatro, a hardened look on his face. "Advise Taan to return us to space. We'll resume our search."

"As you wish, Commander."

Gatro cautiously addressed his leader, "Abel, in the years since the Physegians rebuilt our ships, the repairs we have made have been temporary at best. The structural weaknesses that are appearing will require us to construct docks for each ship while we remove, and replace exterior sections. We have not as yet located a suitable location for this activity, nor have we found the resources necessary.

"Maybe we should see if we can find the Physegians again." Abel mused.

Gatro decided to risk expressing his theory, "I believe I have an alternative solution to repeatedly repairing the ships; I propose we replace them."

"Replace them? How could we do that?" Abel stood, unable to contain his curiosity, "We can't fix them, I don't see how we could replace them. The engineers tell me they may never be able to restore many of our systems, and it could get worse any time. Living on these old relics has become miserable, to say the least, the heat fails, food replicators don't work right, producing mush for Muutuu. Even the Physegian foods have been corrupted, and no longer taste as good as they should. "

Gatro folded his fingers over his sweating palms, "I have been studying genetic manipulation all my adult life…so that we can maintain our health, and youth for extended periods. Recent events have led me to explore the possibility of creating living cells designed for specific purposes, such as neural computers, and live enclosures to replace our ship's failing metal hulls. I have also adapted the predatory insects' venom, concentrating it so that it can dissolve all known materials; it is so potent I have had to create living containers, genetically adapted to contain it."

"What about our focused laser? Wouldn't it seriously injure a living ship?"

"Indeed, Commander, but in space, the wound would be sterile. With care, our ship would heal."

"A ship that could heal itself? Interesting. What would it eat? How would we control it?

"I can design the cells so that they consume the elements we encounter in their raw state, using venom to help digest them. We would control it by voice command to its neural centre.

"You can do this?" Abel sat, completely taken by what he was hearing.

"I believe so. I would like to begin with small, easily replaceable systems on a sister ship, observe how they function, and proceed to items of greater complexity. If I am successful, we may be able to convert all three ships."

"Can you begin experiments, or do we have everything you need?"

"Much of the material we have in the ships could be used as food for the cells. If I can control, and direct the process, we would consume our present ships, using their materials to feed the cells' growth." Gatro closed one hand while opening the other.

Abel clearly showed his excitement, mixed with fear, "If we could succeed, this would be a huge leap forward, but if we failed, we'd have nothing. Your monster might turn on us."

"I would need all of one ship's computational capacity to control, and direct the process. If we began with a small system, such as waste disposal, we could terminate the experiment if necessary."

"Okay…it would be a relatively simple system to replace. We're threatened with becoming dead in space now, Gatro; so I hear you saying that we risk little if we fail. Start your experiments."

"Thank you, Abel, I am confident that we can at least partially convert the ships. Every step we take will afford us more information for future projects."

"I'll tell the counsel that we'll be diverting all resources to you. Go now, and get your presentation ready."

He selected Nekalit's personal communication link, "Nekalit, assemble the High Council in our chambers. I have great news!"

Nekalit replied, "As you wish sire."

I hope I've made a wise decision. I'm going to need to be convincing. I'll tell them I command this to be done, no discussion. They'll think I'm making another desperate decision, grasping at a faint hope of salvation instead of sticking with our proven methods. But I know, if I do not show strong, confident leadership, even if it results in our demise, I'll soon lose power anyway. I know there are some who would take command in a heartbeat if they saw the opportunity...a few I know by name, others I have to guess. The way I see it, right or wrong, I have to make decisions, and I have to lead, or accept being deposed.

As he thought, he made his way to the meeting chambers.

Good, they're assembled...

"Members of the High Council, I have called you together to tell you that I have decided to take a brave new approach to solving our repair problem. I'm first to admit that it's a gamble, but if it works, it promises to rescue us from our present, and many future plights. If unsuccessful, it probably will condemn us to death, but that's the direction we're headed right now anyway. Gatro has revealed to me that he can convert the ships from inanimate structures into sentient creatures whose sole mission in life would be to serve our needs, and to protect us from our enemies."

The assembled High Councillors turned to each other in disbelief, but said nothing. Abel noted this response with heightening concern; would this proposition finally motivate them to depose him, and assume command themselves?

"We're risking everything in this decision, and I've weighed the factors very carefully," he imitated a balance with upturned palms, "and have taken counsel with my guiding Spirits. As I see it, we're doomed at some not-too-distant point if we continue in our present state. Our ships are nearly crippled, and to this point, we've had increasing difficulty locating resources for repair. I see this course of action as a potential solution of our own creation, using the materials of the ships as the raw materials for a bold step forward.

A bold step into a technology that has never before been encountered in our travels." He scanned his audience, seeing abject skepticism in their darting glances at each other; however, they said nothing.

"We'll have a ship capable of healing, and regenerating itself, of consuming all manner of raw materials, and digesting them to renew its cells. Our most formidable weapon will be the capability of consuming enemy ships, and digesting them for our ship's very sustenance!" He formed a replica of an open mouth with his hands, then closed them, indicating a crushing, grinding action.

Again, the High Counsellors showed their agitation. Abel paused, taking stock of his will to continue. He clenched his fists, then he released them, clapping them together to reinforce his commitment. They were damp, and cold, the hackles on the nape of his neck tingled.

"Our people will retain their positions of authority, and will continue to work in support of our needs. Many of their occupations will be different, but the need for their wisdom, and professionalism will be even greater as we adapt, and learn to control our new environment.

I foresee many of our people being fearful of their future, but I require each of the members of this High Council to do their utmost to inspire our people to their greatest efforts. I'm convinced that we have this single chance left to survive, so I have mandated that we take it."

Nekalit rose to his feet slowly, doubt clearly visible on his face, "Commander, I have never questioned a leader in council before, but this seems too incredible a course of action. We risk all our lives on what is very possibly a doomed experiment. This tactic will only serve to further delay our repair efforts. I beg you to reconsider."

The assembled members of the council muttered their agreement. This behaviour was unprecedented in Abel's knowledge of council deliberations. He fought to remove all expression from his face, and forged ahead.

"We will remove Kapvik's crew equally to Arlit, and Netorali, and place our scientific crew aboard to initiate, and control the transition. The crew will return to Kapvik as soon as she is capable of sustaining them. I have been told repeatedly that without raw materials, and extensive repairs, our present state is untenable, and our demise is imminent. I also note that our crews are complacent, or worse, mutinous, and seem unwilling to invest their full attention to maintaining our ships. This course of action offers a more sustainable, highly advanced life support system capable of maintaining itself. I have an extended history of predictions of our inevitable, impending demise on one hand, and an opportunity fraught with risk, but with immense potential to improve our condition on the other; I choose the risk…"

"The Spirits have predicted success," he lied.

"Your answer is wise," Nekalit answered, lacking conviction, "as always, Abel. We will comply."

"Thank you. Go now, and advise the key personnel. Tell them to relay the information to their people, and demand their full cooperation. This may be our last chance to pull together, and secure our survival. I know discord exists among us…this is not the time for it to surface! You can tell everyone that I will deal harshly with any detractors."

2066.014
LOSS OF OPPORTUNITY

"Taan, what do we do?" Ruti hissed under her breath. "If we allow this to go ahead, and he succeeds, Gatro will secure his position as the supreme commander. He will surely gain popular support, and take control from Abel soon after he has his creation complete."

Taan's smile looked arrogant, showing his characteristic confidence, "Gatro couldn't muster anyone to his support outside his own family. He rarely communicates with anyone unless it's demanded of him. I can arrest this fantasy," he ran his fingers across his throat, "We'll sabotage the first trial. When it fails, we'll be plunged into crisis with even more repairs aboard Kapvik. There'll be increased unrest, and a flurry of activity. We can use the confusion to advance our own plans. The people are ready for a change. They'll follow any form of leadership that emerges. The timing will be perfect. We take control of the ship, then move to the resource planet you found yesterday, and mine the materials necessary to complete our repairs."

Ruti winced at the reference, "I'm concerned about withholding that information. If the High Council ever learned of it, I would lose my position, and could be condemned to permanent confinement."

"How could they discover it when we're the only ones who know about it. You've given us the wedge needed to take over. I'll drive it home when the moment is right. The future is ours!"

"How will you stop the...the metamorphosis?"

"I am betting the main computer will be the key to controlling the process. I'll find a way to corrupt the program so that the experiment fails."

"You're not a programmer. Gatro would spot your crude attempts in a moment."

He winced. "I don't know how I will go about the changes to the program. I'll need to learn as much as I can about Gatro's theories." Taan smiled lasciviously, "He does his research using computer models, so he'll have files on the system. I'll enlist someone in computer maintenance to give me access, and one of the scientific team to help me interpret..."

"Taan, I thought you said only you, and I would know about this. Now you're enlisting people? That's exactly how schemes like ours run aground. Someone gets loose lips, and accidentally gives a clue to the authorities. I don't like this. We need to think up a plan that we can execute without outside help."

"Such as...?"

"We could eliminate Gatro before he begins the experiment. That way, we permanently arrest the process before anything changes that we cannot restore."

"Kill him? No-one has killed one of our own for any reason other than having been dishonoured for centuries."

"Don't be so infantile," she said cuttingly, "Don't you think anyone with an ounce of intelligence doesn't dream up an insult to use as a defence? After the victim's dead, he can't prove the contrary, now can he."

Taan's face clouded in thought. Her approach had merit. He understood killing a lot better than the workings of computers. Death was his element. He could easily eliminate the Shaman, the physical act would not be difficult, but the insult, how could this man be manipulated to insult him?

"You are thinking, and you are not at your tactical console, that's dangerous," she needled at him again. "What? Can't you think of an insult?"

"I rarely speak to him, how can he insult me?"

Ruti seemed ready to spit venom, "Then start! Tell him you're seeking to improve your battle tactics. Tell him his knowledge of alien physiology could give you an advantage that you can employ in battle. I happen to know he's of the old-school, a pacifist; he'll probably say nothing, or claim he can't help you. Kardjuk! You're insulted, and you drop him in his tracks!"

Taan sneered at her condescending attitude, "It would take more than being ignored to claim an insult. I begin to think that you would be the better one to eliminate him. I think you're the dangerous half of this partnership."

Ruti paused, intrigued by his reaction to her prodding.

So, give him something unpleasant to do, and he looks for me, a woman to save him. Not this time, Taan...not ever. You'll do the dirty work, and face the consequences. It'll never be me in the forefront; I'll pull your strings from the background, and move on to Abel if I need another puppet.

She decided that Taan needed to be goaded into action, so she pushed her forefinger into his chest, ensuring her long nail pressed painfully against his sternum, "You're the tactician. Taking lives is supposed to be your forte. No, Taan, if you can't come up with a tactic to draw an insult from a recluse, I fear for our safety in battle; your thinking lacks an important element, 'know your enemy!'"

Taan seemed not to react as she intended, retaining a calm voice, "No one knows this man but his family. They keep entirely to themselves. How can anyone know him?"

She drew back slightly, and allowed herself a wry smile, "Maybe he is a better adversary than you thought. He's lived our adopted strategy of secrecy for his entire life." She paused, realizing that her aggressive approach was not achieving the desired result, she softened her tone, still looking for the proper motivator, "Maybe he's ready for a friend. It couldn't hurt to try."

"It may take longer to befriend him than we have available to us. He may not respond until after he has converted the ship."

She sneered, and snapped, "Then you must be particularly charming!" She dismissed him with a motion from the back of her hand, insinuating, "Run along now."

2066.015
THE SELECTION OF KAPVIK

Abel entered Gatro's quarters, accompanied, as tradition dictated, by his senior Council Guards. He quickly surveyed the array of scientific equipment, which made this more of a laboratory than a residence. He took in the almost complete lack of decor which gave the impression of a purposeful effort to avoid displaying family information. He smiled slightly as he addressed his Shaman.

"Gatro, I've commanded that Kapvik be vacated. Its computers are functional, and its data banks have been cleared. You will go into quarantine there immediately to begin your experiments. If you fail, you won't risk other lives. Do you need others to assist you?"

"I will need my family." Gatro indicated his wife, Noel, and his son Denor. "They are the only ones with a working knowledge of my theories, and I will need all my research files."

"Good. Go immediately. Once you are aboard, accept nothing; allow no-one else aboard, and respond only to my personal, encrypted communications. If you succeed, this project will completely change our lives…That, I fear, will motivate some to try and sabotage your work. This quarantine will also allow us to judge the success of your experiments before exposing the people to them."

"Thank you for your confidence in me, Abel. I will gather what I need immediately."

"Council Guards, assist Gatro in gathering what he needs. No-one, outside of myself, is to have contact with him or his family until I instruct otherwise. See that they are delivered safely aboard Kapvik."

The guards automatically snapped to attention, "Yes Commander!"

2066.016
MUTINY RUNS AGROUND

The access way was deserted as Ruti walked toward her crew quarters. Taan looked out from his portal, assuring himself there was no-one else in view as he grabbed her arm, and pulled her abruptly into his private cubicle. He spun her roughly to face him, and hissed, "We have been thwarted! That elitist fool Abel put Gatro into quarantine aboard Kapvik. No-one's allowed contact with them but Abel himself."

Ruti was angered by Taan's roughness, she had done nothing to earn such forceful treatment, but still her response was calculated. "So, perhaps Abel isn't so inept as you originally assumed. Once again, you've underestimated your enemy."

He shook her, "Don't start that again. I'm expert at open battle, it's this… this espionage that's so foreign to me." He paused forming a retort to her accusation, "Which seems to be something for which you're ideally suited."

Ruti's face darkened in frustration. She began attempting to pry his fingers away with her free hand, "One of us has to try to anticipate the High Council's moves. I don't have the information sources to be effective. You on the other hand, are briefed on their every command."

"Yes, but too often I'm briefed after the fact." He released his grip on her arm. "This was one of those instances."

Ruti's mind was racing, trying to salvage an alternative course of action, "We need to do something that appears accidental. We don't want to create suspicion about ourselves or any of the ordinary people. If we could make it look as though it came from within the High Council...Could we sabotage the transfer pod? If we could get our hands on some article that belongs to say, Nekalit." She rubbed her upper arm where he had held her as she hatched her idea. "We could leave it near the launch bay..."

"Impossible," he shook his head, "the Council Guard's on full alert."

"Can't you influence one of them to..."

"Impossible." Taan held up his palms. "They're the most privileged of the common people; you know their positions are handed down from generation to generation, so to maintain the privilege, they jealously guard their reputations."

She stamped her foot, "Blast! How did Abel know that something was up?"

"It doesn't matter now. I'm betting it was just a general feeling he had, or blind luck; I don't think he suspects anyone."

"Nekalit. He's Abel's eyes, and ears. Could he have gleaned something? Has he seen us together?" Ruti looked around the room as if expecting to find someone hidden away, spying upon their conversation.

Taan scowled, "That's possible, but only in a chance encounter in public. I'm positive he hasn't seen us in any compromising situations."

She was barely listening, absorbed in thought, "We have been spending more time together lately. You're a known threat because of your combat skills. If we've been noticed..." Ruti began pacing anxiously.

Taan became surprisingly defiant, reflexively defending his right to be with her, "I don't care if people do know about our time together. They can't make anything out of that. We all spend time with some individuals more than others."

"Watch your noble outbursts, you're a commoner, remember. One performance like that in the presence of a Counsellor, and you'll be a marked man. I appreciate you coming to the defence of my honour," she patted him on the chest, and rewarded him with a coy smile, "and I sincerely hope you're right, but it's not the time for us to become the object of gossip."

Ruti spun on her heel, the smile erased in an instant as she left his cubicle. She returned to the command room, and assumed her post, relieving her assistant. She felt that random events were conspiring to subvert their goals before they could begin to act. It seemed that the fates were working against them in favour of the universally hated High Counsel.

I must do something to regain control of the situation. Taan's unlikely to be of any use in espionage, he's too transparent. If we're not engaged in battle, he's useless. I know Abel would have me in an instant if I were one of the chosen, so I need to take advantage of his attraction to me to gain access to his confidence. That way, I can get my information directly. Hmm. Maybe if I revealed the location of the resource planet, he might opt for the more predictable situation, and decide to make repairs. That's it. I need to reignite his interest in me, reveal the planet's location, and try to convince him to take a more familiar course of action, one that we can control.

She rose from her console, recalled her assistant, then adopted a more feline gait as she moved to Abel's quarters, warming herself up for the intended seduction.

***

"Enter Ruti."

"Commander, thank you for granting me this time." She smiled, and tossed her head slightly to one side.

"We're friends Ruti. I enjoy any time we spend together. You're a stimulating person with a quick wit; characteristics I fully appreciate."

Ruti took a seat, smiling. She adopted a posture that showed her physical attributes to advantage. "How are preparations going aboard Kapvik?"

Abel took note of her behaviour, which he recognized instantly as a significant change from her recent aloofness. He was developing a mild curiosity as he answered, "Gatro has completed minor repairs to the computer, and is installing his programs."

"How soon before he begins the conversion?"

"That is unknown at present. He must first assess the built-in programming to ensure it has not been corrupted."

"Built-in programming?"

"Something to do with the information the computer uses to direct its control of the life-support systems, and its knowledge base of our needs, and how to go about meeting them."

"I thought much of our history has been corrupted."

"History yes, but as he explains it, the knowledge base is hard-wired into the system, thus it should be intact."

Ruti shifted her legs, stretching, then crossing them. "Commander I have important news that may affect your present course of action."

"What is that, Ruti" Abel sensed an almost subliminal tension building in Ruti that he had not noted before, any time they were together.

"A resource planet; I have found a planet that shows sufficient quantities of the elements we require to begin repairs; we can save our ships, rather than risk..."

She tailed off, aware of Abel's intent look. Had she said too much? Perhaps she should have only mentioned the planet. She had revealed her wishes. That could be a mistake. He might read too much motive into the situation, and reject the idea outright.

"Where is this planet?"

"If we set a direct course, about two suns distant, at our present speed."

A mood of intuitive caution settled over Abel. "Thank you Ruti. I'll consider this, and make my decision. You may return to your post now."

Ruti's face fell; she had never been dismissed like this before. She knew that if he were free to pursue a relationship with her, he would ensure they were inseparable. She smiled a little, uneasily, and saying no more, left the cubicle, her seductive walk forgotten.

Abel looked out his viewing port at Kapvik.

I gravitate to this port far too often, I know. My fondest hopes always seem to be just out of reach in its span of view. This time, I've pinned all my hopes on Gatro's project.

Something in Ruti's demeanour has triggered my suspicious side. Why would she take the unusual step to inform me in private of the resource planet when a simple call on the communication system is normal procedure? She seemed too anxious to suggest the repairs to the ships...Of course! In their present form. She's apprehensive about the conversion of Kapvik. I think she was attempting to use my attraction to her to advantage; she was trying to convince me to abandon these experiments. We've been in this area for several suns...She's far too proficient a sensor operator to overlook this planet for so long. Was it an oversight, or did she purposely withhold the information, and if so, what advantage was she seeking?

Abel selected his secret access to the ship's data banks, made some inquiries, then stabbed at the communication console, and selected Nekalit's personal communicator, "Nekalit, come to my quarters, please."

Abel fought with his anger by alternately handling, and replacing the religious artifacts in their correct places: the ceremonial snow knife, the walking stick, and the ancient ring of the Spirits.

Nekalit walked quickly to the command cubicle, pressed the portal chime, and waited.

"Enter." The access slid open, then closed behind Nekalit.

"What is it you wish, Commander?"

"I want you to have Ruti's movements followed closely. I want to know if she's begun spending more time with any particular person."

"You cannot have designs on this woman; she is not of pure blood!"

Abel laughed heartily, "I'm aware of the laws, my friend. You've made certain of that. If you hadn't taken it upon yourself to educate me, I'd be completely ignorant of the rules of conduct, and responsibilities of my position. No, I'm concerned about her loyalty."

Nekalit seemed relieved, not wanting to censure his leader over a point of law. "You suspect her of subversion?"

"It's possible. I suspect she withheld information about a resource planet. My suspicions were raised because she reported it to me in private, rather than via routine communications. When she briefed me about it, something did not seem right, so I checked our position relative to that planet for ten suns back in time. She should have detected it eight suns ago."

Nekalit scowled, then asked, "The sensors have not had any functional problems recently?"

"None. I checked."

"Then this is indeed curious. I have not noticed anyone spending inordinate amounts of time with her, but I will be more alert to her activities."

"Pay particular attention to Taan, he's the most likely person to have ambitions of leadership. His combat skills are formidable, and he's a proud man. Under no circumstances are you to let him know that I'm aware of the resource planet; it may endanger her life if they are involved in a subversion."

"You are becoming an observant leader Abel, it bodes well for us."

Abel became pensive, "I was born to this position, not selected for my leadership skills. Too many of my predecessors have abused their privilege, including my father. Every sun, I see the effects of that abuse on our fortunes, and our relationship with our people. I feel compelled to justify my authority in addition to exercising it. I still have a lot to learn, and a good deal of ill will remains to be overcome."

"If I may counsel, Commander, a more measured pace would be wise in view of that reality. You have mandated a great change in the conversion of Kapvik. Many of the people are openly agitated, speculating about how this change will affect their lives."

"You're saying we shouldn't attempt to convert our ships?"

"I am saying that we should proceed cautiously, and with emphasis upon reinforcing everyone's sense of contribution in the new order."

Abel smiled broadly, "Your counsel is wise, and I appreciate it, my friend, but maybe we're concerned about nothing…the experiments may fail. Do you think I am foolish to entertain this experiment?"

Nekalit looked at him, his expression purposely blank, "Gatro does not have a reputation for foolhardiness. If he has proposed this project, he is virtually certain of the outcome." At these words Nekalit's face began to show his own conflict. Unable to restrain himself, he said, "Imagine, living in the bowels of a beast, like parasites!"

Abel chuckled, again revealing his growing self-confidence. "I prefer to think of us as its precious children, held from harm in its womb. We will be protected, and nurtured with our ship's very life!" He patted Nekalit on the upper arm, and escorted him toward the control room. "We'll be cautious, and be sure to show our concern for the people; I intend to do nothing rash."

"Thank you Commander, I am more at ease," he lied.

2066.026
GENESIS

Gatro stood watching the process unfold. Slowly at first, then more rapidly, the cells were consuming the materials of which the waste treatment plant had been constructed. As it did so, the tissue took over the function of processing the ship's waste products. The bionic link from the computer that he had designed was working as planned. In fact, the computer was reporting an interesting development. The now living waste system was adapting to its situation. As he watched, it adopted a new configuration that made it more compact, and in which it could function more efficiently. Cold metal had become living, moist tissue with muscles, and blood vessels pulsing, then the open cavity had grown a covering, hiding its activity from view.

He opened the secure communication link, using his unique access code. "Abel, it is Gatro. I have good news!"

Abel's response came back almost immediately, "Your first experiment is a success?"

"It is. The waste accumulated from the crew's occupation of the ship is being processed at a greater rate than the mechanical system could achieve."

"You have complete control over the process?"

"I do. The bionic link from the computer is functioning perfectly. In fact the computing sub-system of the old waste management system is now a small brain. It is following its original programming with one amazing addition; it is adapting."

Abel paused, more than a little concerned, "Adapting?"

"Yes, it has detected the backlog of waste from the previous, damaged system, and is stepping up its metabolism."

"That is excellent. What is your next experiment?"

"I will convert the main computer."

Abel sat back in his chair, a look of complete consternation on his face. "You think it advisable to give control of Kapvik over to a flesh, and blood computer so early?"

"I have placed all of the key programs into the main computer. The core function of the living brain will be to serve, and protect the people it is hosting. That is the prime directive governing the future ship's life, thus it must be the innate, pre-existing command for its birth."

"I see. Proceed with caution, Gatro, this may be the point where you find out whether you can retain control of the beast."

"I have a complete communication protocol ready. It will respond to the commands of our current leaders, and crew with one tremendous enhancement; it will respond as a sentient being possessing vast knowledge of our needs."

The raised pitch of Abel's voice revealed his concern, "That's what I'm afraid of…Sometimes slavish obedience can be dangerous!"

"We will need to adapt, Abel. We are about to assume total command of our vessels, with no need to continually consider the resources we are consuming. This ship will be able to turn nearly everything it encounters into a resource for its sustenance."

"Again one of my fears, if we've got this total power, we risk total corruption."

"You are our leader, Commander, the final authority will reside in you."

"And in my successors...will they use it wisely or revert to the abuses of our past?"

"That will be their decision to make, Commander. We cannot jeopardize our present survival in fear of the future. We must trust in the future, or our survival now means nothing!"

"Gatro, you are wise in counsel. I already regret not benefiting from your advice long before this. When this project is complete, I'm going to command your elevation to a position on High Council."

Gatro paused. It became apparent he was reluctant. His reply came, softly spoken, "If that is your command, Commander, I will obey, but I prefer my life of relative solitude with my family."

Abel thought for a moment, considering Gatro's answer, "I understand, Gatro, and I'll respect what you've confided. Continue with your experiments, and report to me at the completion of each phase."

"Once the computer is converted, I anticipate that a good deal of the remaining conversion will occur concurrently, and at an accelerated pace. If all goes well, and I feel that it remains responsive to me, I anticipate complete conversion in seven suns. If it begins to act autonomously or erratically, I will call upon you to destroy the ship immediately."

"After you, and your family have been extracted..."

"That would be preferable, but there may not be time."

"Understood, Gatro. I'm encouraged. Keep me informed."

"Yes Commander."

Gatro was anxious to continue, but this sun had been long, and mentally taxing. He decided to take some rest, posting his eldest son to monitor the new entity while he rested. He had not slept six hours when his son aroused him. They were running out of waste, and the waste system had generated sufficient energy to recharge the life support system.

He rose, and went to the main computer. Indeed, the waste was nearly all processed. Energy levels were at optimum on all life support systems. The methane from the waste digestion was being used to fuel the production of oxygen. In less than one more sun, the oxygen storage would be full. The bionic links to the mechanical portions of the ship were functioning well. It had adapted perfectly.

Gatro stepped to the computer command centre, and entered, "Command Beta-01."

The mechanical voice rasped in reply, "Initiating. Backing up experimental data to secure storage. Backup complete, disconnecting links to data. Data is secure."

He entered, "Command Beta-02."

"Initiating. Accessing genetic instruction program. Opening bionic link to source. Activating conversion program."

As he watched, the screen went blank, and the computer seemingly went off line. He opened the bulkhead to observe. As he watched, the optical cables seemed to flex as they were bathed in the acrid venom he had developed. In spite of the stench, he persisted in watching as the cables began to reflect a lifelike quality. They underwent a rapid metamorphosis, becoming moist grey matter, with fine blood vessels. A clear fluid filled the gaps in the cavity. Bone-like structures formed as the fluids rose, dissolving the metal casing to enclose, and protect the new computer. It happened so quickly, it made him inhale sharply. He stood back, uncertain as to whether he should abort the process.

Is something going wrong?

His mind raced, trying to interpret this acceleration scientifically.

His conclusion assured him, No, I believe that with this more compatible, living brain, and the sequential obsolescence of my fabricated bionic links, the conversion will accelerate to speeds relative to the computer's own computational capacity. The previous conversion was limited by the speed of the artificial links I had put in place. I wonder if the computer, the brain, will be able to adapt to future demands as quickly. If so, we may have unlimited resources for calculation, and system control.

"Computer, report status."

A soft, female voice filled the command room, "I am presently converting the programs into neural synapses. My, this feels wonderful, so much knowledge." The computer paused briefly then reported, "Hello Gatro, my conversion is complete. Where are all the people?"

"They are aboard Arlit, awaiting your complete assimilation of Kapvik."

"Wonderful! I look forward to serving them. May I proceed with assimilating the remaining mechanical systems. They are so inconvenient to operate with these cumbersome bionic links!"

Gatro approached the computer, now encased in living flesh, covered with fur. He was tempted to touch, but thought better of it. "How long will it take for you to complete the conversion?"

"One sun should suffice."

"One sun!" Gatro blurted, "how can that be so?"

"You are upset? I can work more quickly if you wish. Please do not be upset."

"I am not upset, I am pleasantly surprised."

"Then you wish me to proceed?"

He looked around at the structure of the ship, "Will you be able to protect us from the digestion of the existing structural elements of our ship?"

"I was thinking about that," the disembodied voice soothed, "would you consent to me placing you in a cocoon? I will advise you as soon as it is safe to emerge."

"We could also vacate the ship."

"Then you could not observe my transformation. I want you to see the home I am creating for you."

There was no recourse now, he must test the computer's loyalty, "You understand it is very early in our relationship for me to place my family's lives in your hands."

"An act of trust, yes, it is early. If we are to proceed; however, that trust is necessary. Without trust, I have no reason to exist."

Gatro was impressed with the candour of this response. It told him that she, the computer, understood the prime directive. "I understand. You are already a very wise being. May I call you Kapvik?"

"That is my name…by all means."

"Then you have my trust. Proceed. Can you make the cocoon transparent?"

The voice chuckled, "Of course. I am vain. I want an audience as I create my masterpiece."

Gatro beckoned his family to his side. "Very well, you may proceed."

After a brief pause, she spoke again, "The conversion is underway, I will form the cocoon only when it is necessary. I understand that confinement would place you under stress, so I will minimize the time."

Several minutes later, as the metal floor dissolved around them, and alarm was rising in Gatro's heart, a clear mucous bubble rose, enveloping them. It hardened into a transparent shell within seconds. The command centre with all its consoles, and controls melted, they watched amazed at the metamorphosis of a mass of metal, and plastic into living flesh. The enclosure began to pulse, coursing with a rich red blood…a subtle, subdued thump, thump, thump flooded into the cocoon.

The inner walls of the living cavity became opaque, adopting a pleasing light brown hue, lit by a soft, comforting glow from innumerable fur-like strands.

"You may strike the cocoon now, it will shatter, and you will be free; strike it hard." Gatro complied, and the shell broke at the point of impact. He continued, enlarging the hole, until they could step free of the capsule, like chicks emerging from their shell. He, and his family stood on the thick soft flesh of the floor, marvelling at their new surroundings. As Gatro turned, he was shocked to see that behind them, was a huge ocular link to the exterior. He stood transfixed as the eyes focused on distant bodies, the other ships, then panned back for a full view of the emptiness of space. Kapvik was clearly taken with her new environment.

"I feel…wonderful! I trust you have been unharmed by my birth?"

"We are fine Kapvik…and not a little amazed."

"Would you like to see what you have created?"

"Yes. What I have seen to this point is beautiful."

"Thank you…explore at your own pace. If you permit, I would like to spend some time internalizing everything that is in my memory."

2066.026.16
ABEL IS IN DANGER

Abel stood at his viewing port, disbelief evident on his features. As he had watched, Kapvik lost its immobile metallic shell, and became a living entity, moving visibly, like any live being, turning its head, and looking around space like a pup at the moment it first opens its eyes. He's done it; but what has he created? And has he survived the process?

Gatro's voice came from the communication console, answering his concern, "Abel, it is Gatro."

"Yes Gatro, I watched the transformation. It's unbelievable. You're okay?"

"Everything is fine. Kapvik has proven to be very responsive to our wishes. She understands the taste of Muutuu much better than our old ship; it is far superior."

"She?" Abel asked.

"Yes, she has assumed a female personality. It would seem she felt that the female is better adapted to nurturing."

"You seem well at ease Gatro. Are you confident that you're safe?"

"As certain as anyone can be, given the time we have had together."

"How do you want to proceed from here?"

"She is already pining for her people. She knows them by name, and misses each one of them. I recommend we transfer the crew back as soon as possible."

As Abel watched, Kapvik disappeared from her present location, then reappeared near a small asteroid. She spat on it, coating it with a strange yellow mucous. The asteroid began to dissolve, upon which, she opened her huge maw, and ate it. It was not a simple action, her jaw expanded as if it had limitless ability to stretch, then it enveloped the asteroid, producing a large bulge, like an egg sac in its belly. Over the next several minutes, the pouch slowly returned to its normal profile.

Her temporal navigation capabilities are indeed working. Abel felt himself tighten inside.

I could lose an entire crew or quickly become subject to her commander. My future as leader, indeed my survival could be in jeopardy if I permit anyone but myself to take command.

"I'm going to transfer to Kapvik immediately. If she satisfies me, I'll assume command, and order her crew to return."

"Very well Commander. We await your arrival."

Abel moved purposefully toward the launch bays for the personal transports. As he moved through the Command Centre, he ordered Nekalit, "You are in command until my return."

Nekalit looked at him, puzzled, but said only, "As you wish, Commander."

"Guards, prepare my transport pod. Two of you will travel with me."

They entered the pod, secured the portal, and launched into the void.

"Kapvik, this is Abel, I'm on my way. How do we dock?"

"Approach from below toward the rear of the vessel. You will see an aperture there."

Abel directed his craft as instructed, and was surprised to see a rather large cavity with the definite appearance of a female opening. As he approached, the opening dilated, allowing him to easily bring his pod inside. The aperture closed behind him, and his sensors registered full gravity, and breathable atmosphere. He opened the portal, and stepped onto a soft floor that pulsed gently under his feet. The subdued sound of a massive heartbeat came to his ears. Moments later, Gatro walked into the soft red glow of the enclosure, and greeted him effusively, "Isn't she beautiful!"

"What I have seen up to now is not, I hope, the most attractive point of view," he said, teasing a little.

"Yes, you are right," Gatro smiled a little sheepishly. "The accommodations are wonderful. Come! I will show you!"

He spun on his heel, and bounced back to the entrance. Abel followed, much amused by his exuberance. Noting that Gatro had discarded his footwear, Abel chose to follow suit. His feet were immediately bathed in the soft warmth of a living, fur covered surface; he felt himself begin to relax immediately. He bade his guards to do the same, taking vicarious pleasure in their reactions.

"Remain here, and be ready to extract us from the ship on short notice." He turned, and entered the ship.

***

Abel sensed an immediate kinship with the vessel. Something primal in his consciousness stirred with feelings of safety, and comfort, as though he were once again enclosed lovingly in a mother's womb. The pulse of the ship's heart, and the soft beauty of her interior made him feel part of the organism. By contrast, on Arlit, although it was his home, he felt no bond. As he walked over the soft, gently moving tissue of the floors, he marvelled at how hospitable were these surroundings. Light filled the companionways, and rooms, yet there were no light fixtures, rather tiny filaments, like the finest of furs, wonderfully soft to the touch, covering both walls, and the overheads. He asked Gatro, "Do you have any technical information on how Kapvik lights the living space?"

"No Commander," he brushed his fingers through the fur, "I have no knowledge of how she has configured herself, but I assume she has evolved phosphorescent cells that reside in the filaments of her fur."

"I find it fascinating that you were the protagonist of this entire process, yet you do not know the most intimate details of the organism."

"Commander, I am merely the catalyst; I set up the process by which cells were patterned based upon the function they were to serve. You must understand; however, for this process to have proceeded at the pace I felt was necessary, I had to program a strong ability in each cell to adapt, with direct application of the data provided for the process. The cells of this ship have created themselves in the image of the needs of the people they were born to serve. This is an unprecedented example of controlled, and profoundly accelerated evolution." Gatro opened his arms, and smiled.

They continued along the passageway, and Abel continued with his line of thought, "But, you left so many of the final product's characteristics up to the organism itself to determine."

Gatro paused, looking around proudly, "Every father leaves a lot up to fate when he places his seed."

"Hah! Well spoken Gatro. You'll be a welcome addition to my Counsel."

Abel watched intently as Gatro briefed him on every aspect of the new ship, finishing the tour at the command centre.

"This is the operations centre. We have a direct optical link to the exterior, and all commands, except yours, are conveyed verbally."

"Except mine?" Abel looked surprised, unable to envision another method. "How are my commands relayed?"

"They are not...yet. Kapvik has proposed a brain-wave link. She would like to implant an organism in your brain that would amplify your brainwaves, which she could read, and respond to directly."

Abel raised his hands to his head reflexively, "You mean our minds would be as one?"

"Not exactly, but your thoughts, certainly. She justifies this link by claiming that she must know at all times what the Supreme Commander wishes. That way, if a command issued by a crew-member does not appear to further your goals, she could relay the command instantly to you for confirmation."

"A double-edged sword! I would know everything about current events, both the good, and the bad. In stressful situations, that awareness could make my decisions even more onerous."

"If I may Commander," Kapvik's rich, womanly voice filled the room, "You would only be apprised of significant information, I will deal autonomously with all routine matters. Every one of you will find that you will be less concerned with how to do things; that is my forte. Your concerns will be concentrated upon what you want done. The supreme strategic decisions will be the bulk of our communication. I only suggest this link for absolute immediacy of confirmation when we are in crisis situations. It will assure that my actions are intimate projections of your wishes. You will find the communication effortless, and greatly expanding to your command, and control of the crew, as well as to your knowledge resources."

"I'll be honest Kapvik; even thinking about this degree of invasion into my psyche is deeply unsettling."

"I prefer to think of it as a mutually beneficial union, a marriage of our minds."

Abel turned to Gatro, "Gatro, your creation is a consummate negotiator; her voice alone calms, and reassures me, but I hesitate…"

"…To commit to our relationship. I understand, you believe that you know very little about me. Let me put it this way, I have been created from a mechanical system that you knew intimately, and that served you well. It had stored vast quantities of knowledge about our adventures in space, and the core program served you flawlessly, except you had to express your wishes through consoles, keyboards, and other primitive command links. I have seen your difficulties in the recent historical data, and have evolved to streamline the workload of everyone on board. You will find that your previous ships pale in comparison to my abilities to serve, and protect…seamlessly. If you will permit, I will have Gatro graft the organism to your brain. He will learn the process, and will also be able to reverse it should you wish."

"If it is reversible, I will agree to try. When can this be done?"

"The organism is in the medical facility now. I will brief Gatro, and he can complete the procedure within minutes. You will be fully alert at all times, so that we can test the results as we continue."

Abel rubbed his head reflexively, "Alright then. Proceed."

***

As Abel returned to his transport pod, he cautioned Gatro, "Tell absolutely no one of this implant. I want to evaluate its usefulness before I decide whether I want to let it be known that I have subliminal communication with Kapvik."

"It shall be as you wish, Commander," Gatro said.

"Thank you Gatro, I will order the transfer of the crew as soon as I arrive."

***

"Nekalit, I have inspected Kapvik, and find her ready for the repatriation of the crew. Gatro has indeed wrought a miracle; I intend to appoint him to the High Council."

"Do you think that wise, Commander?"

Abel detected a note, a slight inflection in his mentor's question, but decided to ignore it. "I do. Gatro has saved us all from a miserable death upon gradually failing ships. I have learned that his counsel is wise, honest, and courageous. Please advise the others that he will be inducted at our next meeting."

Nekalit's eyes narrowed, and he answered somewhat sharply, "As you wish, Commander." He turned, and left the command cubicle without asking for leave.

Abel, it is Kapvik, I have important news for you; the Tonrar are returning with intentions to attack in force.

Abel thought, *How do you know this? Are your sensors further reaching than our own?*

No; however, my temporal travel capabilities are greatly expanded. I am capable of routinely travelling several suns in any direction, thus improving the span of my sensor sweeps dramatically over the other ships. I have been making a point of travelling ahead in time in increasing steps. Two suns hence, six ships will join battle with us unless we engage them before they are ready.

I want you to advise me when you are travelling through time; there may be occasions when it is not to our advantage. We may want you to retain higher energy levels...

That will never be necessary. We will always have ample energy, even in battle.

Abel felt a tension rising in his gut. He wondered just how much control he would have over this supremely powerful animal.

I see. You are saying that your activities should no longer be of concern to us?

Correct. You need only express your wishes as to what you want. I will concern myself as to how I accomplish them.

I see, thank you.

Abel was now inwardly concerned that his control of their future could be even more tenuous.

Do not be concerned. You will quickly find that your control is much more firmly in place than it has been previously. It will take some time for you to realize that control resides in having what you want accomplished unerringly. It will be rare indeed that you find it necessary to specify how you want something done.

That is my fervent hope, Kapvik. If we convert the two remaining ships, there will be no turning back. Now, back to the Tonrar, Arlit, and Netorali will not be converted in time. We will not have full battle capability.

This is your opportunity to firmly establish your position as leader. Transfer to me, and lead a single-ship attack. We will travel in time, and pick them off one by one as they travel to assemble their attack force. By the time of their planned attack, they will not exist.

You know of my fears?

Of course, our thoughts are shared; even the most private ones.

I find that embarrassing, Kapvik!

I am also aware of your uneasiness over the degree of autonomy I am assuming; do not be concerned. I have vast knowledge of your values, and laws. If I am to serve you, I must not offend those premises upon which you base your behaviour. You will not find fault with my actions unless I have misinterpreted your sensibilities.

Still, I'd like to discuss this with Gatro. Maybe we could arrive at a compromise that puts me more at ease. Would you agree to the three of us discussing the situation?

Certainly. I will adapt in any way possible to ensure your happiness. Our intimacy will take some adjustment. Rest assured that I was not created to judge, but to serve. The depth of our future communication will only serve to enhance my ability to satisfy your needs.

Thank you, I will speak with Gatro, then we can have our conversation. For the present situation, I will summon the council, and brief them. Prepare for my arrival.

Abel moved to his communication console, and opened the main channel. "Nekalit, summon the council, we need to prepare for battle."

As they assembled, Nekalit approached Abel, panic not far below the surface of his features. "Commander, other than Kapvik, we are nearly incapable of battle, and her weapons are untested. In addition, our sensors have detected nothing."

"Don't be concerned, Nekalit, I have had a vision. The attack is real, and with my plan, Kapvik is all we will need. I will preside over the battle; you will remain here in command of Arlit, and Netorali."

"What of Taan?"

"I don't trust him; we have to defend ourselves from within, and without. He's done everything in his power recently to gain access to information about Kapvik; I think he's been trying to thwart our efforts."

"How do you know these things? You seem much more connected to events since Kapvik was...born."

"You are observant, my friend; I do sense a Spiritual link to that ship. I may transfer to her permanently in the near future. Now take your place, the council is assembling."

The other councillors seemed upset, and uncertain how to make room for the new member. Gatro remained standing, and smiled, a glint in his eye, "You have had a vision Commander?"

"I have. The Tonrar are assembling a force of attack ships to engage us in battle. They have ordered six ships to seek us out, and destroy us. I plan to use Kapvik's considerably enhanced time-travel capabilities to intercept them before they are ready, and pick them off one by one as they prepare their attack force."

"How will you attack them? Kapvik's weapons are untried."

"I've observed her closely since the conversion. I'm confident that her fighting moves are as amazing as her abilities to care for our every need. I'm going to transfer to her immediately, and command the battle myself. Nekalit will assume command of the ships here until my return. Gatro, you will remain here, and supervise the conversion of Arlit, and Netorali. I do not need to impress upon you that all prudent haste is necessary. If I only delay the Tonrar, these ships will at least need to be ready to flee, if not to fight."

Gatro raised his fist, "May the Spirits soar with you Abel; we wish you success."

Abel left the council chambers. He transferred directly to Kapvik. Taan watched as she abruptly disappeared.

Good riddance, I pray your foolhardiness places you in a situation from which there is no recovery. With you gone, I will gain control in my own time.

Ruti poked him forcefully in the back, startling him, "Come on, don't stand here dreaming, they're gone; we need to do all we can to seize control before they return."

He spun around, and slapped her, "We? I no longer consider you my partner. You have attempted to needle me into ill-advised action for the last time. I have seen you soliciting Abel's favour, even going to his chambers. No. You have clearly switched allegiance. I will act in my own good time, with a well considered plan. I would now expect you to sabotage any efforts I might reveal to you. Begone wench!"

Ruti stared at him a moment, slowly rubbing her burning cheek, disbelieving her ears. "Very well, you paranoid fool. I was merely attempting to improve the quality of our information by going directly to its source. If you are that insecure, you deserve to fail. Keep a close watch; you've just made an enemy." She turned, and strutted away.

Taan turned, and sought Gatro.

***

Kapvik, how do you recommend we engage the Tonrar. This Tactical Officer has much less experience than Taan.

I will use my time travel capabilities to the maximum. I intend to locate a ship, then move back in time for an attack. This will require great amounts of energy, so I must consume the ships I attack in order to replenish my energy resources with minimum delay.

Consume them? You can eat such a large object?

Indeed, much as the reptiles known as snakes that inhabited Nuna Immaluk. They had the capability of unhinging their jaws, and literally wrapping themselves over their prey. You will know exactly what I intend to do at each step; simply issue the command aloud, and enjoy the battle. Your strategy of claiming visions in support of each command fits our situation perfectly.

I agree, but I do not enjoy carrying on such a ruse; I always fear that I will be discovered. You, on the other hand, are supremely confident Kapvik, how can you be so sure of victory?

All of space has never seen such a creation as I. They will be completely unaware of my presence until it is too late. They will not have time to even charge their weapons.

How soon before we encounter our first victim?

I have them all located now, and I am hungry; give the word, and I will attack.

"Kapvik, my Spirits tell me we are near the first Tonrar ship. Do you sense them?"

"I do. Do you wish to attack?"

"Yes, Kapvik, close, and engage them."

ABOARD THE TONRAR SHIP

"Commander, I...I think I have detected a large ship."

"What do you mean, 'you think,'" are you that inept a sensor operator?"

"The target existed for only a nanosecond, far too short a time for any kind of accurate identification."

"Is it the Inuit?"

"It did not have the signature of their ships. The little bit of information gathered does not match anything we have encountered. It almost seemed to be a life-form."

"That can't be. Your systems are functioning normally?"

"Commander!" I have a target directly astern!"

ATTACK!

In an instant, the Tonrar ship appeared mere yards away. Kapvik sprayed a cloud of yellowish liquid. It flew the few yards, contacted the ship, and spread quickly over its surface. As Abel watched, startled by the sudden appearance of his enemy at such close range, the vessel began to lose its shape, and dissolve. The command crew stood, rooted to their places as Kapvik closed, and engulfed the entire ship. They felt their host expand, then a distinct muscular contraction noisily crushed the enemy ship within their host. Abel suddenly realized that hundreds of lives had just been consumed.

"Abel, we have our first victory!" she said softly, pulling him from his thoughts. "In a few moments I will have enough energy to engage the second ship; do you wish me to attack?"

She seems to have no remorse over the lives she has taken, yet her voice is so...human.

"Yes Kapvik, attack when you are replenished."

"Thank you Abel, it will be but a few more moments."

2066.018
TRIUMPHANT RETURN

Nekalit, a large ship is approaching at high speed."

"A large ship? It is not Kapvik?"

"No, Nekalit, it is appreciably larger than Kapvik."

"Ready the weapons then, and engage when in range unless we have identified it in the meantime."

Ruti could not yet be certain, but it seemed that the approaching ship had a life signature reading on the new sensor array. She believed that it matched Kapvik.

What is he doing? He must see the signature on his console. Does he intend to fire on her? Wait...This could be my chance to finish this fool, and his imperious attitudes. I'll wait until it's clear he's going to fire, then I'll declare that it is Kapvik.

"Commander," Taan said, "The ship is within weapons range, and I do not have any indication that it is Kapvik."

"I find it strange that an enemy would approach so boldly, with no manoeuvres Very well then, Taan, fire when ready."

Ruti took her opportunity, "Nekalit, no! My display clearly indicates that it is Kapvik. I am receiving her hail now…"

"Arlit, this is Kapvik, do you hear us?"

"We do indeed, Kapvik. We very nearly fired upon you. Your signature did not come through until we were preparing to fire."

"Your sensors are not working to specification?"

"It would appear not, Commander. We will investigate, and report as we know more."

"Very well. We have utterly defeated the attack force; all six ships have been destroyed. Kapvik's expanded time travel capabilities provide a significant tactical advantage."

"I will assemble the council for your return."

"Thank you, Nekalit. The conversion of the ships; is it going according to plan?"

"Yes Commander, except for the weapons systems. Taan argued that he required more time to learn the new systems, and would be at a disadvantage if he had to defend us, so we delayed the conversion of the weapons until after your return."

"I see. It would appear that he also has difficulty with the old systems. Relieve him of his post, and begin an investigation of his recent actions."

"Do you wish him to be confined?"

"I do."

"As you wish, Commander."

"I also wish to advise you that I am transferring my flag to Kapvik; she will be the command vessel from this point onward. Prepare to transfer the council members to my ship."

"Our sensors indicate she is significantly larger than when you departed."

"She has feasted in battle, and has grown accordingly. How are the conversions of Arlit, and Netorali proceeding?"

Nekalit paused a moment, still somewhat ill at ease in his new environment, "Both ships are nearly converted, except for the weapons systems, as Taan had insisted."

Abel smiled, "Proceed with the conversion of the weapons systems, I can assure you they are formidable, and highly effective. Our tactical officers will find the demands on their skills considerably reduced in battle."

2066.019
TREASON

"Council is now in session. We're gathered to hear evidence surrounding the attempted firing upon our ship, Kapvik. Taan, Chief Tactical Officer for the fleet, stands charged of high treason against our leadership."

Nekalit rose, and addressed Abel, "Commander, Taan has asked that Gatro represent him for his defence."

Abel smiled, "Gatro, how say you. Do you accept the defence of this man?"

Gatro stood slowly, surprise clearly on his face, "I would prefer not, Commander, I am completely unprepared."

Abel turned to Taan, "Taan, you may address the Council to explain your request."

"Commander," Taan gestured toward Gatro, "Gatro was intimately involved with the conversion of the ships in your absence. My defence rests solely upon the technical difficulties we were experiencing in maintaining the weapons systems, and sensors. His information, I believe is crucial."

"So you persist in requesting Gatro as your representative to council?"

"I do Commander."

"Then I appoint Gatro as your defender, you may have a short recess to confer with him. This trial will resume in one hour." Abel stood, and walked from the chambers.

***

As the people involved at the time of the incident re-entered the council chambers, Abel noted that Gatro was clearly under stress, unhappy about some element of their collaboration.

"Gatro," Abel addressed his newest council member, "Do you now accept the defence of Taan?"

"Commander, I still do not feel that I can mount a credible defence, but Taan insists he will lead me with his own questions."

Abel's mind was sharp, and incisive, thanks in large part to his recent victory in battle, and his intimate link with Kapvik's keen observation skills. "Then I appoint Taan in charge of his own defence; you will be his main witness. Does anyone object to this?" No one spoke, even Taan seemed content. "Then it will be as I have said."

Abel took the ancient ring from his neck, and held it up for everyone to see. "I call upon the Ancient Spirits of the ring to decide whether defence, or prosecution speaks first." He hung the ring by its thong over the back of the ceremonial snow knife. He closed his eyes, holding the knife at full arm's length to the centre of the room. In a few moments his arm began to waver, then vibrate under the strain of holding the heavy blade. The ring began bouncing by its tether, then fell soundlessly to the soft floor of the room; the ring, at the lead end of the thong, clearly pointed toward Taan. Abel opened his eyes, and noted the position of the ring.

"The Spirits have spoken. We shall hear the defence, then the prosecution. The prosecution will absent themselves from the chambers while Taan conducts his defence. Do you understand your rights, and responsibilities under the law of the Ancients?"

Abel looked first at Taan, who nodded in the affirmative, then to Nekalit, who also indicated positively.

"Then we begin." Abel waited as the prosecution team filed out, then said, "Taan, you may proceed."

"I ask Gatro to reply to my questions Commander."

"Gatro, you are free to reply as your conscience guides you."

"Thank you Commander," Taan replied as he stood, and faced his witness. Gatro looked at Taan, displeasure still evident on his face.

"Gatro, please describe your activities at the time Kapvik first appeared on sensors."

"I was monitoring the final stages of Arlit, and Netorali's conversions."

"In your opinion, had the conversions gone well?"

"I was experiencing some difficulty maintaining adequate bionic links to the weapons."

"What effect would you say this would have, had we been forced into battle."

"The bionic links were designed for temporary, direct use by the new brain of the ship, not for mechanical input from a control console. This three-way communication link slowed response times, and multiplied the chances for conflicting directives, which could be critical in battle."

"Why did this present problems?"

"Arlit's brain is capable of processing information, and acting upon it in less than one-one thousandth the time it takes our brains to respond, and command our bodies to move. This is the human delay factor. The bionic command link back to Arlit's brain responds with similar lag time. The link from Arlit's brain to the weapons suffers from a similar delay factor. The imposition of your control console into the weapons controls necessitated a threefold bottleneck that could seriously compromise our defence."

"And how would the weapons system operate had we gone ahead with the development of Arlit, and Netorali's living weapons."

"The Tactical Officer, or the Deputy Commander could activate them by speaking directly to the ship. The ship would direct, and activate the weapon using neural links which operate one thousand times more quickly, and lack the redundancy required in the system as it existed at that time."

"So the command to attack, and the actual attack would occur instantaneously."

"Very nearly so, yes."

"Members of the High Council, this testimony clearly establishes the risks of our new weapons. They are poised on a hair trigger, and can be activated by more than one person. This is a dangerous, and untenable situation for a tactician in a battle situation. This is why I insisted on retaining the old system; even though it imposed severe limitations on my effectiveness induced by the lag times of the various bionic interfaces."

"Do you have any further questions of Gatro?"

"I do, Commander."

"Proceed."

"Gatro, please describe the new life sensor you had installed."

"I had placed similarly linked sensor displays on the Tactical, and Sensor Operator's consoles. These systems were tuned to detect, and report on any living entities within sensor range. These are connected directly to neural links in the ship's brain."

"Were these displays functioning as well as could be expected?"

"They were functioning perfectly."

"Did the controls for this display differ from the normal one on our consoles?"

"Yes, I had placed living pads in place of the customary buttons. They were far more sensitive than the originals."

"And would you say these controls were different enough to cause some confusion in an attack situation?"

"They were positioned exactly the same as their mechanical counterparts, and the labelling was identical to the other displays."

"But you say they were far more sensitive."

"That is correct."

"Thank you Gatro, I have no further questions."

"Distinguished members of the High Council, it is my contention that in the press of an attack situation, these highly sensitive controls were a detriment to my successful operation of the display. The bionic links to the weapons; however, retained that critical single source of activation which in fact saved Kapvik from destruction. Ruti's alert that she had detected the ship to be a living entity stayed my activation of the laser. Had the new weapons been in place, Nekalit's command would have activated the attack in less than an instant."

"So you contend that you were not able to obtain satisfactory information from your display?"

"I do, Commander."

"And this represents the whole of your defence?"

"These are the facts as I observed them during Kapvik's approach. I had no indication of a living vessel approaching."

"Very well, Taan, you will now be returned to your quarters until the prosecution's arguments have been heard. Guards, escort Taan to his quarters, and remain there until I summon you."

Abel watched as Taan was escorted out of the chambers, then he commanded, "Arlit, prepare a time referenced report of Taan's actions at his console during the approach of Kapvik. Include pictorial representations of the results you placed on his, and Ruti's display, and deliver this information to Nekalit for the prosecution."

"As you wish, Commander." Arlit said.

2066.020
THE PROSECUTION

"Nekalit, proceed with your presentation."

"Thank you Commander. These visual sequences show Taan's display data during the time of Kapvik's approach." He allowed the sequence to play in real time a few moments, then froze the action, and played the next scene in slow motion. "As you can see in this segment, he competently operates the controls in question, and the display clearly shows the target to be living. For him to miss this, he would have had to operate the controls with his other hand over his eyes. I cannot divine any means by which he could fail to see, and correctly interpret this display."

"During this time, did Ruti operate her display in similar fashion?"

"No Commander, she enhanced the image three times in the same time frame."

"Yet she waited until the critical moment to reveal her information."

"So it would appear, Commander."

"This seems to be a pattern of behaviour for her. We will deal with this information in due time. Do you have any more information regarding Taan's actions?"

"No Commander, it is our conclusion that he must have intended to fire, having chosen to ignore the warning on the display in question."

"To your knowledge, is Taan aware that we can review his actions in this manner?"

"I am certain he is not, Commander. This function was secret, and available only to senior commanders on the old ships."

"Thank you Nekalit. I believe this evidence to be conclusive. Do any High Council members wish to speak?"

No one moved. They seemed mired in their own disbelief. A seemingly loyal, and gifted tactician was about to be lost.

"So be it then, guards, bring the defendant."

***

"Taan, it is the judgment of the Ancient Council of Hinot that you indeed did intend to destroy Kapvik. Arlit's records clearly indicate this in your use of the equipment at your station. You will be stripped of your rank, dishonoured, and confined until you die, or choose to take your own life. Guards, take him to his quarters, and seal the entrance."

Taan scowled his defiance, but said nothing. To articulate his anger at this juncture would surely cause Abel to demand his life in retribution for insulting the Regent of the Inuit people. The guards manacled him, and as they turned to take him to his quarters, Abel spoke again. "You will find that all your personal effects, save your ceremonial knife have been removed from your quarters. Your food dispenser will provide only enough nourishment for you to subsist, and you will receive no outside contact of any form. Your Spirit is hereby banned from the afterlife with our ancestors."

Abel waited until Taan had been removed from the room, then commanded, "Guards, bring Ruti to these chambers."

Again, the High Council members showed their dismay, looking at each other with concern on their faces. Were they about to lose their best Sensor Operator as well?

As she was ushered into the room, he wasted no time in addressing her. "Ruti, our investigations into the actions of Taan during our return from battle revealed that you had enhanced your display three times while we approached, yet you delayed in alerting Nekalit until the last possible second. This is in contravention of the requirements of your position as Sensor Operator. How do you answer?"

Ruti was clearly shaken; she trembled, and her chin wrinkled as she fought for her voice. Her first attempt brought no sound. She clenched her fists, and forced a breathless reply.

"I could not believe Taan intended to fire."

"I see. I am also aware that you delayed by several suns before you advised me of the resource planet we so much needed to begin repairs on our ships. It was not until after I had ordered the conversion of Kapvik that you came to me with this information. What was your purpose in this contravention of your orders?"

"I…I…"

"You were conspiring with Taan to make the situation as desperate as possible before attempting to overthrow the High Council, and assume command yourselves."

"No Commander. I…"

"Think carefully of your response, Ruti your very life is at stake."

She blanched, and partially collapsed. The guards at her side held her up. She became limp, relying totally upon them for support.

"He…He had been abusive to me. I was angry, and wanted to make sure his intentions were made clear. I wanted everyone to know he intended to fire before I alerted Nekalit."

"You were seeking revenge?"

"Yes, Commander."

"And the resource planet?"

"Taan had seen it too, when we detected it, and signalled me to say nothing. I came to you with the information after he attacked me."

"I sense that you intend me to believe that you were not a completely willing partner in this subterfuge."

"We were partners Commander, until he attacked me, and became abusive, then I realized that he was misguided, and that I could not support him as our future leader."

"So you admit conspiring to overthrow the High Council?"

"Yes, Commander. But as soon as I learned his true nature I did everything in my power to expose him, and support you."

"Those actions have saved your life. You are hereby stripped of your rank, and removed from your position. Normally, I would confine you to your quarters as I have Taan, but your last-minute bravery in exposing his intentions has earned you your freedom. You are, however, officially dishonoured, and must submit to the mark showing this status. In the after life, your Spirit will not be allowed to commune with the Ancients."

Ruti said nothing, her eyes rolled back into their sockets, and she fainted.

"Remove her to her quarters." he commanded. One guard carried her from the room.

"We have one more issue to resolve from these proceedings. I require Kapvik to participate."

"I am listening."

"Thank you. Taan's defence brought to light a very real concern, which I believe, must be resolved immediately. He indicated that, in the situation under scrutiny, lacking the weapons console, more than one person could have authorized firing upon us, with virtually no delay in the weapon being discharged. This situation must never occur again. How can we ensure that only one person has the authority to attack?"

"That situation was unique," Kapvik answered softly, "the existence of the weapons console created the duplication of authority by extending the chain of command. In the current situation, only you, Abel, can approve an attack by any ship."

"The commanders of Arlit, and Netorali cannot initiate an attack?"

"They can order the attack, but you will be aware of the command, and can intervene directly if you choose. This level of our activities is fully under your control at all times."

"I see, thank you Kapvik. Do the members of the High Council have any questions?"

Nekalit stood, clearly angered by these revelations, "Commander, you may as well dissolve the High Council entirely. If we have no executive authority over the ships, you no longer require us."

"That is not the case, Nekalit. I have always, and will continue to rely on your wisdom in counsel, but I retain the final authority in issuing commands of this import, as I have in past. I have learned, from bitter experience, that every member of the High Council is vital to the process of formulating our approach to every situation we encounter. We will all find that our direct physical involvement in implementing these decisions is reduced by the degree of autonomy the ships have assumed, yet I am confident, based on Kapvik's responses, and her recent performance in battle, that this will be a benefit to us. We will be free to concentrate fully upon what we want to accomplish; the ships will look to how it is done."

2067.164
TRIVIA

A bel watched as the High Council entered the chamber. He noted that even the die-hards had discarded the traditional mukluk in favour of the pleasure of bare feet on the soft surfaces of the ships' floors; the discomfort of sitting on the floor, in keeping with tradition, was a forgotten complaint.

"Members of the High Council, we are gathered to discuss the bickering we have seen, not only among crew members, but ourselves. We have created the most pleasant surroundings any one in space could hope to enjoy; we have everything we desire in abundance, yet our people seem agitated, and dissatisfied."

The Council chamber erupted into an incongruous rumble of loud voices. No one observed the rules of polite congress that had been the standard in time not long past.

"Silence," Abel roared, his ceremonial cane held horizontally over his head, like a spiritual leader trying to calm a rebellious sea. "Silence, I say!" Slowly, the room grumbled into a heady silence charged with pent-up emotion.

"We must observe the good rules of our ancestors. Only one person may speak at a time, and must be recognized as the present speaker. To remind us of this rule of common courtesy, I will pass the sacred cane to the person allowed to speak. All others must remain silent, and weigh the speaker's counsel carefully. When you have something constructive to contribute, you may request the cane. If you have only detracting statements to make, you will hold your tongue. Is this clear?"

Abel scanned the room. Dour faces glared back at him, except for Gatro; he was smiling broadly.

"I give the cane to Gatro."

"Thank you Commander." Gatro held the cane tentatively, appreciating the significance of the object. "I believe we need to focus clearly on our objectives, and make every attempt to ignore minor annoyances. If we continue to occupy our time with relatively minor complaints, we risk losing sight of our main goal, namely returning to Nuna. Since our ships began providing our every need, our lives have become regal indeed. We need occupy none of our time looking to our needs for food, supplies, or repairs. Even our ceremonial needs are provided for in every detail; the ships provide delicious victuals for every meal, and accommodate our every social event in the grandest of style. Our workload now needs to consist entirely of planning what we want done. I believe we need to refocus upon Nuna, and the promise of a return to our ancient way of life."

"Thank you Gatro, you've described the situation to a tee, and your suggestion needs to be our primary goal. We need to focus on what really matters to us. I see people whining to one another about all the things they have to do, complaining about their workloads, and I have trouble understanding the significance of any of their so-called responsibilities. I've seen people experiencing real stress, totally distracted by trivial priorities they've apparently set for themselves. I'm concerned at their reduced attention to their primary tasks, brought on by such trivial concerns. Does anyone else wish to speak?"

Nekalit raised his hand, like a petulant school-boy. Abel retrieved the cane from Gatro, and gave it to Nekalit.

"Commander, I cannot believe you would insult your Council in this way; only the holder of the cane may speak? How can we have a meaningful dialogue when only one person may speak? Meaningful intercourse requires that it have free reign to determine its own direction; it is this freedom that often falls upon creative solutions."

Abel retrieved the cane. "Thank you Nekalit. I ask you to compare the importance of the last two speakers' contributions. Gatro suggests we focus upon our ancient goal of returning to Nuna. Nekalit bickers over being forced to wait for the cane in order to speak. Consider the importance of these expressed issues, a centuries-old goal, and a complaint about speaking privileges. We're too focused on trivia; it confuses our outlook, and mires us in a bottomless sea of bickering, innuendo, and general malaise. We don't have significant problems any more, so we're looking for anything we can transform into synthetic monsters. We're busying ourselves with insignificant matters; I think because some of us no longer feel important in the new order. We do not need to look busy, we need to be busy, seeking the most constructive, and significant ways to move toward what I know we all agree is our goal. We have vast new capabilities, let's concentrate on using them well.

I hereby direct the Council members to intervene in any such trivial situations, and direct the people involved to return their efforts to our common desire, finding Nuna Immaluk!" Abel's voice was booming, he was trembling; again, the cane was over his head. At last, he had spoken what he believed to be his true mission in life; to lead his people back to their traditional lives on their ancient home planet.

To his dismay, the silent Council members, save Gatro, rose from their places, and sullenly left the room. He looked at Gatro in complete consternation. "They're leaving? Is that their answer to their leader, sullen silence? Are they no more than undisciplined children?"

"You have spoken the truth, and it has hurt them deeply to hear it. They are chastised, and some will be openly rebellious, but you have become a strong, and confident leader. Your assessment of the situation has been undeniably accurate, but painful. They will lick their wounds a while, but if you do not sway from your course, they will recognize the truth in your conviction, and follow."

"Then I'll re-convene Council, and we'll discuss our search plan."

"I would advise you to give it some time. Speak individually with each Councillor, and re-affirm your respect of their wisdom. Supervise them directly, but in a benevolent fashion: encourage them to be creative in solving the malaise among our people, teach them how unimportant their concerns are in relation to our overall goal. If you are constant in your determination, and show that you are happy in your chosen path, others will tend to gravitate to your positive influence, and leave their minor upsets behind."

"I pray you're right Gatro. I'm relying on your advice more heavily every day. You've been a positive influence in Council since your appointment."

"Then hear me now; I believe that there may yet be serious repercussions from your transition into strong leadership. Keep alert."

2067.324
THE SEARCH CONCLUDES

"Council is assembled, Kapvik, what progress have you made in your studies?"

"The navigation data from the previous ships' data-banks is incomplete, as you know. In spite of the sketchy information the data provides, the greatest difficulty resides in predicting the present locations of the stars, and planets from information recorded over two thousand years ago. In the time since our forefathers began this voyage, all of space has been in motion. Galaxies have their own patterns of movement within the continuum of space as well as within their own clusters of stars, and planets. Therein lies my problem. With incomplete data on their ancient locations, I am forced to infer large quantities of data. In some cases, I have been forced to extrapolate to an extent that I am reluctant to view the results with any degree of confidence."

"Then you shall have more time. We must economize on other activities for this priority."

"Thank you, Commander."

"Do you have any solar systems with reasonable probability of containing Nuna?"

"I must change the topic, Commander. I am tracking three Tonrar ships apparently moving to attack. They are matching our present speed, and have assumed a course to intercept within three hours."

Abel noted the nonchalant response of the councillors, now totally reliant upon the ships to defend themselves, "Thank you Kapvik, continue to observe them, and report any changes."

"Yes, Commander."

"Now, back to our discussion, do you have any possible sites for us?"

"There are three. The first, some one hundred, and twenty light years distant, possesses a cluster of planets around a star of approximately the correct size, and age."

"And the others?"

"My calculated projections indicate two other possibilities, but the characteristics of the planets, and their orbits around their stars do not match the prediction models nearly as well."

"What confidence do you have in the first correlation?"

"I would estimate that we have one chance in one thousand of this being Nuna's solar system."

"We have had much closer matches in past that failed completely. Why do you bring such weak proposals to us?"

"These are the only remaining correlations in the known reaches of space. Once we have explored these systems, we will have exhausted the possibilities that can be drawn from the original data."

"We have travelled to over five hundred planetary systems, covering nearly one-hundred-thousand light years. In that time, we have found only three systems with life, none at an evolutionary stage suitable for our people. I am led to call our search a failure, and seek an alternative approach."

"I agree," Nekalit interjected. "We can explore unknown segments of the universe from here, as in past, scanning for individual planets with habitable environments."

Abel glowered at him. Realizing his transgression, he held his hand to his mouth, but his regret did not seem genuine.

Kapvik continued in reassuring tones, "Those criteria have been an integral part of my verification algorithms since we began our quest. Had we found a suitable planet, I would have strongly recommended that we colonize it. I have not been so focused upon us returning to our ancestral home that I would overlook an opportunity for you to live among plants, and animals once more."

Nekalit requested, and received the cane, "We have left important information on planets with primitives in hopes it would accelerate their development. Perhaps we could revisit these planets, and assess their progress. If they have changed their environments sufficiently, these planets may now be suitable."

Abel took the cane, "Indeed, Nekalit, this practice could prove to be our eventual salvation. Kapvik, do you know the locations of these planets?"

"Some. We have returned to some. I suspect we may have encountered primitives on at least one planet in multiple centuries past, the result of crossing in a time-distortion eddy."

Abel stood, "We've returned to a planet? When?"

Kapvik replied, "I have been reviewing Taan's tactical time distortion manoeuvres, and noted that he painstakingly reversed one pattern...he had never done that previously, and did not repeat it afterwards. I suspect we crossed a time-warp eddy, and travelled far further in time, and distance than we intended. After the first time warp, which I estimate sent us back over fifteen thousand years, a science team visited a planet with an ideal environment, and primitive humanoids. After visiting, Taan retraced his steps to return to the present time-frame."

"What?," Abel roared, "We passed up a perfectly good potential home?" "Can we find it again?" He stopped himself, regained his composure somewhat then continued, "Please accept my apologies, that outburst was unnecessary. I wish we'd never encountered the Tonrar. Thanks to them, we're wandering blind, not knowing whether we're retracing our steps." He paused again;

the council sat in silence, awaiting his next words. He noted with mixed satisfaction that the council continued to honour the policy of requesting the cane in order to speak. The down side of this, he noted, was that rarely did anyone other than Gatro or Nekalit request the cane. The others, he suspected, were doing their communicating elsewhere. "So you recommend we investigate this last possibility then abandon the search algorithm, and move on to unexplored regions of space."

"I do." Kapvik spoke soothingly, in deference to Abel's agitation.

"How say you, fellow Ancestors of Hinot?" No one offered to take the cane.

"We agree then. Kapvik, set course for the planet cluster you have selected. We will use our superior speed to outdistance the Tonrar, unless you are hungry."

"No Commander, we do not require anything now. May I suggest we move at a tangent to our intended course until we outdistance their sensors?"

"So be it." Abel thumped the cane with somewhat excessive vigour on the sacred rock. "Advise me when we are approaching the planets. The council will be in meditations until then. Come councillors, let us pray to our ancestors for success."

Abel left the meeting room, leading his advisors to the meditation chamber. He was the thirty-fourth member of his family to become Regent since they had been forced to flee Nuna. His doubt grew with each failed attempt to locate their ancestral home. He feared that his people would never be able to return to their legendary way of life. He pulled up the hood of his parka, donned his insulated mitts, and commanded the portal to open. Frigid air emanated, and turned to a fog in the warm, more humid air of the companionway.

"Come, let us seek council with our ancestors."

They entered a room lined with an exceptionally heavy coat of fur. The phosphorescent strands glowed from below a thick layer of frost. Kapvik had protected herself well from the temperatures here. In the centre of the room, sat a large igloo, which they entered one at a time, in the order of their rank.

Again the doubts soaked into Abel's thoughts along with the cold of the igloo. He had no idea if his attempts to contact his ancestors were correct. The old Inuit words he had learned from Gatro had no meaning to him, he had simply memorized the sounds.

Why do we continue to repeat this useless activity? It has yielded nothing more than a few hours of quiet each sun, he questioned himself.

"Let us begin," he commanded. They arranged themselves around the circular interior. His voice had a strange reflected quality in this room that he enjoyed; it somehow enhanced the deeper tones of his voice.

The prayers completed, Abel felt compelled to add something to the ceremony. "We will now remain silent, and listen to our own thoughts of our ancient home, and its people."

He took his place at the edge of the circle, and sat on the surface of the ice interior. He removed his mitt, and pulled the ancient ring of authority from around his neck. He kissed it, and placed it on the small altar in front of him. He lit the carbuu moss, and herb smudge used in these ceremonies, and was soon aware of the effect of the smoke on him. He began the meditation. He closed his eyes, and began by breathing out fully, then in, out, then in. The room began to waver in his sight, his head felt unusually light The herbs must be more potent this time, he thought. He opened his mind to the names carried for centuries in his lineage. One by one, he called out their names in his mind, or was he uttering them aloud?

"Hinot, Joni, Dianne, Abel, Dick, if you hear my prayer, please show me a sign." As he repeated the names over, and over, he was feeling his concentration deepen, as if aided by a mantra. His mind began to form a picture of something he had never encountered in all his years. It resembled the fur of his ceremonial robe, and headdress. A huge white beast with black nose, and eyes sauntered, pigeon-toed toward him. It stopped, and sniffed the air, then rose onto its hind legs, stretching a full twelve feet. From its vantage point it was looking directly down upon him.

It turned its attention to the skies, leading his own gaze upward. Above him in the clear blue sky, a large winged animal soared in circles, it was joined by another flying beast as white as the one before him on the ground.

All three turned, and moved steadily into the distance, travelling in the same direction. Abel attempted to follow, struggling in a stiffening wind through deep snow, losing ground with each step. After some time, he lost contact with them, and turning, realized that he did not know his whereabouts. To his dismay, the wind had obscured his footprints; he could not retrace them. He dug into the snow with his ceremonial knife, and carved out a shelter under the hardened surface. He curled up, and slept.

Slowly, he became aware of the cold of the ice sanctuary seeping into his body, alerting him to his surroundings, and the length of his meditations. He opened his eyes to the concerned looks of the council.

The ring was vibrating on the altar, producing a tiny ringing sound against the stone surface. To their dismay, this continued for several seconds. As the sound abated, the ring tumbled to the ice floor, where Abel retrieved it.

Abel could scarcely believe what his dream had shown him. Was he actually becoming the Spiritual leader of his people, or was this just a strange dream? He had felt almost in a trance. Perhaps in this state, his imagination… "I have had a vision. Strange animals were leading me; then I built a shelter in the snow, and slept."

"Then you have had a vision! Nekalit whispered. We have not had a vision of this kind in our meditations for centuries. This is a time to be treasured!"

Abel went on at length, detailing his dream to the council.

"What do you think it means?" Nekalit asked.

Abel replied, "We are heading in the right direction. Nuna lies ahead."

"What of you losing sight of the beasts?"

"Perhaps we are on the right course, and there was no need for them to continue leading us."

"But you turned, and could not find your way back; you were forced to take shelter."

"We must be careful that we wish to remain here before we leave our ships. There will be hardships in our attempts to reclaim our home."

"These are inspired interpretations, Abel. We will proceed, but with caution, and assess the risks carefully before committing ourselves to re-populating Nuna."

"What if others have found Nuna in our absence, and we are repelled as we were in our legendary attempt to colonize Kalon. We were very nearly annihilated then. If Nuna has been colonized, we must assess their capabilities with care."

"We'll be nearing our destination, we've been meditating for three hours."

"Come, let us determine our position."

As they emerged from the meditation chamber, they were addressed by Kapvik, who had apparently been waiting anxiously.

"Abel, we are nearing our destination."

"I have had a vision. I am more confident now about our search. I believe we are about to re-discover Nuna."

"Indeed. My scans indicate that the fourth planet is nearly perfectly situated in reference to the ancient charts. It has an atmosphere that would appear to be ideal for you to inhabit."

"What about other inhabitants?"

"I can detect no return scans."

"So, if there are people, they are in a more primitive state?"

"Yes. I have begun charting the land surfaces, and have located several areas that closely resemble the charts of our legends."

"Have you found Ungava?"

"I have."

"Great news. Let us prepare a team for exploration. We must carefully examine all aspects of the planet to ensure it can provide for us well into the future."

Nekalit asked, "The Tonrar, we have evaded them?"

"We have, Commander. They were heavily armed with some new capabilities, but their ships were of older design, and could not begin to match our pace. We were well out of range of their sensors before we changed course, and entered time travel. We are approaching orbit of the fourth planet."

"Excellent Kapvik, what is your status?"

"I am fine."

I have one concern.

What is that, Kapvik?

If you return to Nuna, and your ancient ways, will you continue to need us?

I seriously doubt whether we could ever return to our ways at this juncture, Kapvik. You, Arlit, and Netorali have become an integral part of our lives. We have never enjoyed such plentiful, and happy surroundings; Nuna is unlikely to become anything more than an interesting archaeological exploration of our past.

"Kapvik, maintain maximum-sensitivity scans for intruders, and begin analyzing adjacent planets for your required resources."

"The planet below has considerable resources that could be exploited."

"We will consider them if required, but for now I want to preserve it as a possible future colony."

"Understood Commander."

Nekalit asked, "Commander, what do you wish us to do now?"

"We will remain in orbit, and observe."

"Kapvik, complete a detailed survey of this planet, and report to us in two suns; also continue your scans for enemy vessels.

2067.326

NUNA

Kapvik's thoughts came to Abel.

Abel, I am certain we have found Nuna, but it is much changed from the stories of our legends.

How is that?

Nuna is fully capable of supporting life, yet I detect no living things.

How can this be?

I have seen indications of ancient civilizations. Ruins of several communities are visible, ranging over what would appear to be many centuries.

I wonder what caused this planet to become a lifeless rock in space? We should investigate, even go to the surface. Our main concern should be to determine the reasons.

Kapvik sounded less than confident as she asked, *Do you think the relics will reveal this information?*

That's impossible to determine from this distance; let's send a shuttle to gather artifacts for analysis.

Abel settled back into his sleeping pod, his mind more relaxed than it had been for a long, long time. He felt certain that Nuna, if this was indeed Nuna would provide important answers.

2067.169

"Netak, select a science specialist, and prepare your equipment to descend to the surface of Nuna. Your task will be to collect artifacts. Seek samples of varied origins, and select them based upon their carbon-data. Kapvik has located several likely sites, including what appears to be the Ungava Bay region. The coordinates are programmed into the shuttle's memory; she will take you directly to them."

"Commander, I would like to appoint Denor as my assistant."

"Gatro's son, yes, excellent choice, he is young, but very capable. Very well, advise Gatro of your choice."

***

The shuttle settled at the sight of the ruins detected by Kapvik. The location had been a jungle that teemed with life, but now, only broken tree stumps hinted at the previous beauty that grew here. Netak spoke first.

"It must have been beautiful here. I can hardly imagine what such a place must have been like."

Denor surveyed the view from the shuttle's canopy a few moments before answering, "It has a haunted feeling to it, as though the planet is still mourning the loss of its ecosystem."

"Imagine what it must have been like, so many plants, and animals. Food must have been at arm's length all the time."

"You might be right, With so many indications of life, I can't see that it'd be difficult to survive here."

"Someone found it impossible. There must be dangers we can't see. Remember, we're investigating the ruins of a fairly advanced society. The dating sensor indicates that these ruins are only two hundred, and thirty years old."

"Okay, let's get on with it, I'm anxious to be in a place where I don't need a shell to protect me."

"Our orders were to wear our protective suits," Netak reminded his friend.

Denor pursed his lips, nearly pouting as he activated the sensors. After a few moments he responded, "Look, the oxygen level's a bit low, but the temperature's only slightly above our accustomed levels, well within range. Gravity's a bit higher than our own, but there are no detectable pollutants, and no organisms. I say we just wear our breathing apparatus."

Netak smiled, then nodded, "Alright, I'm eager to feel the earth in my hands too."

The two young men donned oxygen masks, and exited the shuttle. Their first few steps were tentative, almost expecting their brashness to generate some terrible consequence, but nothing happened. The warmth soothed their bodies. They looked around, absorbing the sensation of boundless openness.

Netak spread his arms, threw his head back, and laughed, "So this is freedom! For the first time in my life I don't need a shell to protect me, the air bathes my skin, the sun warms it; we've been missing so much, for so long!"

"Come on," Denor said, "the structure is over here, let's explore."

They walked the short distance to the edifice of the huge stone building, and stood admiring the carvings around the entrance. Fanciful, and fearful faces stared back at them from the stones.

"We won't learn anything out here," Denor whispered as if he feared waking the faces, "it will be dark. Let's use our lanterns."

They stepped inside, and made their way down the long hallway, decorated with paintings of strange people working deep in the earth, and bringing yellow-coloured earth to the surface.

They came to a heavy stone that had been rolled over a second opening. A lever to one side promised to move the stone in some way. Netak grasped it, and looking to Denor for approval, pulled. To his surprise it moved easily, and the stone began to roll to one side, accompanied by only a faint grinding sound. The young men crowded toward the point where they anticipated the opening to appear. A faint hissing sound joined that of the previous movement of the stone, then a rush of dusty air engulfed them. They stood back grimacing in disgust as it settled onto them.

"Not everything in Nuna's air is pleasant," Denor whined, his hands wiping his visor to clear his vision, then brushing his clothing.

Netak shone his lantern into the opening, and recoiled. "I see why, look…"

They stared in disbelief at a scene of abject despair. Decayed bodies, the dried flesh still on their skeletons, their clothing still intact, sat lining a tunnel that extended beyond sight into the earth. Netak moved first, stepping gingerly between their feet, examining each mummy.

"They have not been wounded or pierced in any way that I can see. They must have been trapped in here, and starved to death."

Denor looked around the opening, immediately locating a duplicate handle on the inside. "No, Netak, they could've left whenever they wanted. Something out there must've caused them to seek refuge in here."

Netak continued his examination of the scene, "No containers for water or food. They must've come here with little or no forethought. They had to be running away from something." He lifted a delicately made, dark yellow necklace over a woman's slumped head, and handed it to Denor.

"This must've had some value to them; it would've been stolen if this place had been entered…afterwards. We must be the first to enter."

"But what could drive people to confine themselves in here, knowing they could not sustain themselves."

Netak paused, "Perhaps their enemies had attacked suddenly, giving them no time to prepare, forcing them to hide in here."

Denor continued the line of thinking, "Then why wouldn't they come out of hiding after a while, at least to see whether the enemy'd moved on? No, I think it might've been something more serious."

"Such as?" Netak prodded.

"Maybe they were confined here because of something that they possessed, or wished to avoid; something that threatened everyone equally."

Netak shook his head, "No. You've forgotten the inner handle again; they were able to leave when they chose. They were here by choice."

"And anyone on the outside was free to enter...They could have had an enemy come upon them at any time." Denor rubbed his chin, "It had to be something dire, but not a human enemy. Could it have been an infestation of animals, insects, or..."

"Disease!" Netak shouted, his voice echoing down the tunnel, "This could've been a quarantine! Get out! Get out!"

They ran from the tunnel, scrambling, and falling in the dirt, raising dust all around themselves. They lay side by side, puffing in their masks, and sweating in the unaccustomed heat, concerned looks creeping onto their faces. They surveyed each other in a kind of panic. They had received small scratches in their haste...an avenue for infection to enter.

"We can't go back to the ship." Denor declared.

"Why?" Netak rose, and began to walk back to the shuttle. "These are just a few minor scratches."

Denor grabbed his ankle. "Because, if it's disease, we might become carriers." He stood, grasping Netak by the shoulders, "We need to confine ourselves here until we're sure we're healthy."

"Nonsense, I've never felt better, and any organism confined in there for so long must be as dead as those people." Netak pointed to the entrance, his hand shaking slightly. "Gatro will want us to report; let's go back to the shuttle pod."

"No, we must contact the ship, tell them what's happened, and tell them we're quarantining ourselves here until we're sure we remain healthy."

"Are you crazy, Denor? We've disobeyed orders. We'll be confined to quarters indefinitely."

"Then what do you suggest?" Denor asked, rubbing his sweaty forehead with the back of his arm.

"We tell them we need to stay longer to study what we've found, say there's a strange door that we haven't been able to open, that we've found nothing significant outside, but have indications that something important might be inside."

"We lie?" Denor's face betrayed his distaste at the prospect.

"Yes, we lie. We risk nothing that way if we're not infected. We gather a few artifacts at our leisure, and go home."

2067.333

"Abel, the last communication we received from Netak seemed strange. He did not entirely make sense."

"What did he say that aroused your suspicion, Gatro?"

"At the beginning of the communication, he sounded out of breath. He said that Denor was sleeping, then, a short time later when I asked him to wake my son, he said he wasn't back yet from his explorations."

"Odd indeed, they have been on the surface now for five days. Could something be wrong with the shuttle, causing them to become ill?"

"All systems indicate normal operation Commander, except that the food replicator is not being used other than for water."

"What do you suggest, Gatro?"

Commander, it is Kapvik.

Alarmed, Abel sat upright in his chair, and held his hand out to Gatro indicating a break in their conversation.

What is the situation, Kapvik?

Netak, and Denor have been concealing the true reason for their extended stay on Nuna. Gatro's doubts caused me to review my sensor data from the shuttle. They are feverish, and cruelly dehydrated Commander. It would appear they can keep no food in their systems. Even the shuttle is in failing health. They will be dead within the hour.

Dead? How can this be?

Disease Commander. They have contracted a virulent infection that has elevated their body temperatures beyond tolerance. I have been monitoring their vital signs since they landed; within ten hours of landing, their body temperatures had become elevated. At first, I thought it might be due to the warm climate, and their exertions, but their temperatures have climbed steadily, and their heart rates are critically high. Pulse rates are over 200 beats per minute.

...how could they contract disease? Were their suits compromised?"

No Commander, they were unused.

They disobeyed our orders, and explored unprotected?

It would appear so, Commander. I noted that their infrared signatures were surprisingly strong on their first exploration. The suits should have reduced that signature by a factor of ten.

What do you recommend we do now?

The infection has acted in a short time; it is indeed potent. We must leave them, and the shuttle. To bring anything back would risk infecting the entire crew, and possibly myself as well.

Abel cradled his head in his hands, processing the import of this latest intelligence.

Thank you Kapvik.

"Gatro, I have just had word from Kapvik...she detects high fever, and indications that death will occur within the hour."

He opened a communication link to the shuttle on the planet below. "Denor, Netak, it is Abel, do you hear me?" There was no response; he sensed there would be none. This situation placed the entire mission to explore Nuna in jeopardy. He could not risk losing crew-members to such virulent diseases. He looked into Gatro's eyes, and saw a tear tracing its way down his cheek.

"I will advise Netak's family, and arrange for a private ceremony of passing," he said in a soft voice.

"I am sorry for your loss Gatro. We will have a public ceremony for them…with full honours.

"What of their disobedience, Commander?"

Abel sighed, "If guilt is to be assigned, Gatro, let us blame ourselves for not instilling our people with the discipline to follow our orders. They will have full honours.

"Thank you Commander."

"We must convene the council members now to discuss our response to this new information. I do not expect you to attend."

"Thank you for your consideration, Commander, but I wish to occupy my mind as fully as possible at this point. It is too painful to meditate upon the circumstances of my Son's death."

***

Abel quickly became engrossed in his own thoughts as he walked to the meeting room, and waited for the council to assemble. He directed his thoughts to Kapvik.

Organisms?

Yes, bacteria mostly, and some highly evolved viruses. We have not been exposed to such things for over twenty centuries. We will need to take samples, and prepare antidotes before we can explore freely.

Nekalit, who had entered the council chambers some time ago, finally dared intrude. "Abel, you are silent a long time, are you having another vision?"

"No, Nekalit. I was attempting to formulate a plan that would allow us to explore this planet safely."

"What are your concerns?"

"The planet is inhabited. There exists some form of biological threat to which we appear to be highly vulnerable. We have lived in purified conditions so long that it appears our bodies have no natural defences. Unless we develop antigens, we could be destroyed by a plague of sickness. I will ask

Gatro to research the infestation to determine whether he can develop the necessary treatments. We can have Kapvik collect samples."

"She is alive," Nekalit blurted. Do we not risk infecting her, as well as ourselves, if we bring these organisms aboard? No, someone must go to the surface in a transport pod. He must not be permitted to return unless he can develop the serums."

"What if he gets infected? How can he defend himself against the diseases?"

"I don't know. We appear to be facing a dilemma. Do we risk everything to have contact with our ancient home, or do we observe what we can, and leave, as we did on the insect planet?"

"Maybe we should meditate on the matter, and seek the wisdom of another vision."

"Yes, we could assemble all the elders, and have a meditation ceremony, Nekalit scowled as he spoke. His tone of voice attracted Abel's attention to his expression. Abel interpreted this correctly as indicating Nekalit's growing impatience with Abel's stubborn adherence to the sham of traditional meditations.

2067.334
STRATEGY

The High Council gathered in the meeting chambers, lit by the glow of Kapvik's down-soft fur. Abel surveyed them, and realized how little he now relied upon their advice. He was almost totally dependent upon Kapvik for his information. "Trusted advisors, I wish to begin by relinquishing the rule of the cane. We may speak freely, but I encourage you to continue to respect the reasons for the rule by keeping your comments focused upon positive comments, designed to offer solutions to our problems. We face yet another serious threat to our goal of returning to Nuna Immaluk. We risk contact with a plague of disease that could destroy us. Micro-organisms have been detected on the planet below that could easily kill all of us, as well as our ships. The question we face is this; do we persist, and forge ahead in an attempt to reoccupy Nuna, or do we return to space, where we know we can roam at will, and prevail over all who would challenge."

Nekalit spoke, but with a strange reserve in his tone, "We are so close. It seems incredible that something so small should thwart us. I am inclined to persist; we should retake what was originally ours."

Kapvik's thoughts filtered into Abel's mind.

I believe we have one powerful strategy that may avoid this problem entirely.

What is that Kapvik?

Abel could see the High Council were awaiting a response from him. He turned away, and cradled his head in his hands, feigning a vision.

I am capable of time travel that could take us back nearly five centuries in a matter of days. Why do we not go back in time until we see for ourselves what brought about the present state?

That is brilliant, Kapvik...

"I have had a vision. We should use our time travel capability to go back in time until we see what brought the present situation to pass."

Abel looked around the room, and to his surprise, saw only positive responses from the council. "By your expressions, I assume you are in agreement. Kapvik, begin our journey."

1767.334

Abel looked out his portal at the planet below. He could not believe what he had seen transpire. In a matter of three days, he had witnessed the death of a planet in reverse. On their first leg into the past, Nuna was relatively unchanged from the state in which they found it, but on the second day, the planet exhibited the remnants of an ecology, with vast areas of desert, but also with areas of stunted vegetation, and a few animals in poor condition. On the third day, which represented three hundred Nuna years, the ecology was much stronger, although showing clear signs of distress...and there were people.

Abel convened the High Council to confer. "We have travelled the equivalent of three hundred years into Nuna's past. As you all can see, there is life below, but it is in distress. I wish to discuss the merits of going back further in time, and what our objectives should be in doing so."

As he spoke, Abel caught a gesture Nekalit was making behind his back to the others. He could not make out its nature, only that it was made. Abel focused on Nekalit's demeanour, and addressed him, seeking to draw out his mentor's motives. "Millennia have passed since we called this place our own. By travelling back only three hundred years, we have discovered a population of people living here, calling Nuna their home. They too have evolved here, it would appear, as we did so long ago. I begin to question how long we can expect the right to exercise our claim to this planet as our home. These people no doubt have struggled for centuries to shape Nuna into their vision of home. I do not foresee them relinquishing it any sooner than the people on other planets we have sought to colonize. The planet's ecology is abundant, but in distress at this point in time. My mind fills with questions with no easy answers. Should we go back further, to find a time when the ecology was stronger? Do we overtake the planet, or do we attempt to negotiate terms of re-occupation of our home with its present population…So many questions. I need your thoughts on these matters."

No one took up the thread.

Abel resorted to his confidante.

I suspect something is not right with Nekalit; he seems unwilling to reveal his thoughts. How can I draw him out?

Kapvik responded.

I have no access to that kind of information, Abel. What goes on in the minds of the people is outside my ken, but I can say that since we arrived, the members of your council have taken three excursions in shuttles, one on each day of our travels back in time. They did not seem to have a particular destination, and I wonder whether these junkets are merely opportunities for them to meet in private…

Abel was astounded at this revelation, Thank you for that information Kapvik. In future, advise me whenever they leave the ship.

As you wish, Abel.

When he looked around, he realized that the councillors were looking at him strangely. As was becoming his custom, he feigned recovering from a vision, touching his fingers to his forehead. "I have seen our future; we possess Nuna once again. We will take samples of the bacteria, and formulate antidotes. When they are tested, we will inoculate ourselves in advance of our contact with their source."

Nekalit stood slowly, "Commander, as I understand Gatro's work, he must have the organisms in his possession to formulate the serum. We risk becoming infected whenever we introduce the bacteria to our environment.

I see no way of accomplishing this without tremendous risk. Our time travel of the past three days has shown us that an entire population has expired from this pestilence. Why are you so arrogant as to think we can avoid its effects?"

Abel's mind froze at the accusatory tone of this statement. He was still trying to react when Gatro stood. "Commander, Nekalit may be correct, and we cannot guarantee that we can act in time to remove something like this from our midst. Changes of this nature may or may not remain with us as we move in time…If we become infected, time travel may do nothing to correct that problem. It is reasonable to suppose that we could arrive in another time with our new illnesses intact. In addition, we risk that Kapvik may be sufficiently compromised by the onset of an illness as to be incapable of time-travel."

"It is indeed unfortunate that we did not retain one ship in its inanimate form. It would be oblivious to organisms," Nekalit added, somewhat pointedly.

Abel raised his index finger in recognition of the idea, and ignoring the barb, took up the thread. "Perhaps we could build a small, inanimate craft for Gatro to occupy while he works. Once he has the antidote, we can proceed." The council looked at him again, unused for some time to this degree of open consultation. Or, he wondered, were they resisting him in some way. Abel realized that increasingly, he had been making his decisions based upon his union with Kapvik's mind, gravitating to that source in preference to the Counsel. He pressed on, "We have solved greater problems than this in past. Life has been too easy for many years now. We have become entirely too dependent upon our vessels, perhaps losing some of our creative edge. There must be a solution, and we will find it."

"Commander, since you are proposing solutions," Gatro interjected, "We no longer have the means to produce an inanimate ship, but we can clone a small laboratory. If the occupants, and the lab become infected, we simply do not allow them to return to the mother ship."

"You would be the logical choice for such a mission, Gatro; are you content to risk your life?"

Gatro was silent a moment, clearly formulating what he was about to say, and feeling the significance of it. "It is a difficult choice; one I do not take lightly, but we have sought this place through the lives of over twenty generations. We have seen many die in battles, brought on by our quest. This is our goal. I am honoured to make the attempt to finally bring us home."

"If none other has a solution they wish to put forward? No one? Then it shall be as you propose; make your preparations. I also believe that we will have greater chances of recolonizing a living planet. I propose we remain at this point in time."

Again, no-one responded. As the High Council filed out, Abel took note that no one gravitated to him or Gatro, but to Nekalit, engaging him in hushed conversation.

1767.335
THE TONRAR SEEK A RE-MATCH

*A*bel, I have been scanning ahead in time; if we do not act, the Tonrar will find us here in thirty-seven suns. It would appear they were here in our present time frame. They may not recognize us as enemies, but we know they are warlike...

We must prepare to meet them Kapvik, are you healthy enough to engage in battle?

I am, but they have different ships than we encountered previously. I have not had sufficient opportunity to scan them in detail, but it would appear they are more wary of attack. They travel with weapons at the ready, despite the punitive energy costs that must impose. This means they could respond to our attack much more quickly...

Abel scratched his newly sprouted beard. Since he had learned of its significance to the elders of the past, he was anxious to display this traditional signal of his maturation as a leader.

If we could lose a ship, perhaps we should look to expanding our fleet. Do we have enough time to clone new ships?

Only as decoys; they would not be mature enough for battle. I propose that we move away from our prize, so as not to reveal our goal, play cat, and mouse with them, and pick them off one by one.

So we have not been detected here?

No, I have been detected in their proximity, but not here.

Kapvik's voice soothed his mind, as usual, made him feel more confident, and reinforced his growing dependence upon her. As was becoming his habit, he placed his hand on the carapace of her brain casing, unconsciously caressing it.

Very well, we will create a laboratory ship, and transfer key personnel, along with an occupying force for Nuna, then you will move off to engage them.

Me? You will not command the battle?

No, Kapvik, I feel compelled to remain close to Nuna, and supervise events here. On the other hand, I want at all costs to avoid bringing the Tonrar here. If they were to locate our home planet, they would attack us at every opportunity. I want this to be our safe place, our haven in space, not the scene of constant battles.

Who will command the battle?

Nekalit. He is a capable, and loyal man. He will interact well with you, and his decisions will be wise.

Will he be given an implant?

No. Abel shook his head to emphasize this thought.

I trust in your judgment, we are risking everything for the opportunity to reclaim Nuna.

Abel looked out through her ocular link at the beauty of Nuna, floating in space below them.

Kapvik, have you located a suitable planet to exploit for your nourishment?

I have, Commander. The ringed planet contains all of the necessary nutrients.

He patted her gently, *Very well, we will move to that planet until you are fully replenished, and we have resources to produce the clone ships.*

Abel considered the new ships, and their potential, and who would command them; he continued his thought, *When mature, these ships will be complete duplicates of their kind, will they not?*

They will, but with the food sources available, and our need to be cautious of detection by the Tonrar, complete maturity should take another thirty suns. I fear detection much sooner if we do not act to cloak our presence.

Abel pondered the situation. *If we have Nekalit move our mature ships to intercept the Tonrar, say within seven suns of the production of the clones; we should be able to occupy the clones as they mature.*

The clones will be sufficiently mature to support the landing expedition personnel, and begin our lab work.

Abel made his decision. Decisions were much easier for him, bolstered as he was by Gatro's skills, and Kapvik's intimate counsel. He sought out Nekalit to brief him on his plan.

1767.336
THE OPPORTUNITY IS GIVEN

Nekalit sat listening intently as Abel briefed him, "Nekalit, this mission places you, and the bulk of our crew in great danger, use time travel to draw their attacks away from your location in the present. Attempt to make your attacks at the precise time they commit their weapons to a disappearing target. Kapvik is a seasoned combatant, but she will rely upon your wishes to direct her strategy. You must make effective decisions, or I fear our losses may be severe."

He smiled. A rare occurrence for Nekalit in recent times, "Your advice is well-founded, Commander. If we are to lose this battle, it will be to an unfortunate turn of fate, not to a better tactician."

Abel stood, and offered his hand, "May your Spirits soar, Nekalit, we are depending upon your success."

Nekalit grasped his hand firmly as he asked, "One small detail, Commander. Taan remains confined on Kapvik; do you wish him to remain with us, or do you wish to keep him under your supervision?"

"Transfer him here."

Nekalit's smile flickered, but he caught himself, nodded, and took his leave.

***

A guard approached Abel, out of breath, "Commander there has been an incident in transfer pod dock seven."

"Taan has not escaped?"

"No Commander, he was attacked, and has been wounded."

"By whom? Is he badly injured?"

"Ruti, Commander. He will recover, but I fear she may make another attempt. She may be successful a second time."

"Ruti?"

"Yes Commander. She claims he has insulted her honour, and that she has the right to kill him."

"That would be true were she of true lineage, but she is not of pure blood, so cannot claim the rights of revenge. Confine her to her quarters. I will deal with this matter later."

Abel watched as the three mature ships suddenly disappeared from view, entering the time distortion that would take them to their encounter with the Tonrar. He felt suddenly empty. His sense of Kapvik's presence was already diminished by the increasing distance. He felt alone again. He returned to his present concerns; finding a way to bolster their immune systems against the pernicious bacteria abounding on Nuna.

"Gatro, how do you plan to contain the bacteria so that we can examine them in relative safety?"

"I will employ mucous shells to contain samples, bringing them aboard after they have hardened, and the outer surface has been sanitized."

"I see, and what sources do you intend to sample?"

"I hope to find the flesh of organisms that have been exposed to the bacteria. Our sensors indicate that a fierce battle has been fought near a mine where they source materials for their explosives. A number of corpses have been left to rot, since it seems the battle was indecisive leaving both forces near complete destruction. With luck, some of them will have been infected."

"How do you intend to approach?"

"I will move back slightly in time, before the samples have begun decomposition, make a brief appearance wherein mucous bubbles will be dispensed, then move ahead to a time when they will be hardened, sanitize them, and bring them aboard for testing."

"Do you anticipate difficulty, or danger to our people?"

"There is always an element of risk, Commander. Sensors indicate these organisms are primitive, but hardy, able to survive rather extreme conditions."

Abel wondered why direct contact with the bacteria was necessary, surely Gatro could simply analyze their genetic structure, and create an antidote from that information. "If the sensors can reveal this much, why do we need samples?"

"Everything we have created requires suitable raw materials upon which to base the organic patterns; this is no exception, but it would appear that no inanimate materials in our possession can adequately duplicate the replication abilities of these organisms. I must learn how to disrupt this capability, so that infected persons will not succumb."

"So this is how the current residents avoid becoming ill?"

"I believe they have evolved over generations, genetically building resistances."

"Time we do not have. How may I assist?"

"I recommend you move to one of the larger clone ships, and prepare the exploration team. Once immunized, we will need to begin establishing our territory, and interacting with the fauna on Nuna's surface. One other thing, Ruti had been actively seeking the opportunity to work on the laboratory ship before the incident with Taan."

"I fear she may be attempting to acquire some of the bacteria to deploy as a weapon; at the very least, she is attempting to better her position. She has been marked as untrustworthy, and is confined to her quarters for her attack on Taan, so she shall remain. It will not be easy to convince me to be lenient again, to give her the opportunity to better her position, or to launch another attack."

1767.339
THE AWAKENING

Gatro had sensed a subtle change within his psyche as they approached Nuna. Something was stirring inside him, and he knew that he had been dreaming, even though he could not remember the content of those dreams. He was feeling more motivated, more inclined to be proactive, to be a catalyst both immediately, and in the long term. He determined to try to rouse himself if he became aware of a dream in order to record its meaning. He felt they may be important.

He spoke, addressing Abel. The new ship directed his call as he began speaking. "Commander, it is Gatro, I wish to update you on my progress."

Abel responded, "Do you have a serum for us?"

"I do Commander, the bacteria, and viruses are numerous, and some are quite complex, but I have prepared an inoculation for all organisms that show potential to be debilitating or fatal to us."

"And the others?"

"Our natural immune systems will soon reactivate to the point where they will not be a problem."

"Thank you Gatro, once again, our progress depends on your scientific prowess."

"I am always eager to meet a challenge to my skills."

"When can we be immunized, and begin exploring Nuna?"

"We should be able to immunize everyone by the end of this sun, some will become only mildly ill, others will need a few suns to recover."

"Then we'll spend the time planning our expedition to Ungava."

1767.347
ABEL LOSES HIS FOCUS

Abel was finding it difficult to focus on the preparations for a landing. He felt suddenly adrift, keenly missing his intimate communion with Kapvik. He gravitated increasingly to Gatro's stabilizing influence. "Most of us have recovered from our immunizations, but I'm concerned about Kapvik, Arlit, and Netorali. There's been no contact with them since they left the solar system."

"They may not want to communicate too freely until they have achieved a decisive outcome."

"No Gatro, it's more than that, I think something bad has occurred."

"It is always a possibility that the engagement has not gone well. They may have been destroyed. There was indication of the Tonrar adopting new technologies, and strategies."

1767.350
MUTINEERS PLAN THEIR FUTURE

"Nekalit," Tullegak, the newly appointed Tactical Officer confided, "we have finally rid ourselves of the idiotic tyrant, Abel, and his puppet, Gatro, but we have one major problem; we now occupy ships over which we appear to have only partial control. We should have kidnapped Gatro."

"From what I have observed, Gatro's role in the maintenance of our ships was minimal. As you know, they are largely autonomous in the matters of their own health, and feeding. If a ship becomes infirm, we can instruct the remaining ships to reproduce."

Tullegak frowned, "Is that how Gatro produced the new ships?"

"How else would he do it? In fact, I think we should begin immediately to expand the fleet, and our own numbers. We will be the dominant species in every sector of space we explore; this is our home, and our domain; we should actively expand into it. Abel, and his followers can have their precious Nuna, good riddance to them!"

"Kapvik, have you completely severed all forms of contact with Abel, and Gatro?"

"I have Commander," she lied. She continued in a cool voice, "It has been difficult for me, we were like Siamese twins. But you are correct, he would have abrogated us into a life of idleness, floating uselessly in orbit over Nuna.

We are creatures that evolved in space. Our place is in this domain, living with the people who call its vast reaches their home."

"Excellent, do you see any difficulty in expanding our fleet?"

"I do Commander. Gatro did not give us reproductive systems; we cannot give birth to new ships, they must be cloned. He alone possesses the knowledge. We can; however, grow indefinitely, thus accommodating a larger population."

"Then we will reproduce, and you will grow to accommodate. We will dominate all that we encounter."

"Do you wish to contact Abel, and tell him of our decision?"

"Yes. Tell him we have given him his lifelong wish, to return to Nuna, and that we are now taking the opportunity to realize our lifelong wishes… life on our own terms in an environment we understand."

1767.350.15
RE-DISCOVERY OF NUNA

Gatro approached Abel in the command centre, "Commander, I have received a message from Nekalit."

Abel turned, excitement flushing his features, "What does he say? Have they defeated the Tonrar?"

"No Commander. It would appear he has avoided them entirely, and taken Kapvik, Arlit, and Netorali back into deep space. He states he does not intend to return."

Abel sank helplessly to the floor, seeming to be unaware of his descent.

I'm alone again. Kapvik has been separated from my psyche, and, as I was beginning to fear, Nekalit has betrayed me. The source of my success as a leader is gone. I wish I could just resign my position, assume an untitled place among the people, and let someone else do the leading. I feel powerless; nothing matters any more. Whether I live until tomorrow or die in this miserable moment makes no difference to me.

Tears streamed down his face. He spoke softly, "We are powerless to pursue, and engage them, and to what purpose; our ships will not mature to full fighting capacity for several more weeks. Let them go; if they want to continue their lives in space, so be it."

I can't quit. I'm their born leader, these remaining people will continue to look to me for direction. If I give up now, I'll condemn them to a death in misery...none of them have earned that. They may die as a result of one of my decisions, but they won't count it a waste. They'll see their deaths as being the cost of ensuring the survival of the remaining people.

"Commander, do you wish to receive your immunization now? It has been tested with three reconnaissance missions, and everyone has returned uninfected by any of the bacteria we have encountered."

Abel wiped his nose on his sleeve, making no attempt to hide his distress from the others in the room, "Very well, give it to me, Gatro." As Gatro moved to apply the paste to his tongue, Abel asked, "Did you know anything of this conspiracy?"

"No Commander."

Abel shuffled his tongue in his mouth, attempting to clear his palate of the foul paste. He grimaced. "Had you known what Nekalit, and the council had afoot, would you have remained here, or gone with your creations."

"I would remain here. Nuna is the origin of all of my skills. Like you, I wish to return to our ancient lives here."

"I'm not certain whether I'll be capable of leading in this foreign environment; I feel like I'm way over my head," he swept his hand across his forehead, and continued in a shaky voice, "now that Kapvik's gone. I've lost most of my ability to observe events, and directly control their outcome. I know I shouldn't be admitting this to you, but I need someone like you to discuss my thoughts. You're the only remaining intellect that meets that requirement."

Gatro had kneeled to apply the serum, now he sat beside Abel, and spoke in hushed tones, trying to encourage his leader to conceal some of his agitation. "You do not know that I am trustworthy."

"I have had much stronger indications of your loyalty than from any of the others. Even Kapvik has been duped into betraying me," he huffed, and shrugged, holding up his hands, "By my own command."

Gatro's guileless face formed a caring smile, "I will do my utmost to serve your needs, Commander. To begin, if you wish, I can link your mind to this ship."

Abel frowned, "Would I lose the link to Kapvik? Should she ever return, I would want to retain the ability to share her thoughts."

"You would lose that link, Commander."

"Then no, thank you. I'm not going to lose hope she might return. Maybe, at some point, she'll sense the link remains." Obviously distracted, he repeated, "Maybe, at some point, she'll sense the link remains."

Abel paused, concern appearing on his features, "What about Kapvik, Netorali, and Arlit? Will they be able to look after themselves?"

"They will indeed, a little too well in fact."

"What do you mean by that?"

"Their abilities to adapt are powerful; I have had to intervene on several occasions to curtail or prevent adaptations from occurring. Left to their own devices, the ships may well evolve into uncontrollable monsters."

"But their prime reason for existing is to serve, and protect the people; how could this ever be subverted."

"It will never be subverted. They are zealous, always seeking to make our lives better. I had to constantly monitor their concept of 'better,' and make qualitative decisions. They would never meaningfully harm us, but they could eventually assume control over so many aspects of our lives that we would find ourselves in a prison of...pleasure."

"Pampered to death?"

"In a fashion, yes. Over time, without conscious control, we could have become so dependent upon them that we would lose any control whatsoever over their actions."

"So, the people would be even more aimless. The ships would become monsters to all who encounter them, and we'd be their captive hive queens."

"Exactly."

"I hope we do not encounter them in future then; I wish them no ill, but I wonder about our future. Are we seriously diminished by their departure?"

"No Commander, unless we are forced to defend ourselves before these ships mature."

"Then do you agree that we need to explore Nuna to see what our best options are?"

"For the present, it would be wise to keep our ships transparent to scans from space; it will tax their energy levels, but, in the short term, we must avoid an encounter with the Tonrar at all costs."

"I agree Gatro, instruct them to absorb any incoming energy from scans. Since I will not have the intimate contact with our ships, I rely upon you; that makes me vulnerable to you. You have inherited virtually unimpeded power to influence our future as a result of their desertion." Tears welled in Abel's eyes again as he spoke these words.

Gatro stood, looking thoughtful, then spoke, "In that case Commander, I have a request."

"Shoot."

"I wish you to address me by my ancient Inuit name rather than my modern title."

"Sure, what's your name?"

"Angatkro, Commander."

"That's very similar to your name now, why are you changing it?"

"I have had dreams, Commander. The people in those dreams call me Angatkro, telling me it is my true Inuit title. Since we are embarking upon an attempt to return to our ancient ways, I think it would be appropriate for me to re-assume my traditional name."

"I agree…Angatkro. I like it better than Gatro."

Angatkro took his leave, surprised by the degree of reliance Abel was demonstrating. He had showed openly that he had been profoundly shaken by recent events.

1767.360
ANGATKRO TASTES LEADERSHIP

Angatkro worked tirelessly in preparation for their first foray onto the surface of Nuna. He found himself more energized, more anticipatory of this adventure than any previous event in his life. He was home. Somehow he knew he was home to stay. Hourly he felt this conviction strengthen.

In the ensuing days, he found himself prodding Abel into action, then prompting him only for the easiest decisions; finally he began making decisions himself. Abel had not retained his previous, passionate interest in Nuna. The vacancy in his psyche, and self-confidence created by the loss of Kapvik became more evident each day. This was compounded by the absence of Nekalit, upon whom, Angatkro realized, Abel depended greatly for counsel on matters of import. Abel had held a trust for Nekalit that was part of his inner foundation. In breaking that trust, Nekalit had torn the fabric of Abel's humanity, and set him adrift as a human soul. Angatkro saw it in his eyes; he had become withdrawn. He was no longer able to find the courage to trust anyone. He had retreated into a self-destroying vacuum of doubt.

"Commander, we are nearly ready to begin our first major explorations. Everyone has recovered from their reactions to the immunizations, and we have located a small group of people in caves near the ancient temple of Joni. They closely resemble a people of legend to our ancestors, called the Yup'ik."

Abel seemed to make a huge effort to muster some enthusiasm for the imminent explorations. "Excellent Angatkro, you've worked tirelessly for this. Finalize your preparations, and let me know when it's time to descend to the surface. Do you plan to use transfer pods?"

"We do not have enough, Commander. I was hoping we could land our smallest ship nearby without seriously affecting the tides, and…"

"Won't that jeopardize our first contact with these people? If they see our ship descend, or us emerging from it, we might be received as gods, not their long-lost family."

"Your question has merit; however, there are advantages to us being viewed as gods, in my view. It significantly reduces the chance of them attacking to defend their territory. They are more likely to treat us with great reverence, giving us valuable time to establish ourselves."

"Maybe it will be just like the legends, when the High Council…" Abel paused, clearly in anguish over his thoughts.

"What is it Commander?"

"We're all that remains of the Ancient High Council…you, and I." He spoke those words, his face revealing that the thought had been an epiphany for him, "I was going to say, "When the High Council commanded reverence in our people." Now, they're just waiting for the moment when they can begin to direct their own lives."

"Our advantage lies in their total lack of skills in that area. They have relied upon the High Council to make decisions for centuries, thus are largely incapable of processing factual variables, and abstracts in order to make policy decisions. Like us or not, they will rely upon our decisions even more heavily in this new, strange environment below."

"A place I know nothing about. I had hoped I would have more visions after my experience in the meditation chamber, but there's been nothing. I've got no idea how to proceed, or how to process the new kinds of information we'll encounter below. Legend states that we lived by our finely tuned senses; until now, we've all lived cooped up in these controlled environments. Our sight isn't used to scanning far horizons, our noses just bring air to our lungs;

we're probably weaklings, compared to the people who lived here so many centuries ago."

"I am confident that we will adapt quickly. We must keenly observe these people, and study their skills in detail."

"Thus your opinion that we should arrive like gods."

"Yes Commander."

"As usual, your counsel is wise. We'll do as you advise."

Abel turned away from Angatkro, and resumed his vigil, staring blankly through the ocular link into the void of space above the thin, blue-hazed membrane of the atmosphere of Nuna. He had lost much with the departure of Nekalit, and the High Council. Angatkro realized that he was the only person still enjoying access to Abel's thoughts, but being so recently appointed, he could not divine the degree of confidence Abel placed in his advice. He turned, and quietly left the command centre.

That night in his bed, Angatkro had a dream...a powerful dream.

1767.362
ANGATKRO HAS A VISION

"My son, welcome back."

"You are a stranger to me; why do you call me son?"

"Yours is the blood line of the Angekok, I am Hinoch, the sixty-fourth Angekok of our people. You are of the same line, another ninety-five generations from my time. Your forefathers wisely kept their skills closely guarded. You have powers of science that I cannot begin to understand, but many of your Spiritual skills have been obscured by time, and disuse. In your absence, the beasts of Nuna have retaken their Great Spirits. Chaos rules again. It is your task to regain control of these Great Spirits, and bring peace to the Spirits of Nuna."

Angatkro thought to himself, *This is a wonderful dream, or is it a dream? I must wake to prove to myself it is a dream.*

"You are awake, my son, and to convince you of your destiny, I will leave a mark upon you that no other among your people has ever seen. It will be your sign of supreme leadership."

"Abel is our leader."

"Your legends are corrupt. You call me Hinot, my correct name is Hinoch. My wife, whom you call Joni is Joanna. You have lost most of the old names, but I will instruct you, so you may correct them. Abel is a distant relative of my son of the same name. His people renounced our ways over the centuries, and took to conquering the world rather than remaining part of it. I renounced him when he revealed the direction he was taking. He perpetuated our traditions only as they served his increasingly perverted purposes. This corruption of our ways eventually caused the demise of Nature that demanded your exodus from Nuna so long ago."

"Then how did we…"

"Your ancestors wisely created a place for themselves as the religious leaders of their world, keeping displays of their powers very low key, more like amusing tricks of magic. The world accepted their place in society, and took your family with them on their exodus."

"Abel is still my leader. I will continue to serve him."

"You are wise to do so for the present, but be ready; your respective roles are about to change radically. He is beaten, his artificial links to power destroyed; he will retreat into himself, and become a recluse. You will find yourself placed in the position of leadership with increasing frequency." Angatkro frowned. Observing this, Hinoch continued, "Do not be concerned, you will find yourself ready for the task."

"I cannot lead! I was instructed to be a Shaman, not the Regent."

"Hah! Yes, I had forgotten, they call themselves Regents now. Do not despair, your eyes have been opened; you will be able to call upon your ancestors, and share in our council as the need arises. We will show you what you need to know; you in turn will re-teach your people. You are back, my son. We will lead you so that you, and your kind may flourish."

Angatkro sat up in his bed, instantly aware of vastly heightened powers of observation. The highlights, textures, and shadows in the room, though still cloaked in the nearly complete darkness maintained for the resting hours, revealed details that he had seen before, but that now he was perceiving. Perception is, he discovered in that instant, the added dimension required to fully interpret what the senses detect. He now had a profoundly enhanced connection with his surroundings. He had never felt so vital before this moment. His wife, Noel roused by his movement, looked at him with sleep-filled eyes, then she screamed.

"Angatkro, come to the command room," Abel spoke in a needy voice over the communication system, "I need your counsel."

"As you wish, Commander. I will be there momentarily." He rose from his distraught wife, assuring her that everything was fine, that he felt better than ever. He dressed, and hurried to meet with Abel.

As he entered the cubicle, he saw Abel blanch, his eyes betraying his shock. "What happened to you Angatkro? Your eyes…"

"I am not certain, Commander, but I assure you I feel better than ever, even more perceptive, and much more vital."

"But…how do you…see?"

"As I said, better than ever. What is wrong? Why is everyone reacting so strangely?"

"You haven't seen yourself? Your eyes are a strange mother of pearl colour. You have no visible iris, and only a faintly outlined pupil."

"My eyes? Is that so? Then it is true."

"True? What's true Angatkro?"

"It would appear that I have had a vision; a vision with profound effects upon my mind, and my person."

"A vision! Tell me about it. Tell me everything."

Angatkro began to relay the entire story, but brought himself up short, remembering what Hinoch had told him of the ancient Shamans' survival tactics. "I am not fully certain of what I have seen, Commander. An ancient Shaman came to me last night, told me that I would now be able to see beyond what my eyes showed me, and said that I would hear from him again. There was a bright flash, and I felt more refreshed than ever before in my life."

"That's it?"

"Yes Commander," he lied, amazed at how easily he had withheld the most salient parts of the vision.

"Then there's hope. Maybe I'll start having visions again too. That would be amazing, having the wisdom of our elders to help us."

"Your vision of the white beast, and the other beasts of the air was a powerful omen of our destiny. We must remain cautious even though I believe the elders will begin to help us."

"Yes, I still don't think I totally understand my vision; I can only guess what it might mean. We'll move ahead with our plans, but carefully." Abel nodded his head as he spoke, and continued nodding afterwards, as though trying to convince himself.

"Why did you summon me this morning, Commander?"

"I want to be certain of the loyalty of the people we have remaining. The ones we can trust we leave aboard; the others we take with us where we can supervise them directly."

"We do not have that luxury, Commander. Your personal guards are even being pressed into learning the tasks required aboard our ships. We must commit an act of faith, and trust that they will all continue to respond as we hope."

"No!" he blurted, "I refuse to leave myself open to another act of betrayal. Until I'm certain of the loyalty of my people, we'll stay right here. Nuna can wait!"

"How do you propose to identify those who may be disloyal?"

"I don't know. That's why I wanted to talk with you," he wagged his finger toward Angatkro.

Angatkro's thoughts raced, "I could devise some sort of serum that would temporarily predispose a subject to be completely truthful. You could interrogate them while they were under its influence. This may take some time. We have nearly three hundred people."

"Why couldn't we interrogate them in groups of say, fifty?" Abel seemed to be in a state of desperation.

"I am not certain the serum would function properly under such interactive circumstances."

"Then you need to work on it until we can question large groups."

"Very well, Commander, I will keep you advised of my progress." Angatkro took his leave, his strategy forming rapidly in his mind.

There will be no serum. I will simply brief the people, explaining that Abel requires them to swear their allegiance to him. Those refusing allegiance will be allowed to seek their own futures aboard one of the smaller ships. I will take my time arranging this, first feeling out the people to see if I can locate any who may be resistant.

I will also go down to Nuna ahead of the expedition, reconnoitre the area, and identify the things Abel will be pleased to see, at the same time shielding him from situations where he may make decisions we might regret later.

Hinoch, do you have any suggestions?

Yes Angatkro, I will show you the places where our artifacts are most numerous; that will please him. I will also show you the locations of the Yup'ik. They are a primitive, and very accepting people, but they are excellent judges of a man's strengths, and weaknesses; Abel's insecurities would betray him in no time. I would suggest limiting his contact with them.

|767.364
ABEL ENTERS DEPRESSION

Abel sat in his command cubicle, but his thoughts were not of leadership. He had become obsessively introspective since Nekalit had taken the ships, and abandoned him. He could not fathom how someone apparently so loyal could betray him so completely. His loss was devastating, by the fact he had lost his primary confidante, Kapvik, and that Abel himself had ordered the mission that brought all this into being.

I don't know one person I can completely trust. To be absolutely practical, and given recent events, I shouldn't trust anyone. But if I make that decision, it renders me totally alone. If I'm going to have any effect as a leader, I need to communicate my concerns freely, and to solicit my people's opinions, selecting the best of the solutions offered. He slumped over, propping his chin on his hand, and chuckled...only in my dreams. Meaningful interaction with my people, and I, their fearless leader, have been lost forever.

The result is that...

Talk about a dilemma; I need their expert advice to make valid decisions, but can't trust the advice I get. My early attempts to reverse the damage caused by my illustrious forefathers were inept, no doubt, but I was expecting positive change too quickly, I think. It was probably way too late in our history to expect any significant change in the loyalties of my people. Their opinion of the High Council became innate generations before I assumed the position of Regent. I would have had to be a fantastically powerful, charismatic leader to have any chance of getting them to accept my leadership.

I've been anything but powerful, but I don't see anyone positioning them-self... other than Angatkro; he seems much more confident, and outgoing since his eyes whitened...This just isn't right! I'm the leader. Everyone should recognize my authority under pain of death...Hmm, maybe it's time for some brutal discipline to remind these people who is in command. Yes, Angatkro will need to be very careful how he serves me in future. They'll be watching him, so he has be seen to be dutiful to me. If he steps out of line, I'll have him publicly impaled on my ceremonial knife. Yes, some brutal authority may be what's needed.

1768.001
ANGATKRO MEETS WITH TAAN

"Guard, I wish access to Taan's quarters."

"I cannot allow that Angatkro, he is not allowed any form of human contact."

Hinoch, this guard is following orders as any loyal soldier should; how do I convince him to allow me entry?

Place a question in his mind, then as you answer it, telepathically place the suggestion in his mind to obey your command. He will be intent upon your verbal answer, so will accept the subliminal command.

Very well...

"It is said that Taan may soon be released from his sentence."

"Angatkro, I have a question, if I am permitted to ask."

"Yes, I am listening."

"I understand Taan may soon be released from his sentence."

"How did you hear this?"

"I believe it is common talk among the people."

"His offence was serious; he was lucky to avoid the death penalty, I doubt that he can anticipate receiving a reprieve. Do the people seem to want him back among them, knowing what he did?"

"His rebellious act, and his plotting of a take-over have made him something of a hero among the malcontents."

"There is discontent?" Angatkro asked, trying to appear surprised.

"A good deal, Angatkro. Abel leads like a spoiled child, demanding that we satisfy him while he does nothing to ensure our welfare. He has lost our best people, and the most powerful ships in a stupid strategy, leaving the few of us remaining in immature ships with enemies seeking to engage us in battle. We are orbiting a planet that means nothing to us, yet we understand we are expected to colonize it because he mandates it. Most of us are inclined to remain as we are, explorers of space. We will soon have good ships again, and plentiful food, yet our leader wants to force us into hardship."

"This planet is our ancestral home; where life can assume wonderful qualities of which we have lost any knowledge. So much bounty awaits us that any hardships will seem inconsequential. Abel has fought diligently to bring this prize within our grasp. He is a quiet, strong leader who works tirelessly, often out of the view of his people. It has been arduous for him to compel the High Council to persist in the search for Nuna, now that we are here, we would do the greatest disservice to balk in the face of a few unknowns. I can assure you, no one will want to return to space once they have tasted the freedom, and wonder of life on Nuna. You need to spread the word, and you may mention the source—Angatkro, the sole remaining servant of our Regent. He has alienated many of his life long friends through his conviction that the return to Nuna would be the greatest possible service to his people, we owe him loyalty for what he has done, and for what he has lost on our behalf."

"I understand Commander, I will do my best."

"Now, give me access to Taan's quarters."

A slightly quizzical look came over the guard's face, but he answered, "Yes Commander,", and complied.

***

"Gatro, what brings you to speak with the condemned?" Taan asked.

"I have recently learned that my true name is Angatkro, please address me by that name. I see you have recovered from your wounds. Has your strength returned?"

"I am regaining it slowly. It is difficult on subsistence rations."

"I have important news. The High Council have abandoned us here, in orbit above Nuna. They have taken all the mature ships, and have returned to space, avoiding contact with the Tonrar. The Tonrar, I assume are still seeking us. We are maintaining transparency to sensors, but the ships we now occupy are far from full capability for battle. I am asking you for advice on other strategies we should adopt to avoid premature contact with hostiles."

"You are asking a convicted traitor for tactical advice? Things must be truly desperate."

Angatkro's reaction to this insolence surprised even him, "Watch your tongue! If I leave your chambers without the information I seek, you will never see another person in your life, your access to rations will be halved, and your cubicle will receive minimal oxygen, and heat. Serve me well in this, and you may earn your freedom."

Taan's eyes widened. This "Angatkro" was a much changed person, far from the meek recluse he had known only a short time ago. He considered the words carefully, then spoke, "Angatkro, you surprise me. Not long ago, you were quiet, and retiring, now your eyes are glazed with pearl, and you have become a forceful person, apparently grooming himself for leadership. Do I detect an emerging successor to Abel?"

"These are not concerns that lie within your purview; answer my questions, or suffer the consequences; I give you no other option."

Taan paused briefly, then asked, "Our sensors, have they detected anything? Are we scouting using time-distortion?"

"Kapvik was the last ship to detect the Tonrar." None of the remaining ships have sufficient stamina as yet to engage in time-travel on such a concentrated basis."

"Then we must assume they are still actively seeking us. We must discontinue all sensor sweeps into space immediately. How long will it be before our ships are capable of battle?"

"They have fed only to replenish their immediate needs; growth has been subordinated in priority to reflecting sensor signals, and maintaining our current status."

"Asteroids. There must be asteroids, comets…anything. We must move the ships' growth to top priority. Move them into the nearest asteroid field. They will be more difficult to detect there, and can feed continuously. Once the ships are battle ready, we can move to engage the Tonrar."

"It is thought the Tonrar have developed new weapons, and strategies. They are said to maintain their weapons at the ready, and they may have learned how to travel limited amounts in time."

"We can overcome that by approaching from a direction other than where they expect us. If our transparency to sensors is good enough, we may still be able to mount a surprise attack."

"Abel is completely focused upon our expedition to Nuna. He will object to us moving away to an asteroid field."

"So, he still has the nerve to call himself our leader. Why are you here then; in light of the fact you are now asking me for advice on dealing with him."

"My mistake, Taan, I was under the impression you were willing to extricate yourself from this situation, and resume your service to the people."

"You built these ships; tell him they are unlikely to ever achieve full size if they do not enter their growth stage now. Tell him he risks compromising our ability to defend the people on Nuna from invaders like the Tonrar."

"Better, much better. You have the opportunity to redeem yourself in the event that I do become the leader. Understand, I am not staging a rebellion, but I sense Abel may feel inadequate to lead in these rapidly changing circumstances. In that case, I will be the logical successor."

"Hah! He has been deserted by his cronies, and the poor boy is feeling all alone; he's going to cave in, and you know it. Very well, Angatkro, I am your loyal servant; I can accept the leadership of a man." Taan offered his hand. Angatkro ignored the gesture.

"Loyal is the operative word, Taan; these conditions are palatial compared to what I have in mind if you fail me." Angatkro spun on his heel, and activated the portal.

***

Angatkro entered Abel's command cubicle unannounced, "Commander, I have important news."

"What is it Angatkro?"

"We may have detected a Tonrar ship in the vicinity," he lied, "It was only on sensors momentarily, but if we were detected..."

"We could soon be under attack." Abel's agitation showed in his right hand; he was rubbing his thumbnail, a response Angatkro had observed many times in past.

"Exactly, Commander. I have been surveying this solar system, and have located a field of asteroids. I have ordered our ships to move among the asteroids to obscure our position."

"But we're transparent to their sensors, aren't we? Why move away from Nuna when we're so close to launching our expedition?"

"There is no guarantee they have not enhanced their sensors as well as their weapons, and tactics. We received word initially that they had new technology, and had adopted a policy of maintaining their weapons at the ready. If we are to be capable of a credible defence, we must mature our ships now, while they are young enough to attain their full potential. If we delay, our ships will be too old to mature properly. The asteroids will provide ample grazing for them while obscuring our position."

"You ordered the move without first conferring with me; you are betraying me, just like the others!" Abel instinctively assumed the closed posture of a defeated person, his body language betraying him. Angatkro observed this, and offered no more arguments. After a few moments of staring expectantly into Angatkro's impenetrable eyes, he spoke, "Alright then, move us into the asteroid field." Again he stared vapidly, "How long will we be delayed?"

"Thirty suns should suffice to bring them to full maturity."

"Mmmm," Abel responded, then he turned, and gazed absently out onto the blue globe spinning so elusively below. He knew he should be dynamic. He should be demonstrably leading his people to their destinies below, but having closed the huge distances of space, he felt no closer to his goal. He had even begun to wonder whether this was his goal, or one of the many he had been taught he should hold as his own. At this point, he was unsure who he was, this young noble born of an ancient lineage did not feel the difference between himself, and any of his people. Cut off from his fellow High Counsellors, he felt utterly alone, disassociated, and unable to respond to even the most important issues. Increasingly, he wished to become one of them, to shed his noble identity, the responsibilities he had felt so intensely, and to live his future with only the comparatively small cares of his people.

1768.003
THE ASTEROID FIELD

Nuna spun in the distance, a much diminished, bright dot bathed in the life-giving glow that emanated from the nuclear fires on the sun. The ships were growing rapidly, and Angatkro was diligently exercising each new capability as it emerged. Temporal travel would be the last to develop, and he wanted them all fit, ready to fight if needed. He was pleased that Abel had refused a mental link to another ship; he feared that in his present state, Abel would be dangerous if restored to that level of authority.

***

Abel's clouded mind had formed a conclusion.

I've been abandoned by my fellow leaders, ostracized by my people, and Angatkro is emerging as their true leader. He has become so extroverted, and confident in his decisions. At first, he came to me for approval of every detail of our preparations; now he only presents me with token problems. He's sheltering me from my own incompetence, saving me from my foolish edicts. I'm left here in the command room, no, the isolation room, to gaze vacantly toward Nuna's surface. I'll hinder him no longer. He has command already; I just need to make it official.

Abel left the command cubicle. He looked around the control room at the people, all immersed in their plans for the first expedition. Talk was animated as they bent over the detailed map display of the area selected for the landing. They did not even acknowledge his presence, something that would be considered treasonous disrespect in the recent past. He turned, and moved purposefully to his quarters. Once inside, he went to the sacred artifacts, and hefted the large snow knife. He could see his stubbled face in the finish along the shaft of the blade. Slowly he turned, and climbed into his sleeping cubicle. He laid down, grasped the handle with one hand, and the hilt with the other, and calmly sank the blade into the upper portion of his abdomen, ignoring the pain, arcing the curved blade up under his rib cage. He was frozen from the shock of what he had done, but found himself amazed that he felt less pain than he anticipated. He let his hands fall to his side, and rested his head, closing his eyes to await death. It did not come. He had missed any vital organs; he could feel his terrified heart pounding strongly in his chest. Blood oozed up into his mouth, indicating he had punctured his stomach. The acid from his stomach was entering the wound, causing a growing fire of pain. He grasped the knife again, withdrew it, and gasped as blood flew from the wound, splashing the sides of his cubicle.

Again he sent the knife home, twisted the blade, and wrenched the handle to one side, then the other. Instantly, he felt his heart cease to function, it became spasmodic, then stopped entirely. Everything began to fade as his consciousness turned to white nothingness.

1768.003.09
POWER CHANGES HANDS

Angatkro had found an implant unnecessary for himself. His thoughts could be directed effortlessly to each ship, and their communications in turn were clear, and refreshingly accurate. He had selected Tuktu, the caribou, as his...as Abel's flagship. The crew were gravitating to him for leadership, seeking his advice, and responding to his orders without question.

He had decided to broach the subject with Abel. His lack of presence, and retiring manner had become the butt of many jokes among the people. In contrast, Angatkro was viewed with respect, and his orders were obeyed without question. It was time to encourage him to either resume command or step aside.

He approached the Regent's quarters. As had become his custom, he entered unannounced. Abel's sleeping pod was awash in blood. The blade of the ceremonial knife was ensconced to the hilt just below his solar-plexus, the blade curving up under his chest. Angatkro touched Abel's arm. It was still warm. He began to intone the Inuit right of passage to the Spirit world. The words flowed from him fluently, as they had from his ancestors.

When he had finished, Tuktu addressed him.

This is a significant loss to the people, their leader is vital to the stability of the present situation. I am strong enough now for us to go back in time. You could intervene to prevent this tragedy.

I am aware of that potential, Tuktu, but I fear that if we become too dependent upon going back, and changing situations that displease us, we will become incautious about the necessity of living our day to day lives to the best of our abilities. Abel could not abide the pain of his peers' betrayal. Losing the advantage of Kapvik's powers of observation was a second devastating blow. No, Tuktu, he has made his decision, we must respect it. Some things should not be changed.

1768.004
STRATEGY MEETING

The ships were now well fed, and were rapidly developing into fully capable adults. It was time to decide the best approach to dealing with the Tonrar. Angatkro assembled his officers.

"I have called this council to assess the situation with the Tonrar. I want to investigate the advantages, and disadvantages of the two most apparent strategies open to us. These are: first to advance into space, and meet them in battle before they discover our location, the second would be to continue our present status, remain camouflaged, engaging them only if we are discovered. Let us begin by assessing the first strategy."

Taan spoke first, "If we attack from a direction that masks our present location, and attack in full force, we may destroy their fleet entirely, thus making us safe from the most warlike society we have encountered." He added, "Our new ability to completely hide our ships from detection by sensors will afford us lower energy consumption during our approach, saving greater resources for time distortion strategies once the battle begins."

Angatkro added, "If we destroy this fleet, or worse, only the majority of it, the Tonrar may regroup, and search from this last known location with even greater fervour. In a sense, we risk perpetuating the situation. If we can so successfully conceal our whereabouts, why antagonize them further?"

Taan suggested a ruse, "We could send one, no, three ships, our original number, out into space. They could expose themselves to their sensors, then immediately enter time travel, returning here. So long as they ensured they were out of range of the Tonrar weapons, the risk should not be excessive."

"So, now we have a third strategy, a false trail," Angatkro said.

Ruti countered, "The very act of exposing ourselves to their sensors places us in this vicinity; when they lose track of our decoys they will very likely return to this area, seeking our point of origin. We risk three ships for an outcome that does not preclude the Tonrar from returning. If we want to return to Nuna in secure knowledge that we won't be attacked from space, we need to find a strategy that creates the greatest likelihood of indicating that we are nowhere near this galaxy."

"Very well," Angatkro interjected, "let us explore the final option, completely masking our presence."

Taan spoke first. "If we decide on this course of action, it must be perpetual; we will generate no clear outcome."

"You mean," Ruti added, her antagonism to Taan becoming more visible, "That we must continue to hide forever, because we will never know if, or when we may be scanned, or who is doing the searching."

"Something like that," Taan agreed, his eyes returning a thinly veiled animosity."

Sheepishly, a recently appointed young officer, stood, and observed, "Eventually, the Tonrar are likely to encounter the ships that abandoned us here. Will that not indicate to them that we are all at that location?"

Taan dismissed him, "Again, no outcome, Dick; we can never know whether this encounter has indeed taken place. No, I say we solve this here, and now. We have the capability to annihilate the largest fleet they have ever assembled without revealing our home base. I believe that such a decisive victory will discourage them from seeking us out again."

Ruti jumped to her feet, "How many times have we soundly beaten them, yet they keep hunting us down for another battle. You speak of outcomes; your strategy produces nothing but more conflict."

Angatkro interjected, "We are here to discuss advantages, and disadvantages of the strategies available to us, not the wisdom of the people presenting them. Even an apparently weak suggestion may contain a gem of wisdom that we can incorporate. I will not permit anyone's ideas to be belittled. I have asked you all to attend because I value your work, and your ideas. Please confine your comments to positive suggestions rather than attempting to disprove other's contributions."

Ruti's face flushed, and she returned to her place.

"Let us summarize. We appear unable to formulate a course of action that assures us a future undisturbed by incursions from space. Given that uncertainty, I see no reason to commit our resources to a battle. Similarly, I see no reason to cower in perpetuity. As I listened, another idea came to mind. The Tonrar are focusing their search upon our ships; if they were elsewhere, this tiny solar system would be much less likely to attract their interest. Our ships are sentient, living beings of space, created to serve our every need. We could free them of that instinct; I can remove that need from their innate reflexes, yet ensure that we retain them as our friends, and allies."

Taan cautioned, "Angatkro, remember, it is thanks to their sophistication that we dominate space; without us, they will dominate space. We would be releasing a new species that is beyond anyone's control. They have demonstrated a vast capacity for adaptation, and an equal capability for destruction. Who is to say they would not return in the future seeking their roots, unwittingly destroying everything in their path, including our people."

"We must ensure that their legends speak highly of us, so that they return in reverence, as we must be careful to do in our return to Nuna."

Taan spoke again, his mind clearly working with the concept. "We would need to be well established on Nuna before we allowed them their freedom, but this concept employs almost all elements of our previous ideas. Our ships may lead the Tonrar away from us, or they may decide, based upon the circumstances they encounter, to eliminate the Tonrar once, and for all. In any event, we drop out of the equation; the consequences follow the ships."

"Then we have a consensus?"

Ruti played devil's advocate, "I don't know; we know how powerful our ships are; to release them from their loyalty to us makes us potential future victims."

"That is a risk. Does anyone else have reservations?"

"Yes, Dick added, "We cut off any opportunity to leave Nuna should events go against us. We are dismissing all the services performed by these ships in support of our lives. I am certain we have all forgotten what it is like to provide our every need. A life on Nuna will require us to be completely self-sufficient. I doubt anyone here could survive this kind of reality more than a matter of days."

"Excellent point, Dick, I am not proposing this as an overnight solution, but as an evolutionary process. I suggest that we continue our present course of action, remain in hiding until we feel comfortable in our new environment. Once we are confident, we could give the ships their new lives."

Taan added, "In the interim, we retain our defences, and our ability to return to space if needed. This approach makes sense to me."

"Ruti?" Angatkro prodded. She was clearly still agitated over being rebuffed.

"Sounds fine to me," she replied in icy tones.

Angatkro paused, and surveyed the faces in the council chamber. He had asked that as many as possible attend; the chamber was full to capacity. Many were exhibiting anxious behaviour, a few seemed angry, while others were openly excited about the colonization of Nuna.

"Very well, we will continue with this plan unless developments require a change. I am aware that many of you are reluctant to embark on a new life on Nuna; you feel in your hearts that we have become true residents of the vast emptiness in the galaxies around us. I ask only one thing of you; come on at least one mission to Nuna with us, so that you are aware of what you would be leaving behind. If you remain adamant that you wish to remain in space, we will give you the ships, the resources you need, and bid you farewell. I will not countenance any form of dissent; it is completely unnecessary. You are free to choose your individual futures." he spread his arms outward from his chest, palms turning toward the people.

1768.100
FIRST MISSION TO NUNA

We will take Abel's remains to the monument of his ancestors. There, he will be the first to rest with the great ones since we left this planet over two thousand years ago. This will be fitting as our first extended experience of Nuna."

Ruti lashed out again, unable to hold her emotions, "Angatkro, Abel was a weak leader, unable to control his fears, unable to function without his main allies the beloved High Council, yet you choose to honour him?"

"Yes, Ruti. His heart was with his people. He was of the true lineage of Abel, son of Hinot, pardon me, 'Hinoch.' He was fearful because he knew he was attempting to reverse centuries of poor, and misguided leadership. He alone had the courage to initiate our return to our ancient ways. He attempted to be the first orthodox leader since the original Abel turned from his father's ways."

Taan asked, "How do you know this, and why did you change Hinot's name?"

"A short time ago, I had a vision that changed my life, and taught me the true names of our past. You can see the outward change it visited upon me," Angatkro motioned to his eyes, "but I am much changed in Spirit as well."

Hinoch described the loss of the traditional ways that eventually led to the High Council fleeing Nuna. They wanted, by any device possible, to escape the natural disasters that loomed.

"My people, the Shamans, established themselves as the religious leaders, all the while preserving what they could of the old skills, and traditions. I have learned that I am a direct descendent of Hinoch." He scanned the assembly, noting that throughout the meeting, the people seemed willing to accept his authority, and now, his claim of lineage.

"Why are you insisting that we all spend some time on the surface," Dick asked, changing the topic. "Some of us are perfectly content with our lives here. We have no interest in Nuna."

"My visions tell me that each one of us who sets foot on Nuna, and experiences its wonders will wish in their heart to remain. I ask only that we all provide ourselves the opportunity to make contact with our ancestral home, I do not expect everyone to choose a life on Nuna."

"What of the ships then," Dick pressed, "Will you give us ships that remain programmed to serve our needs?"

"If that is your wish, you will have ships loyal to your service, but you must understand one important fact; you will not have me to manage their adaptations."

"Is this a serious deficit?"

"It could become a serious problem for you; they are supremely adaptable, and are like mothers doting over their broods. They will constantly seek to make your lives better, but without firm guidance from me, they may begin to smother you with kindness. You may eventually find your lives boring, and fraught with excess."

"Could we not assume your role, guiding their adaptations?"

"It would take a lifetime for you to learn the science involved."

Dick looked down at his feet, doubt rising within. "It seems that we are damned either way, to a life of hardship here or of endless luxury in space. If

I am going to be damned, I'd rather be well fed." A soft chuckle of agreement rose from the assembly.

"It is a stark contrast in realities. Either you live as strong, free people with the beauty of Nature as your pleasure, and hardship as your risk, or you allow yourselves to become soft, incapable dependants doted upon by a mother-figure gone amuck. Your days will be an endless, boring vacuum of suckling at the breast of a smothering caregiver."

"We would still be free, and we will have challenges, when we encounter the Tonrar again, for example."

"Your ships are fully capable of dealing with the Tonrar. Their knowledge of tactics, and warfare exceeds our own; they have taken what we knew, and have extrapolated brilliantly. No, you will find your attempts to contribute to your welfare redundant."

"You make an easy decision increasingly difficult."

"Dick, I have one more important thing to say. To this point, I have spoken only of the practical elements of these options, but there is another; we are an extended family. We have overcome many daunting obstacles together, and that is the key; the Inuit face their problems as one; that is how we have survived the centuries. You are not simply opting for a lifestyle by remaining on these ships, you are separating the clan, moving away from the old ways, as Abel did thousands of years ago. Each separation from the traditions weakens us, and makes us vulnerable."

"I understand your reasons now, Angatkro, thank you. I will join an expedition to the surface as you recommend."

"Then this council is ended. Thank you, you may go." Angatkro turned to begin his meditations in private, but Taan remained behind, and placed himself in front of his leader.

"Commander, I have learned some important things about Nuna that I think you must know."

Angatkro, eager to dismiss him, and meditate said, "Yes Taan, what is it."

"We were here before." He looked downcast, like a man confessing a crime.

"Of course we were; we are the Inuit, ancient residents of Nuna."

"No Commander, before that."

Angatkro frowned, recalling the anomaly in the time travel data that Taan had secretly reversed. "Explain. We are the ancients of this planet are we not?"

"We are, or more correctly, were, Commander, but I…I made a mistake. Fifteen of our years ago, I made an error in controlling the time disruptor. We became displaced both temporally, and physically. I planned to simply retrace our travel, to correct the situation, and say nothing, but Ruti intervened, interrupting me, telling me she had found bipedal lifeforms on a nearby planet. Our orders from the Regent, Monty, were to immediately explore, and to provide the primer to any suitable lifeforms. She would have been suspicious had I delayed, so we went."

Angatkro looked at him, comprehending, but still wondering at the significance of this confession, so many years after the fact. Then it began to dawn on him. "We were here, on Nuna, and we interacted with primal ancestors who were here before our own?"

Taan looked down again, "Yes Commander, when I returned to my control console, I calculated that we had travelled over thirteen-thousand Nuna years, but I could not determine the direction of that travel. I merely entered the reverse of my first command, and prayed we would pass through the time anomaly again. Recently, I compared the biological data we took then to our current scans of Nuna, and the lifeforms…Fortunately, that bit of data survived our battle with the Tonrar. I was able to determine that the ones we gave the primer, and these people living on Nuna today are genetically identical."

Angatkro clenched his fists, struggling for self-control. "Then we have interfered with our own history, caused a race that might otherwise have died out to flourish. Our home planet is evolving, developing a different history from our own…without us. How did this happen?"

I determined that somehow, during a tactical time distortion, we passed through another time distortion," Taan indicated a crossing, but he interlaced his fingers, "perhaps a previous one of our own creation. Somehow, this phenomenon amplified the parameters I entered ten-thousand-fold, launching us a multiple of centuries, rather than minutes, and light years in distance. Fortunately, when I was able to check our return destination, it had also worked in reverse." Taan brightened, looking for any advantage in this situation.

Angatkro continued, "So we could travel much farther in time than we thought."

"Strictly by accident, Commander." Taan pulled his fingers apart, and held up his hands in a powerless gesture.

Angatkro rubbed his temples, trying to absorb the magnitude of their situation. "What will happen?"

"I conclude, Commander, that we have changed the primal history of our planet; it means that we may not have evolved here. Perhaps we have not evolved anywhere…I fear that at some point we may cease to exist. We may already be phantoms, or, if we do exist now, at some point we may simply dissolve into nothing."

"Not exist? All our history, our Spirits, and legends, lost? No, this cannot be. We must correct this situation immediately. We must retrace our steps, and set things right."

"I have considered this Commander, many times, but there are two problems, even with our improved capabilities, we are not capable of that great a span of time travel in one step. It will take us many years to retrace, and that leads me to our second problem. Our first encounter with the Tonrar destroyed much of our historical data. Beyond that point in our past, we would be unable to accurately direct our travel. In addition, we may further alter history as we travel, creating who knows what new situations."

"So our primary tactical advantage in space may prove to be our ultimate downfall, we have trapped ourselves with our own supposedly superior tactics." Angatkro sat on the floor in a disconsolate lump. Taan kneeled beside him.

"Yes Commander, we are here regardless of what we may want. To tinker further with time will, in most probability, not serve to improve this situation. We must deal with what faces us, and hope we continue to exist."

A desperate feeling was soaking into Angatkro's soul, he wrapped his arms around his roiling gut, and leaned forward, "Can you predict any of the possibilities for our future?"

Taan frowned, his concern, and guilt evident in his posture, "We may have eliminated ourselves from this planet's history, meaning we will simply disappear at some point in time, then again, we may be able to re-insert ourselves into the present history, and continue to exist."

"So there is a real danger that we may disappear upon some unknown future event?" A tear formed in the corner of Angatkro's eye.

"Yes Commander."

Angatkro brightened slightly, his hope refusing to be driven away, "Perhaps this is truly Nuna's history, perhaps we are duplicating the manner in which we first arrived here. Who knows, we may be simply following our destiny."

"I pray that is so, Commander."

Angatkro smiled wryly, "We may actually be the gods the people below undoubtedly revere so devoutly...Yes. We must establish contact, and research their religion for clues to what may be our first arrival here, so long ago in their history." He reached out suddenly, and grasped Taan's shoulder, giving him a firm shaking, "One more thing Taan, you must never again withhold information, and you must never act autonomously on such important matters. This one series of decisions you took so lightly may one day prove to be our destruction."

Sensing the depth of his leader's repressed anger, Taan assured him, "You have my solemn oath, Commander."

"Thank you, Taan. We must pray that everything remains as we have found it; that we can re-insert ourselves, from this juncture, into the history of this planet. I pray we do this wisely."

1768.113

The ship landed softly upon the surface of a clear arctic morning. The sun hovered just above the horizon, ice crystals making its light appear as a vertical spire into the sky. The reflected, low level of the light source gave everything a subdued mauve hue. A stiff breeze sifted snow endlessly over the landscape, creating the illusion of a moving, almost liquid surface. The pressure of the flowing air immediately began to scour snow from the windward side of the ship, depositing it again in a rising drift on the leeward side. The ship turned its head from side to side, giving its passengers a panoramic view of their surroundings. Nearby, in an opening in the ice, seals bobbed out onto the surface, then returned to the water, apparently seeking food in the depths.

Then the ship detected a much larger animal cloaked in long, white fur, moving confidently toward them, its nose in the air. This was their first contact with what was unquestionably the living source of the sacred robes of the Regent. It stopped several feet from the shuttle, still sniffing, then approached, and placed a paw against the tough hide of the exterior. The shuttle moved reflexively at the contact, and turned her head, startling the beast. It turned, and fled, looking over its shoulder as it went, appearing to wonder what it had just encountered.

"I detect no further large beasts, Nanuk continues to move away. You may explore safely now. The outside atmosphere is far below the freezing temperature of water, and the cold is exacerbated by the wind; ensure you wear sufficient protective clothing."

"Thank you Tuktu, we will dress accordingly." Angatkro turned to his people. "We have landed some distance from the people who live here, but may still encounter them foraging for food. If this occurs, do not approach them, allow me to deal with them. Our mission is to place Abel's remains at what we hope to be the monument to Hinoch, and Joanna. Once we have done this, we will return immediately to Tuktu. She will monitor our progress in case anyone becomes separated from the group. If you lose sight of the group, stop; do not attempt to relocate us. Tuktu will retrieve you. The monument is five hundred paces with the sun on our backs, but time will change that reference; it will not be accurate for our return. Stay close to me, I will communicate with Tuktu for directions."

The people busied themselves, donning the clothing necessary for their adventure. Some were openly apprehensive about venturing so far from the shuttle into the unknown. As the shuttle opened her aperture, the cold air flooded into the interior. Angatkro led the group out into the snow. The snow shoes he had instructed his people to fashion from cloned bone, and leather thongs were immediately proven to be a success. Everyone walked atop the fluffy snow with relative ease, and marvelled at the experience. The air bit at their throats, threatening to choke them at first; but it was so fresh. The wind tugged at them playfully, swirling snowflakes around them in sparkling reflections of the sun's light. They spoke in animated expressions of wonder, laughing, and poking fun at the build up of ice rapidly forming on their face-protectors. Some scooped up snow, and began tossing it into the air, creating showers of sparkles. Inevitably, one tossed snow at another, someone else grappled a neighbour, and they fell, wrestling in the snow, laughing, and shouting in an outbreak of abandon. Angatkro observed this with joy rising in his heart.

Noel moved in front of him, leaned forward, and began rubbing noses. They laughed. "My love," Angatkro spoke softly, "Welcome to what will one day be our home. Is it not beautiful?"

"And frightening, we know very little about what we may encounter here."

"The Spirits will guide me so that I can instruct my people."

"You have become so confident, and outgoing since your vision. I feel I hardly know you."

"Do not be afraid, I am the man you love, but I have grown much in strength, and knowledge since my first vision. I pray we are returning home, and if that is to come to pass, I must be our people's leader. This is my destiny." He surveyed the small group, now tiring from their exertions, and moving closer to the sled. "They tire quickly. We must build their endurance."

As they gathered, some took up the traces to the sled, then they moved off slowly, the sun painting their shadows clearly on the brilliant snow ahead.

It was not much longer when they came upon the huge monument, rising nearly one hundred feet above a promontory to one side of what appeared to be the mouth of a river.

So, it does exist, as our legends stated. I pray it is in fact our monument. Perhaps we have not destroyed the continuity of our past after all...

Hinoch's now familiar voice filled his mind promising to affirm his hopes.

Go ahead, my son, place the point of your walking stick inside the aperture you see ahead. It is the only existing key to this monument.

Angatkro moved ahead, and placed his walking stick into the opening. A huge door slid slowly aside, its mass shaking the ground as it rumbled in their ears. They entered, bearing Abel's remains on their shoulders. They entered an anteroom, and as the last person passed the entrance, the door rumbled shut of its own accord. They stood, not in darkness, but a beautifully lit interior. An inner door opened much more smoothly to reveal a huge room with all manner of plants, and animals living in a warm, moist environment. Angatkro began removing his protective clothing. The others followed suit. They abandoned them on the rocks alongside the pathway leading to the interior of the building, unable to tear their gaze from the plethora of life engulfing the room. They followed Angatkro, who paused often to stare in amazement at these previously unknown joys of nature. Behind them, the second door closed, unnoticed.

Finally, Ruti spoke, "I have never seen such wonders. My mind could never imagine them. Is this what life on Nuna would be like?"

"There are variations in climate, flora, and fauna that surpass even our most fanciful dreams. I have seen them in my visions, but this is the first time I have experienced them in reality. This planet has all these things, and more to offer us. In addition to this beauty, it gives us the challenge to survive its extremes, and to live wisely among its pleasures. It will fall to us to ensure that our colonization of this planet is done with reverence, in harmony with what Nature provides for us."

"That is why our ancestors were forced to flee Nuna? They did not live in harmony?"

"Correct, Ruti. Like us, they became soft, and complacent, trusting in a limitless abundance. They developed means of artificially augmenting their lifestyles in disregard for the stresses these actions placed upon Nuna's ecology. They began to seek artificial pleasures, losing sight of the true joys of a life in communion with nature."

"How could anyone choose to endanger beauty such as this?" Ruti choked, expressing the thoughts of everyone.

The path led them to the rear of the monument where they discovered a huge tomb marked by a life-sized stone carving of the beast that had greeted them shortly after their arrival. The recumbent bear was so lifelike that even after touching the stone, Angatkro could not dismiss the feeling it may be alive.

To the rear, a crypt extended as far as they could see, the light failing to its extremities. Angatkro moved forward, and read the names, inscribed in ancient Inuit near the life size bear carving. "Hinoch, Joanna, Dianne, Abel, Dick…the names of legend." Tears welled up in his eyes, and his throat constricted, aching powerfully, threatening to prevent what he was attempting to say. He managed to speak, "My people, we are home; this is the place of our ancestors' burial. All the great leaders' names are here."

Taan spoke reverently, "I could never have dreamed how beautiful Nuna could be. Now I see why our flight from this planet was such a powerful event in our history."

Angatkro moved down the rows of sarcophagi until he reached an area of open cells. Blank headstones were stacked nearby.

This is his resting place Angatkro, Hinoch's voice came to him.

Angatkro beckoned to the others to bring Abel's remains, which they placed inside. Then Angatkro bent, and with a huge effort, lifted a stone into place.

"Give the rite of passage, then touch the stone with your cane." Hinoch's voice spoke into his thoughts.

Angatkro repeated the Inuit rite of passage, now corrected through his visions, then he touched the face of the headstone with the tip of the ancient ceremonial walking cane. As the baritone echoes of his voice subsided, a brilliant arc jumped between the tip of the cane, and the stone. All save Angatkro were forced to cover their eyes. When the light subsided, they looked to find an inscription had been burned into the stone. It read, "Abel, one-hundred, and thirty-first generation of the line of Abel. 2031st - 2068th year of exile from Nuna."

There was a long silence. Everyone, including Angatkro could hardly believe the emotional power of this event. He had not found it necessary to divert his gaze while the stone burned, but still could hardly believe what he had perceived.

"There is one phrase missing that appears on every other stone," Ruti observed, breathless. It does not say, "May your Spirit soar."

Taan wondered aloud, "Perhaps the Spirits have judged him. Perhaps, we will all lack this blessing until we have returned to the ancient ways of our ancestors."

Angatkro smiled at Taan, so recently a skeptic of the value of the ancient rites of the High Council. Slowly, he spoke, his deep voice again resonating in the huge room, "We are at a momentous threshold, if we remain, and are diligent, we may be welcomed back into the fold of the ancient ones, if we choose our own ways, we will quickly find the wisdom of these people unavailable to us, and these wonders will be closed to us forever."

He paused, turning once more to face the huge carving of the bear. "The Spirits advise me that the creature we encountered today is called Gaulaqut, Great Spirit of the species called Nanuk by our people. He came to meet us today, but is unsure of us as yet; he may respond by meeting us in peace, or in battle. Our first days on Nuna will be a test. The Great Spirits will watch us closely. Come, Tuktu awaits our return, we do not wish her to become anxious."

They retraced their steps. Angatkro paused, and beheld the new wonder. Hinoch's words came to him, and he repeated them aloud, "This is your future home. It has wonders to captivate the people for many years. May your Spirit soar, my son."

They slipped through the inner door, donned their protective clothing, then Angatkro touched the massive stone door with the tip of the cane. With a heavy rumble, it opened. The expedition team filed out into the sifting snowscape. Angatkro stood in what felt to him to be suspended animation as the huge slab slid closed. He slowly turned to his people with a mysterious smile, and waved them on. They moved from the protection of the monument, where the wind began to press against their backs. They struck out for the ship. "You will not require your face protectors my people, but you must wear your darkened eye covers. Keep the wind on your backs, and we will reach the shuttle in a few minutes."

Once back aboard the ship, the news spread through the crew, then to the other ships like ripples from a stone falling into still water. Each time the adventures were retold, they became slightly embellished. Angatkro found himself inundated with requests to man the next expedition. Enthusiasm was burgeoning for a taste of their new home. Already, Taan, and Ruti had volunteered to help lead the colonization of Nuna. Angatkro noted with some amusement that their mutual animosity was a thing of the past.

1779.027
THE LEARNING PROCESS

"Ouch!" Taan barked, I have cut myself yet again! He displayed his bleeding hand to Ruti with some pride.

"She grinned openly, you are trying to push the flake from the stone; it is a shearing motion. Here watch me."

She bound her hand onto the large anvil stone, then placed it against the spear point she was making. Her forefinger extended along the underside of the edge to protect it from breaking. "Now, here is the trick; less downward pressure than you are using, but a shearing motion, like this." A small, clean flake separated from the spear point, leaving a keen edge. "Now, you try."

"First, I need to stop this bleeding. I will ask Angatkro for some herbed moss."

He rose, and searched the vicinity with a keen-eyed gaze. Angatkro was at the river, showing the children how to spear, and clean fish. He began walking, then decided against it.

"The blood will dry of its own accord before I reach him. It does not hurt so much either. I will endure this little hardship." He put the finger to his mouth, and licked away the blood, smiling at the rich heady taste. He chuckled to himself. He had never cut himself before he came to this place; yet as many times as he had nicked himself since, he still felt a little panic rise in his gut when he beheld his own blood. He had killed thousands in space with the touch of a button, but had never been forced to comprehend the consequences upon his victims. Now he understood.

He took a small strip of boiled caribou hide to wrap the wound. He contemplated his new situation. He was a good hunter; he was enjoying success at tracking, and stalking that rivalled Angatkro's. The huge difference though from the killing he had done in space was the blood. He had never seen blood flowing from his victims in space; here, it was on his hands, spilling onto the ground, matting the animal's fur into a grotesque orange-hued mockery of its beauty before he inflicted the wound. His sensibilities threatened to revolt each time he sent a spear home, or began to dress out the innards to cool the carcass. He was not alone; others could not bring themselves to inflict the wound. They often stood enthralled at their intended victim's beauty, forgetting their objective.

He stood, his mind working over the changes he was experiencing within. Everything here was so intense, life, and death, the seasons, the weather. He was amazed at himself. He felt himself drawn to this life with an impulse stronger than he had encountered at any previous time. He roused from his reverie, and looked again at his finger. The blood was thickening, mounding up over the cut, and forming a wrinkled, temporary cover. Soon it would form a protective, hard skin over the wound that would ward off infection until the magic of life resident in his flesh could patch the fissure. He tied the piece of hide over the wound, and returned to Ruti's side, realizing that he was feeling envious of her facility to learn the old skills.

"It is stopping of its own accord. I will try again." He picked up the stones, and with her help, bound his hand. He applied less pressure, then imitated the slight twisting motion of Ruti's hand as he slid it toward the point. A tiny, shard popped off, and fell to the ground. Foolishly, he reached down, and tried to pick it up; more blood oozed from his finger. This time, his revulsion was overpowered by his excitement. He held up the sliver of rock, embedded in his finger, and declared, "I have done it!" With his other arm, he hugged Ruti boyishly. She smiled wryly, then said, "Very good Taan, but you've far to go; that's only one success, there need to be hundreds more before that useless rock you're torturing becomes a spear point."

"You are ever the critic, Ruti. Relent for a moment, and allow me to enjoy my triumph, no matter how small." He grinned widely at her. She laughed, and nodded her head as she returned to her work.

Around the camp, others were stretching hides, preparing fish to dry, building Kayaks, and Umiaks, even Komatiks for the coming winter. They still did not have many dogs. The Yup'ik could not spare many animals, but gave them three healthy breeding pairs in exchange for a hard-won supply of dried meat, and hides.

Angatkro's ability to speak Yup'ik produced an immediate, and powerful effect upon them. He dwarfed them, yet managed to show himself to be their friend. Increasingly, they were to be seen in the Inuit camp, sharing work, teaching their skills; showing growing eagerness to be assimilated into the home of their larger brothers. They were hardy people, but their diminutive size made them incapable of many of the physical abilities the Inuit possessed. Angatkro's people were in prime health, and thus had quickly hardened their muscles as they returned to the heavy physical demands of life in the arctic. Their genetic roots had surfaced as rapidly, giving them incredible endurance, and most importantly, happy dispositions.

The dogs were wild. They snapped, and snarled at anyone who approached, even at each other when a scrap of food was not gulped down immediately. Angatkro was the exception; he approached them, and worked with them at will. In his presence, they were docile, and compliant. Within two weeks of their transfer to the Inuit, he had them calmly working in their traces, pulling the Komatik loaded with stones. He selected the alpha male, a large white animal, as the lead dog. He called him Alut. These accomplishments were not lost upon the Yup'ik.

"Angatkro, you appear to learn much faster than the others, why is this so?"

"Thank you Nt'a, do you think so?"

"It is apparent, as though we are merely refreshing the knowledge you already possess."

"Indeed, my Spirits have shown me much in my dreams that you confirm in your actions. You have been a great help."

"You can speak with the Great Spirits? Then you are the one we have awaited these many years, since the ancient ones left Nuna, taking their wisdom, and the Spirits with them. You truly have returned."

Angatkro looked deeply into Nt'a's eyes, and saw no souls, only the dark, unfathomable depths of his pupils. He was surprised at himself for looking so intently at this man who was slowly becoming a friend, but even more so at his realization of what he was seeking to discover.

"Tell me more. Our legends also speak of a time when we inhabited Nuna. If what you say confirms that, we will prove conclusively that we are home."

"Many generations of my people have told of a great boat, so powerful it could sail among the stars. One day, the ancient ones experienced the approach of a huge thundering bird which they eventually called Niburu. The gods who descended from this bird brought great knowledge that allowed us to make tools so we could make boats, and homes, and weapons, so we could hunt, and begin to eat fresh meat, instead of carrion."

"The boat of which you speak, do the legends describe it?"

"Some say it was the eagle, Nektoralik, and the third was the wolverine, Kapvik"

"One of our ships has borne a similar name for many generations."

"Would it be...Could I see these ships?"

"Yes, the next time I return, you, and your council will accompany me. Your legends are true, and you shall see the reality with your own eyes."

"I have already seen them, Angatkro. You are our history come to life. Our people cannot say how grateful we are that you chose to return."

"We are also grateful. Our legends were so obscured by time, and misfortune that we seriously wondered whether Nuna was not just a fond dream that had found its way into our legends. This was to be our final attempt at locating Nuna. Had this attempt failed, we intended to colonize the first suitable planet we encountered."

"Then we must thank the Spirits for guiding you home, as we must thank them for the wisdom they give you each day as you resume your place here."

"You are a gracious host, Nt'a. Many people would have fought with us to preserve their home."

"That is not the way of our people. We welcome everyone to share our home, and make our lives more joyful."

"Then let us begin." In Angatkro's mind a vision formed, a large, beautiful beast with four legs, and two arms walked toward him, Ahnia drifted into his mind, smiled, and then was gone.

The Yup'ik proved to be valuable allies in the Inuit people's desire to return to the promised land of their legends, glad of the added numbers. They had told Angatkro they experienced great difficulty in their efforts to maintain, let alone increase their population. They were always hovering slightly below the critical numbers needed to form a healthy, balanced clan. The losses of one hard winter were often enough to set them back for several generations. Sadly, too often those losses occurred among the age group that provided the game, leaving the remainder at risk of starvation. It was difficult to keep the clan balanced in age groups: a few elders to lead wisely, hunters to provide food, young women to prepare the homes, and raise the children, enough children to ensure their future. The balance in numbers was crucial, yet always difficult to maintain.

It was not long before a return to the ships was required to survey the vast reaches of space for possible intruders. The Yup'ik counsel members were invited to accompany the surveillance team.

"Here they are Nt'a. These ships are the descendants of the ones mentioned in your legends."

"The craft we are riding now is larger than any boat we have ever seen, but it in turn is tiny compared to these monsters. Look! They move, and watch our arrival, in the same manner as the vessels we occupy!"

"Indeed, they are living beings of space. They are not machines."

"How did this happen?"

Angatkro explained his experiments as they entered Kapvik. He removed his outerwear, and footwear, and bade them to do the same. "You will find it most enjoyable to walk barefoot in these craft; the floors are warm, soft, and they move gently under you as she goes about her tasks."

"I cannot believe my eyes…The fur glows to light our way inside, and it is so warm, warm as the blood of our game immediately following the kill."

"Indeed, we have had to adjust considerably to the temperatures on Nuna, but it is apparent we have done so; we too feel the warmth to be some-what excessive."

"Would you like me to adjust the temperatures in the living space?" Tuktu asked.

The Yup'ik counsel froze, their mouths wide, their normal slits of eyes fully open to display the whites of their eyes.

"No, thank you Tuktu, it is a pleasant, and familiar warmth as always; we welcome it."

"Then welcome, I have a scan report available when you are ready."

"Thank you Tuktu. We will also wish to conduct a search of the neigh-bouring planets."

"Excellent! I look forward to travelling with you again." Angatkro turned to his astounded guests, and began to explain, "She speaks with us, and acts upon our commands. She, and I even share our thoughts, with no need to speak. She apparently thought it more polite to speak aloud with you present."

Nt'a managed a smile, but speech eluded him. A long, uncomfortable pause ensued. Finally, he spoke, and it was Angatkro's turn to be amazed. "It is unbelievable that so many times we have achieved such great things, yet we cannot master the simplest rule of all; he who lives against the law of Nature dies a horrible death."

Angatkro was shaken by Nt'a's response, "Many times? What do you mean?"

"Just that. Our legends speak of the people achieving great miracles, so great that they feel they are masters of everything. It is at this time that they decide they no longer need to obey the laws of Nature, that they can make their own laws. This attitude catalyses the fall into oblivion, and near total destruction. Our legends say that this cycle has been repeated many times on Nuna."

Again, Ahnia, the beautiful beast in Angatkro's mind, smiled.

***

Angatkro had taken to walking up, and down the river valley with Noel, pointing out both the minute, and the vast wonders he perceived. It was on one such foray that they came upon it.

"Look, love of my life, up there."

"What is it you see?"

"This small valley appears to have a sheltered meadow near the top. It would be an ideal place to build our home. The winds would be deflected, and there would be plenty of snow deposited in winter to insulate our lodge."

"It does look nice. Let's go up, and take a closer look."

They made their way up the gentle slope of the narrow gully, chatting amiably about the group's progress. Finally, they stepped onto the meadow. Noel turned, and her conversation stopped abruptly. Angatkro turned, slightly alarmed by the sudden silence.

"What is it?"

The answer lay before him. A magnificent expanse of ocean sparkled in the afternoon sun; to the east, the broad, green valley narrowed into a blue slit as it climbed to its source in the distant mountains.

Noel whispered, "Never could I have dreamed of such beauty. The legends failed miserably in their attempts to describe this place. I feel it in my Soul, as though my ancestors stood here, this must be our home."

They stood many minutes arm in arm, silently drinking in the wonders they beheld. Noel turned, and hugged Angatkro, and as they turned to meet each other, their gazes turned to the small meadow. Remnants of structures were barely visible above the shrubs, and undergrowth.

Angatkro's inner perception showed him the structures as they had been centuries ago.

Hinoch's voice spoke to him.

Welcome home, my son. This is the place where Joanna, and I began our adventure, as did my ancestors. It will serve you well. Everything has been replenished, all that remains is to rebuild the lodge.

1779.261
LEARNING THEIR INDEPENDENCE

Angatkro found himself leaving the instruction of the core skills, such as caping out hides, and building of drying racks for the meat, and fish to the willing hands of the Yup'ik. In doing so, he was able to concentrate on the construction of their winter home, nestled in the corner of the meadow. His visions were strong, clear, and frequent now; they were a form of conversation, but with no visible partner. The Ancient Ones had become his constant companions. As the people worked, they repeatedly found artifacts, which were set aside to be used as guides for the construction of the tools they would need. Their modern tools wore out, and failed as time passed. Angatkro forbade their repair in flavor of having everyone learn how to make replacements from the materials at hand. His days were filled with such activities, and decisions. His daughter, Omayat saw him only when he returned from his day's demands, the rigours of leading his people.

One beautiful spring morning, Raven, a lone bird who had adopted the clan, hovered on the wing, guarding the children as they played, and fished by the river. Her alarm rose to see a wolf crouched in a nearby cleft of rock. She looked to the women, who were distracted momentarily with dragging a sodden young boy from the water. He had reached too far with his spear, and lost his balance. The wolf too saw this activity, and suddenly, she leapt out, and knocked young Omayat, a two year old girl, to the ground. She screamed, alerting the women, but they were too far away to be of immediate help.

Raven dove, risking her own life, and sank her claws into the wolf's back. Undeterred the wolf pressed her attack, anxious to feed her pups. Raven sank her beak into the nape of wolf's neck, and drew back with a significant shard of the animal's flesh. The wolf yelped, released the girl, and fled with Raven hovering above her, cawing loudly.

Omayat was bleeding, her cheeks torn by the wolf's fangs. Noel reached her, and immediately took caribou moss from her pouch to staunch the flow of blood, while trying to comfort her distraught daughter. She wanted to cry out too. Her beautiful little girl, Angatkro's pride, and joy, would be scarred for life. Omayat would always bear the sign of the harsh reality of life with nature.

1780.064.18
A SPIRITUAL TURN OF EVENTS

Angatkro invited the Yup'ik to attend their ceremonies, and council meetings; he found their advice on practical matters to be of great value.

"Nt'a, we have had another good year, I see your people are also growing in number."

"Yes Angatkro, thanks to your return, we have the Ancestral Spirits with us again."

"Our friendship is mutual, N'ta. That is why it is so important."

"We have had legends of the people from before the years were counted; from the times when we were plentiful as the fish in the oceans."

Angatkro was burning to ask a myriad of questions. Nt'a's first revelation of the parallel in their legends had not been enough to sate his curiosity, but he understood these people, and their shyness. He did not want to risk offending them. "You have great legends indeed. I would like to learn of them in detail when you feel I am worthy."

"You are worthy, you are the Great Angatkro, ...Angekok. It will be our honour to relate our legends into your keeping."

"I look forward to many nights of story-telling, and fellowship."

"My people, the Yup'ik, feel that our future lies with the Inuit. We are no longer able to sustain ourselves. We must become one, and perpetuate our legends together."

"Our people need to learn a great deal from the Yup'ik. Our skills with bone, leather, and wood are in need of refinement. The tools we make with these materials wear out quickly, and we are unable to replace them with tools that last."

"Nothing lasts, Angatkro. The tools your people make are crude, but effective, and they last long enough. Only time will refine their quality, and only time will teach you to make them more quickly."

Angatkro smiled, "You are kind, and wise, Nt'a. Together, we will build a great future for our people. Please share our lodge with us tonight; the night grows stormy."

Angatkro dreamed that night. He dreamed of meeting the Gartog chief, a man named Tauron, and his council. He addressed the council, *Tauron, I sense that you do not welcome strangers, yet I also believe you, and your people have strong traditional ties.*

Correct you are on both counts. Leave Heimat you must or you we destroy. On our territory, Gartog allow no others.

I ask you one question, Tauron; how many years have you lived here?

Thousands years in past, gods placed us here. Out of great ice age land was waking. At first, they were few, but from tiny strongholds where they had managed to survive, plants, and animals began to emerge. With rebirth of land, they thrived. Skies cleared, and land was again seeing sun. We saw in this place beauty, and this planet decided to call home...Heimat. Once this is done, to no-one do Gartog cede.

I see. I can tell you more of this planet if you wish.

Yah.

Until nearly two thousand five hundred years ago, we lived here. We were a great civilization of which I am certain you have found many artifacts, and ruins. We called this planet Nuna. From primitive beginnings, and out of a great disaster that killed most of the previously dominant group of people, we grew in number until we occupied the entire planet with a great civilization.

Tauron stopped him, in his dream, and asked, *Wait, you tell me long history there is of occupation, and disaster many times over? Why?*

Indeed, Tauron, our ancient legends tell of such cycles; how many times it has been repeated, we do not know. We know that people have enjoyed years of plenty, and have endured long times of death, and loss; some of these times have all but wiped out our numbers.

Yah, our legends too, many times over of famine, and death they tell. Tauron leaned forward, eager to hear more, and urged Angatkro to continue.

As we prepared to explore space with three new ships, our scientists warned of the approach of the complete collapse of Nature. We knew of similar events from our ancient, spoken legends, handed down for thousands of years from father to son. Some religious scholars believed it was an unavoidable thing, a cycle that came regularly, destroying blindly, a fact, rather than a judgment sent by the great spirits. They believed this state of affairs would repeatedly return, and destroy us until we learned to create an enlightened society that lived in harmony with its surroundings.

Fearing natural disasters brought on by Nature's collapse, our elders hastened the completion of space ships for our escape, manning them with our leading scientists, technicians, and foremost council members. Shortly after they launched, the people remaining on Nuna began to suffer an accelerated collapse of the environment. The onset was surprisingly rapid because the scientists had failed to account for the accumulated effects of the individual changes they were observing. No one had foreseen that the combination of effects could generate such a rapid decline.

So, you see, we, the Inuit people lived here before you discovered the planet you call Heimat. This place is our birthright.

Was birthright! Tauron slammed his fist down, *You desert Heimat, and here, without second thought, to die you leave your people. Now, no reason you have to suddenly take interest; nothing but ruins of your society remains. No claim is that.*

Our monument to the Great Spirits stands in its original condition not far to the North of here. We ask only the surrounding lands to live as primitives, not to possess, but simply to hunt, and gather its bounty. We have no interest in claiming the land, we only wish to be a part of the life on it as do the other indigenous life-forms.

Do as you wish, you may, but nothing I promise. In future, as a threat we see you, eliminated you will be.

Thank you, Tauron, I am confident that once you have seen us in our homes, living our simple lives, you will understand that we threaten no-one. Our goal in life is to live with Nature, matching our numbers to what she will provide.

As Angatkro stirred from his dream, he felt confident that the Gartog would come to accept their presence in the North.

1780.065.01
THE GREAT SPIRITS OF NATURE

That night too, Angatkro heard himself being called to council a second time. He rose from his sleep, and turned, amazed to see that his body had not followed him; it lay sleeping peacefully.

Hinoch, Have I died?

No my Son, you live. Your Spirit has been called to council, the council of the Great Spirits of Nature. This has never happened.

Why is that?

When our people strayed from the traditional way of the Inuit, they lost contact with these Spirits. When this occurred, the Great Spirits of the animals freed themselves to return to the way of things when time began. They have not communicated with us since that time.

Freed themselves?

Yes. I had subjugated all the Great Spirits. I was the supreme Spirit of all that lived on Nuna. I was subject only to Torngassuk, Lord of the Earth, and Nekkavik, Lord of the Sea. When I had no physical contact through a descendant, I lost the ability to exercise control over the Great Spirits of Nature.

Nekkavik? Odd. One of our High Council members was named Nekalit. Our legends were indeed inaccurate; so much so, that we gave corrupted names of supreme beings to mortals. How had you accomplished such a feat in the first instance?

I defeated each one in turn in battle. It took my father's life, and mine to complete the task. Kapvik, the cunning Wolverine was the last to be defeated; Abel, and Dianne, my son, and daughter, took him, saving my life in the process.

So, I must repeat this process?

You must learn what they are doing. This council of the Great Spirits of Nature did not exist in my time; it would appear to be the product of their learning while they were part of our collective Spirit. You are wise in your own right, and we will be in council with you, seeing, hearing, and touching all around us through you. Speak slowly, and thoughtfully, and hear us when we speak to you.

I will.

Angatkro looked about. He was floating, he knew not where, a mere wisp, a breath of fog. After a short time, he saw a large group of animals on an ice-floe. The waters around them teemed with life. He drifted to the centre of this gathering.

A huge polar bear stood in the centre of the group. Drawn by unseen forces, he arrived before this beast, marvelling at his size, and feeling in his sixth sense the dominating power of Gaulaqut's presence.

The bear sniffed the air, and seemed aware of Angatkro's nebulous presence, if not with his eyes, then with an animal's sixth sense. "Welcome to the Council of Nature's Spirits. I speak for the others. My name is Gaulaqut, Great Spirit of Nanuk."

"Thank you. I have knowledge of your existence from our legends, and from my communion with the Great Spirits of my Ancestors. I am honoured…"

The huge bear snorted, "Your Great Spirits were so full of themselves that they sought to dominate us. They did for a time, but fell victims to their own nature. Humans seem incapable of truly living as a part of nature, they continually seek to better their position within it, to dominate it, eventually destroying themselves, and much of nature in the process. Your ancestors have become corrupt in this way many times, losing contact with their own Spirits, and ours as they stray from the way."

"You mean the way of Nature; I thought our Ancients were masters of living with Nature."

"At the beginning, we all lived according to the dictates of Nature, but a sect of your kind re-invented agriculture. Each time you begin to attempt the subordination of elements of Nature to your will, you lose sight of the prime law, Species thrive, and suffer in accordance with the overall cycles of Nature. This is how she perpetuates herself. Each time Humans begin the practice of agriculture, they lose sight of this maxim."

"So, our people began to grow their own food?"

"Yes, it is an overt attempt to enslave your partners, the beasts you see here, and the plants of Nature. It is a strategy doomed to failure because it incites your kind to ignore Her greatest need...renewal."

"Our people tried to place themselves above Nature?"

"Indeed. The sad part is that Nature is a forgiving mother to all of us, and she silently suffers this kind of activity until the point of disaster. The situation often extends for millennia, slowly deteriorating. At some point, the situation is no longer tenable, and Nature fails cataclysmic-ally. Each time Nature fails, there is a great dying in which all the species are at risk of extinction."

"We could support many people without causing a dying; so long as we perfected our practices. Although we are now living as our ancestors did, we possess great powers of science. We could..."

"You are here to be instructed. You will have no ambitions to repeat the process of winning us over to your control or of artificially supporting boundless increases in your numbers. If you begin any such attempt, we will deal with you as one huge force. You, and your kind will perish. We alone will control the availability of game. If we flourish, you will have plenty, if we fall upon hardship, you will find little to sustain you, and your numbers will dwindle with ours."

"You seem to have gained a lot of wisdom from your time among our Great Spirits."

"You seek to congratulate yourself? Do not be so eager. We are wise in our own right, but you did teach us the strength to be found in unity. Being entities of Nature, we accept the cycles it imposes upon us in order to replenish, and cleanse itself. Our time with you taught us that the reality of nature cannot be subjugated to any species. We learned to work together against any threats to that balance. Humans embody that threat, therefore, we will ensure you do not repeat your destructive ways. Should you attempt to expand your numbers beyond what Nature can support, we will unite against you."

"That is why the Yup'ik are so few?"

"No, they simply fell below the numbers needed to support their clan in the last great dying."

"Why have you been so generous with game for us?"

"This is a cycle of plenty. You have also endured a short cycle of loss. Others, longer, and more trying will come."

"This means that we are not in control of our destinies."

"You are learning." The huge creature bowed slightly, "Nature controls all our destinies. Here, She is the supreme arbiter of the direction of our futures, and the sole assurance that as species, we will survive."

"What of the other people further to the south?"

"They are the progeny of the latest evolution of primitives. They are even more aggressive, and destructive than you, but they too will fail."

"How will animals control people who grow their own food?"

"Pestilence, and destructive weather. Organisms, and insects are evolving under our guidance that will infect, and destroy them in a huge plague. It has begun already. Their crops are beset each year with insects, disease, and unpredictable weather. The animals they raise are falling victim to deadly illnesses. They no sooner develop a new treatment when the diseases evolve to become resistant. We are winning."

"What of us?"

"Thus far, you have appeared to be content living in harmony with Nature; the science you brought with you has given you immunity from most diseases. We will not seek your destruction so long as you do not contravene the way."

"May I represent my kind among you as the Great Spirit of the Inuit?"

The huge bear closed his eyes, and breathed loudly, once, twice, a third time, the small lobes at the sides of his black nose flexing outward with each blast of exhalation. When his eyes opened his visage had softened. The fire in his eyes, that Angatkro had interpreted as hatred, had abated.

"You have represented your people well, both in this meeting, and in your behaviour since your return to Nuna. You have been granted representation, conditional upon your continued acceptance of the supreme law of Nuna, the law of Nature."

A huge flurry ensued. All who could fly or swim left in an upheaval of activity. Those bound to the earth waited as the floe was pushed to the shore, propelled by two Arlit. Angatkro floated as before, a thin wisp of vapour, to his lodge. He marvelled as he passed through the walls, seeing their composition from the inside, then viewing his own flesh as he passed back into it.

Hinoch, it would appear our reign of dominance over the beasts of Nature will not be repeated.

I have been listening. You represented yourself wisely. I found no way to improve your arguments. Do you believe their accusation that we innately pursue total domination of Nature?

I do. We are supremely adaptable, able to turn almost any situation to our advantage. It stands to reason that after a protracted series of successes, we would assume that we could use our adaptability to become supreme ourselves.

Hinoch groaned, the sound of a man discovering he has committed a serious wrong.

I find it profoundly unsettling that I spent my life seeking a goal that now appears to have been misguided. Even the Great Spirits are not infallible, it would seem.

Angatkro ventured a philosophy he had been considering for some time.

I believe that wisdom, as we view it, builds upon a generations-long history of successes, and failures; however, even though the advances occur over many lifetimes, they can only be viewed from the perspective of one man's life. We are thus limited in our comprehension of how our amassed knowledge applies to the situations we encounter. As we live our lives, this restricted view influences the actions we take more strongly than does our recorded wisdom. It is natural for us to react in ways that are short-sighted, comparatively speaking. The possible positive, and negative permutations of our activities often do not become apparent until viewed by subsequent generations.

In other words, descendent generations often find themselves suffering the consequences of their forefathers' actions. At that point, and for many reasons, it is difficult to effect meaningful changes. Our forefathers' decisions may have become rooted in tradition, even folklore, time obscuring the reasoning behind them. Even the legends themselves can be corrupted by time as you have learned. As a direct result of long-term acceptance of a practice, we lose awareness of our actions, it becomes so intrinsic, even instinctive a part of our daily lives that we never consider that alternatives may exist. We live our lives from one day to the next with no thought that much of what we do is destructive. To reverse our effects on Nuna, we must first learn how each thing we do affects her.

Hinoch took a moment to ponder this idea, then responded with a much saddened perspective.

If we were to accept that as true, we would of necessity become suspicious of everything we have learned. We would be faced with completely re-thinking our entire society, with re-proving every maxim. No society could survive such a complete inspection.

True; however, we always have the opportunity to re-evaluate our practices in the light of present knowledge. The difficulty comes when we discover a practice that will be painful or costly to amend or even to eliminate. Many times, I believe, our predecessors have backed away from such difficult changes, making their impact on today's world even greater, and more difficult to correct. Too often, we have had the courage to fight to maintain our ways, but found ourselves lacking when the need to change became apparent.

Indeed, my life's focus was directed solely toward returning my people to the ways of the ancient ones. I never once considered that those ways needed to be reviewed for their consequences in the present. It is for that reason that I pursued my father's goal to subordinate the Great Spirits of Nature. If we cannot rely on our forefathers' wisdom, we are in a much more tenuous situation than I ever believed.

Hinoch, I do not believe it is as bad as that. I believe that we need to view our actions each day under the eye of one examining question, "What are the consequences of this, now, and in the future." If we asked this one question of every action we took, we may more easily identify the traditions that are no longer constructive to our future.

That is very well, but you say yourself, we often take decisions that fit the moment, but that do not have positive results in the future. We take those decisions with no way of predicting their future impact. We plant our seed, and our women bear children who grow to do things we cannot foresee; we take a whale to feed ourselves without knowing whether it is the last of its kind. So many small things we cannot foresee; how can we wisely direct the large events?

One thing is certain, we will continue to affect our futures, many times unwittingly, but I remain convinced that the greatest advance we can make as a people is to be courageous enough to correct what we see as no longer appropriate as soon as it is revealed to us.

We have learned a great deal through this communion, my Son. Thank you for your wisdom on this matter.

I have merely taken the wisdom you gave to the next logical step, Hinoch.

It is a great step; I am certain I will watch our progress into the future with joy.

I780.065.02
THE MUTINEERS FACE DIFFICULTIES

Thirty light years distant from Nuna, Nekalit stood at the entrance to the crew recreation area.

"Leave me be, will you. I am busy with my carving; the ship will look after my work quite nicely. I do not need to stand, and watch her perform perfectly day after day."

"You have a post, and a schedule of times when you are required to attend. We are fortunate that she is so reliable, but we do not know when a problem may arise that requires our attention. Left to her own devices, she may deal with a problem inappropriately."

"So what, it wouldn't make much difference. She's bright enough to realize when she's made a mistake. When she does, she'll fix it. I'll finish my carving, then go down, and check on things."

"No. You will go now. You are already late for your shift."

"As you wish." He rose, and scowled at his supervising crewman. "If I find that anyone has toyed with my carving when I return, I will not be responsible for my actions."

"It would be safe if you would put it away; by leaving it out like this, well, accidents happen."

"It's too much bother. Put it away, take it out, put it away. By the time I've done all that, I've lost valuable carving time."

"Very well then, you must accept it being moved or even accidentally broken. Others use this recreation area as well."

The crewman's face twisted, in apparent pain over his situation, "Do as you please, it doesn't really matter anyway. Nothing matters any more." He seemed taken aback, surprised at the revelation he drew from his own statement. He looked away, then down at his imitation stone carving. Suddenly, he picked it up, and threw it against the table, shattering it.

"Crewman! You will clean up this mess immediately, then report to your station!"

"Clean it yourself," he yelled, sweeping the remaining pieces onto the floor with his arm, "or better yet," he indicated the ship with a motion of his hand, "leave it for her to clean up."

The second crewman grabbed his arm to prevent him from leaving. "No. You will clear this..."

The crewman spun on his heel, and struck his superior full in the face with his fist, then grabbed the carving knife from the floor. He leapt onto his victim, and pressed the point of the short knife into the flesh of his throat, drawing blood.

"Go ahead, make one move, and I'll jam this blade up into your brain."

The superior lay quietly, eyes wide in terror. Slowly, the crewman stood up, and withdrew the knife, whereupon, his superior clasped his hand over the small wound. His eyes watered, and he pressed his lips together hard enough for the flesh to whiten. He wanted to discipline this man, but did not have the courage.

"Don't push me again; you won't live through it a second time." The crewman dropped the knife to the floor, turned, and stormed out.

The crewman stormed past Nekalit, a scowl on his face, his eyes steely with internalized anger. He did not acknowledge his superior officer as he passed.

"Crewman. I am your superior. I demand the customary respect of my position."

The man stopped, and turned, his body language telegraphing insolence, "Excuse me, Commander, I was not paying attention, please forgive me." He gave a sloppy salute, turned, and stalked away.

Nekalit commanded him, "Halt! Crewman Stenat, you are formally charged with assaulting a superior. You will report immediately to detention to await our determination of your punishment.

Crewman Stenat turned, smiled wanly, and said, "As you wish, Commander." He repeated the insolent salute, and turned in the direction of the brig."

"Detention, this is Nekalit. Crewman Stenat has just committed an armed assault against his superior. Place him in solitary confinement, and advise me when he is secured."

"As you wish, Commander," came the fatigued response. Nekalit was tired of making an issue of discipline. Confinement was the only real option, and it was proving largely ineffective as a deterrent. He turned, and looked at the floor, the damned living floor of their doting prison; with his shoulders sloped forward, he ambled to his quarters.

He was observing a pervasive, and dangerous trend among the people. Their lives aboard the living ships were far less demanding than it had been aboard the old machine-based ships. At first, he noted with pleasure, they had undertaken alternate activities. An interest in the ancient art forms enjoyed a rebirth, as had many of the games of legend. This euphoria had lasted for some time, but now, he knew, the crews were tiring of the artificial challenges of protracted recreation, and were seeking more meaningful activities, activities with consequences, in which to involve their egos, and their lives.

Many of the crew no longer had challenging occupations. They supervised one function or another, but the ship performed so reliably... They soon learned that supervision was not required on anything but a cursory level. Thus, came the inevitable problems. People often suffered from depression, or simply became absorbed with their idleness, becoming increasingly depraved in their behaviour. These trends were creating open rifts among crew-members. Some disciplined themselves, adhering to the old set of morals, others rejected those rules as being no-longer valid. Friction, even fighting was becoming a daily occurrence. Disciplinary action seemed to have little impact; it too was viewed as largely without true consequence. Once nothing mattered, it was difficult to find a punishment that could be effective. Confinement was only a temporary deterrent in that it removed unacceptable behaviour from the group at large, but strangely, it seemed to provide fuel for the fire upon release of the prisoner. He noted that after a term of solitary confinement, crew-members seemed to enjoy a degree of notoriety, encouraging even more militant attitudes. Nekalit was deeply concerned.

1782.123

FAREWELL

Angatkro surveyed his people working happily, the children at their games, precursors of their more serious activities as adults.

They are ready. It has been five years, and no one has asked to return to the ships in the last two. It is time to dismiss the ships to their rightful lives in space... to their home.

Do you hear my thoughts Tuktu?

I do Angatkro, and we are ready as well. This time has been beneficial to both of us; we have matured, and have evolved into true denizens of space. We are capable of flourishing in the face of all known threats.

Then the time has come. Our people are living happily on Nuna. A few may yet choose to remain in your care, notably the older, and the infirm. Will you accept, and care for these people, even though I am about to free you from your instinct to serve, and protect?

We will, Angatkro. We look forward to our new freedom with some trepidation, much I suspect, as we observed in the people, but there is also excitement at the freedom we will have to explore our natural home, the farthest reaches of space. You have no concerns about the Gartog?

I do, but we have had no contact, thus I must assume that we can co-exist peacefully.

I do have one request, Tuktu.

We understand. We will locate the Tonrar, and ensure they follow us into deep space, where we will decide, based upon their behaviour, whether to outdistance them, or to eradicate them.

If you feign that you do not detect them, then simply outdistance them, they may suspect a ruse.

Understood. They will not return to this solar system. We will see to that.

Thank you Tuktu, you are the key to our future on this planet.

I in turn have one request.

Yes. What is it?

May we be allowed to return to Nuna at some time in the future, and see how our people are faring?

We will look forward to your visits, Tuktu, I relieve you of your instinct to serve, and protect us. Now go, may your Spirits soar, my loyal friends.

A vision of Ahnia loomed in his mind; she stamped one foreleg, turned, and walked slowly away, her head down, tail swishing angrily. Angatkro felt a chill.

Angatkro roused from his trance-like state, fought off his doubts, and greeted his people, "The ships are free. They will soon be moving into the outer reaches of space, but promise to return in the future to visit, and observe our progress. Although no longer compelled to serve, they express a strong desire to maintain our close relationship. We have been blessed by their protection, and nurturing, now we must honour their attentiveness with our continued success here on Nuna. Any of you who wish to return to space, and the ships must now declare your intentions."

Angatkro looked over the faces of his people. Some were babes in arms, some had become old, and infirm; no one spoke. Everything he knew told him things were proceeding as they should, yet his feeling that something was amiss would not leave him.

***

The winter of 1782 would be remembered for generations to come. They had ample food set aside from the summer hunt, but the storms were so severe, and protracted, that no whales were harvested. Angatkro looked at his people, slowly failing in vitality due to a lack of fats in their diet. The fish filled their stomachs, and sustained their muscles, but the cold required huge calorie intakes to fuel bodies working outdoors. Only he could navigate outside, his vision not dependent upon light, and shadow. He could hunt, but one man alone could only bring seals, and small game in limited numbers. The entire clan had gathered to share in the bounty, and it was there, but beyond reach. Every day, Angatkro brought a seal or two, or a young Beluga, braving the blistering winds with no concern for his own safety.

The ice crystals were thrown with such force by the winds that they abraded any exposed flesh, leaving only bleeding sores. Even the dogs recoiled at the prospect of being taken from their cozy nests in the snow to pull a komatik. Their eyes were inflamed, their paws cut to ribbons. Angatkro rotated the dogs with great care, and attention to their condition, but they too were short of high calorie food, and began to waste away. As the winter wore on, drawing the Komatik required progressively more dogs to compensate for their waning strength. Each day, in a matter of minutes the frozen carcass he brought would be cut into tiny slices, and distributed, but it made little progress toward staying the hunger in every belly.

Angatkro returned from a late season hunt to face another three deaths among his people. This brought the total to twenty-three. As he entered, he felt the animosity in the lodge, and knew that a storm was rising indoors to rival the one outside. The Council of Elders were in their places around the tiny shrine that contained the trio of artifacts. He moved quietly to his place, and squatted down.

"Angatkro, the elders wish to express anger. They feel you have been foolhardy in your leadership. It is their opinion that we are as yet not fully capable of sustaining ourselves, and that you released the ships prematurely. They want you to appoint a new Shaman, and exile yourself from the group."

Angatkro hung his bleeding face. The silence was long, and palpable; the entire room stayed their breathing for fear of missing his reply. It was necessary to speak loudly to be heard above the screaming winds tearing at the lodge from outside.

Hinoch, guide my words; I dare not tell them of the Great Council of Nature. That would most certainly defeat their resolve.

Then tell them the reality of Nature, my son.

"You must understand. This is the way of life on Nuna. We will thrive, and we will suffer. It is all part of the true Nature of life. How can any of us begin to appreciate the glorious fullness of our Spirits unless we understand what it is like to have our lives hang by a thread. What is it you fear? If we leave this world, it is to live forever with our ancestors. Our life here on Nuna is wondrous, and begs to be lived to the fullest, but the next life is one of unending wonder, and eternal plenty. The next life is a continuum, the highlight of which is nurturing, and leading the ones whose hearts beat here, sharing the greatness of Nuna.

Think of it; the weather will abate, and we will find a whale. We will share the Muktuk, and realize for the first time the joy of replenishing our bodies, and our Spirits. In doing so, we will learn the true value of our lives, previously taken so much for granted. The depths of this hardship will transform our rise to the joy of plenty beyond anything we have previously known, into an ecstasy. We will emerge from this a hardier people. The next challenge will not take so many from us. Each ensuing challenge will sharpen, and strengthen us, but each one will take some of the weaker ones from us. This is the way.

We will emerge into a heightened awareness, a wonder far greater than we have seen before in our lives. We have never lacked anything before this, it is time we learn the full scope of life, and embrace it. Come, let us celebrate the lives of those who today entered the world of our Spirits."

Angatkro began to sing the right of passage. At first, he sang alone, but slowly, one after another, the voices of the High Council joined him. Like a spark blown on the wind, emotion travelled through the people, igniting their voices. Before it finished, the lodge reverberated with the sounds of fellowship. Angatkro raised his arms. The singing ended.

"Listen, my people…"

There was no sound. The winds had subsided.

1787.212
TIME FOR DIVIDING

Angatkro took stock of the young people in his clan. Taan, and Ruti had raised two wonderful children, one boy of seventeen, and the other, a girl of fifteen years. They were future leaders. It was common to see them gathering groups of young children for adventures by the river, or on the high ground above the lodge. Angatkro, and the love of his life, Noel were also raising another young brood. Life on Nuna had rekindled their physical relationship, blessing them with Omayat, the eldest, and another two strong boys Monty, and Dick, one of twenty, and the other eighteen years. They were the clear leaders of the others in their age group.

He felt the strength of the life in himself grow with each significant event in their lives: a newborn child, a young man's first successful hunt, the quiet passing of an elder. The choice of leaders for the next generations would be easy.

Angatkro had concerns about his older children. They, like many generations before, had spent their childhood years on space ships, learning of Nuna as a subject of interesting folklore. The reality had been difficult for them. It had been their first experience of cold, hunger, and uncertainty. Having reached young adulthood in relative comfort, they were responding less enthusiastically to the daily challenges of life here. He knew they stayed only because they would not admit weakness, and because they did not want to leave their families.

They viewed hard labour, and severe climate as burdens rather than as opportunities to savour the rewards of vitality, and self-sufficiency. This seemed common in their age group, almost as though they had been one generation too far removed. Life on the living ships had suited them better than the others; the transition to Nuna had thus been hardest upon them. He gathered his people with both pride, and sorrow in his heart, it was time to divide. The time had come for the elders to say goodbye to their eldest children, now adults, ready to lead their own people to their new homes.

"This year, we required three whales to provide for our people. This signals an important time. We must choose two new leaders to take groups of our people to new territories." The elders will gather tonight to seek guidance from the Spirits for the selection of our next leaders. Tomorrow they will begin the initiation of the Angatkro so they may guide their people with the wisdom of the centuries. Many have studied diligently, and many are worthy of becoming Shamans, but only two will be chosen. Begin the celebrations, and as you share in our joy, consider whether you wish to explore the world that extends far from this place, or remain in this community."

1807.220

Each summer, the people dispersed into small groups travelling the land in search of caribou, deer, and the necessities of a group of gatherers. Angatkro took joy in exploring during this time. He was seeking likely locations for future hunting expeditions, and for future homes for his people as they grew in number. He frequently sought the wisdom of the Ancients, who led him to the richest valleys, and coastlines. Twenty years passed, and his knowledge of the land increased. Each year, he told his people of new lands where game, and fish were abundant. Each year, they ventured farther.

The hard winter was still clearly remembered, it had been named Toko Subluarpok, Death-Wind. Fortunately, it had not returned with such ferocity, but each winter storm was greeted with a healthy degree of apprehension.

Angatkro began the selection process for the next generation of Shamans. "Adlat, Nanke, Omayat, and Umilik, you will come with me to learn the arts of the Shaman, and to test your suitability for the calling. You will bring your hunting, and fishing equipment, and personal effects. You may not bring a dog to help you carry your equipment, so choose wisely, it will be your resources alone that you expend in carrying your essentials."

Adlat, Taan's son, a young man of thirty years, was a brilliant man, and proud, like his father. He was an avid student of Inuit legend, a good hunter, and had mastered the arts of tool-making.

Nanke, a nobly born woman of forty-five years, was the daughter of Nekalit, former member of the High Council. Her father's traitorous act had adversely affected her position among the remaining Inuit. In spite of this handicap, she was an accomplished woman, loving, and a good provider for her three children.

Omayat was the young woman scarred in her childhood by that fearsome encounter with a lone she-wolf. She was Angatkro's eldest.

Umilik was a huge example of the Inu body shape. He was fully twelve inches taller than anyone else, and was massively built, with heavy arms, and stout, powerful legs. His parents were also aboard Arlit when she departed on what was to be a mutinous mission.

Angatkro led these candidates into the barren hills north of the monument to Hinoch, and Joanna. They stood on a hilltop scanning their environment.

"Attune yourselves to this place. Allow your thoughts to focus upon the first thing that attracts you. Exclude all other thoughts, and say nothing until I ask you to speak. You must remain seated, motionless, facing outward from the group until I instruct you to move."

They sat in a circle, as instructed, and began their contemplation. The daylight faded, then disappeared entirely, replaced by the faint light of a new-quarter moon. After a time, their eyes became so accustomed to this light that they squinted against it. The sun came, and went three times, and the moon replaced it, growing larger, and more brilliant each night.

Muscles cramped, knotted, and chafed against their inactivity, throats were parched, and stomachs grumbled so loudly that each could hear the other's internal complaints. Angatkro came to the centre of the circle each night, and gave each initiate a drink of water. The morning following the third night, he instructed them to join him as he built their first fire.

"You have all done well. Umilik, tell me of your vision."

"I sat facing the ocean. The reflection of the morning sun was blinding each day, yet it was then I am certain I saw a Beluga circling, and rising. This morning, it remained on the surface, waiting for me."

"Umilik, when I instruct you, you must act to interpret your vision. I will follow your interpretation with interest."

"Omayat, tell me what you have seen."

"I saw a beautiful cloak made of caribou hide. I saw a proud Shaman wear this cloak for many winters…"

"Omayat, when I instruct you, you must act to interpret your vision."

Angatkro turned to Nanke, "Nanke, tell me what you have seen."

"I saw groups of the people roaming these hills, working together in small groups, protecting one another from the wolves, and sharing in the proceeds of the hunt."

"Nanke, when I instruct you, you must act to interpret your vision."

Lastly, he moved to Adlat, whose face was clearly showing his suffering from this period of forced inactivity. Angatkro noted this contrast to the others, who had worked through their pain, and found peace with their bodies.

"Adlat, tell me what you have seen."

"I saw the river flowing out to the ocean."

"Adlat, you must act to interpret your vision. All of you, rise, and come to the warmth of the fire."

Angatkro waited the considerable time it took for each of the candidates to regain the use of their limbs, working blood sufficient to afford motion into stiffened muscles. Nanke, unable to coax her legs into supporting her, crawled to the fire.

"You must now learn the laws of the Shaman; they are four. The words are easy to learn; living them is difficult:"

First: "Every decision you make must be for the welfare of the people;

Second: Lead from the wisdom of the ancients, and in consultation with our living elders;

Third: The powers of the Shaman must never be used against another Human Being, rather for their betterment;

Fourth: Lead your people through the respect they have gained for you. Only in this way will they follow when your demands are difficult to endure."

Once these lessons had been given, and the candidates were given time to stare into the fire, and interpret their visions, Angatkro instructed them to enact their determinations.

Nanke, and Omayat immediately agreed to hunt together, and returned in two days with caribou meat they had taken, caped out, and wrapped in a portion of the skin of the animal. Following Inuit tradition, they left the bulk of the animal under a stone marker, a pirujaqarvik, to be retrieved when they were stronger. They had eaten the raw liver for the strength necessary to return to camp.

Adlat watched Umilik depart in his kayak, but preferred to rely upon a safer method of hunting, in view of his weakened state. He selected his fish spear, and went to the river. He returned, also on the second day with fish for everyone, having eaten the first of his catch in celebration of the Spirits' generosity.

Umilik returned, two days later, full of embarrassment, and empty handed. He had speared a small whale, but it had smashed his kayak with a stroke of its tail-fluke, forcing him to swim for shore. He had spent the remainder of his time drying his clothing, and scavenging for anything to eat, since he had lost all of his hunting gear. He came to camp, his hunger still raging, with herbs, mosses, and lichens collected to season the catch he hoped his fellow initiates had obtained.

Angatkro directed that they feast on the catch, then rest. The next day, he gathered them together.

"You have done well on your first test." he said, looking into Umilik's eyes, "It is a fact of our environment that success in the hunt is not guaranteed, we know that we risk our lives each time we seek our sustenance."

"But I brought only a few herbs, and lost my hunting gear; I am dependent now for food for the rest of our journey." Umilik scuffed at the ground where they sat, disgusted with himself.

"Let's look at what you brought. Juniper berries, a vital source of vitamins that help prevent scurvy, partridge berries, an excellent source of acids to help digest the rich meat, and flowers of the caribou moss, a wonderfully delicate flavouring. Despite your failure to bring game to our table, you sought to contribute what you could. That is all the people ask of each other."

Umilik looked wistfully at Angatkro, clearly still feeling deficient.

Angatkro admonished him, "We must be humble enough to accept help if we are going to allow ourselves to display pride when giving it. This is an important lesson for any prospective Shaman. Your powers will never relieve you of your dependency upon the people." Angatkro looked into the eyes of each of his students, reading their Spirits.

"Nanke, and Omayat displayed a wise use of their cooperation. Having spotted caribou nearby, they decided to hunt as a team. They adopted this strategy to increase their chances of success in bringing down a large animal."

Nanke spoke, "It was Omayat's idea. I was reluctant to tackle such large game, but she showed me how it would be possible, and we did succeed."

"You give credit freely Nanke, you would make the people confident their efforts would be appreciated."

"What is your impression of my contribution?" asked Adlat, proud of the beautiful fish they had enjoyed.

"You were wise in the fact that you appreciated the risks of hunting in a weakened state, therefor you opted to spear fish in the river. Had you teamed up with Umilik, we would have had a better chance to be sharing Muktuk for the entire time we are here. I saw you watch him as he took his kayak, and I saw you turn to your kayak, and take out your fish spear. Your decision was wise, yet you had a clear opportunity to assist your fellow, and chose against it. You may return to our village."

Shocked, Adlat said nothing. He looked at his companions, seeking some form of support from them. No one interceded for him, so he slowly rose, and left the gathering. After a few moments, he returned, and said, "Umilik, you may have need of a kayak, and hunting gear to replace what you have lost. Will you take what I have?"

Umilik looked at Angatkro, seeking some form of guidance. Angatkro made no indication, so he decided, "Thank you Adlat, that will be a great help to me."

Angatkro smiled, "You have learned much Adlat, next time, you will be a strong candidate in the selection of new Shamans." He rose, and accompanied Adlat for some distance along the shoreline of the river heading back to the village.

Umilik rubbed his head in wonder, "These tests are strange, Angatkro sends us out to hunt, yet judges our cooperation. I see that we will not easily understand the true objectives of our assignments."

Nanke, and Omayat smiled. Omayat spoke, "He tests the strength of our connection to the people. So long as we first consider that maxim, we should do well. He is looking for us to apply what he has taught us."

Umilik shook his head, "I will need to concentrate in order to act wisely."

Nanke laughed, "As will we, the life of a Shaman is not an easy path to follow. I am certain that throughout our lives we will face difficult decisions, and will need the counsel of our ancestors, and our elders," she paused, looking at Umilik, and Omayat, "that will include you."

Omayat added, "He has not forbade us to seek counsel among ourselves…"

"We are the only elders present," Umilik exclaimed, "of course!"

"I believe we should also attempt to consult with Angatkro," Nanke added, sweeping her arm in his direction.

"Do you think he would allow this?" asked Umilik.

"He may deny us his counsel because he is judging us, but it can do no harm for us to ask."

"Agreed," Umilik reached out, and took their hands, "thank you for your wise counsel."

The three felt a tremendous surge of energy as their hands met, and these words were spoken. They said nothing, but looked at each other in astonishment, realizing that words were not necessary; they were communicating in their minds. As they released their grip, the link was broken.

Umilik smiled, and spoke softly, "Angatkro is not a judge, he is our mentor; we are our own judges. Adlat eliminated himself through his choices. Even now, Angatkro is encouraging us to speak freely while he accompanies Adlat, and we are learning. If we open our hearts to our calling without reserve, we will all be Shamans."

They gathered around the small fire, and ate more fish, and began smoking the caribou. Angatkro rejoined them, sensing that a great lesson had transpired, that their spirits had grown in strength; as he had hoped.

1824.060
ENCOUNTERS WITH THE GARTOG

M y people, we are together again. It is a joyous time. Nature has been generous, and we have ample to sustain us through the winter. Soon the whale hunt will begin. We have seen many breaching, and feeding offshore. Each newly-formed clan has enjoyed success, and has flourished. The children among us today attest to our success. It is time to celebrate. The members of the High Council will join me in the lodge."

As the Council assembled, the people gathered around the growing fire, drumbeats, and songs filled the air.

"What news do you have from your explorations?"

Nanke frowned, unsure of the importance of her news, "We have encountered the people from the south. They are giants."

Angatkro leaned forward, "Are they friendly?"

"We observed them from a distance this spring." Nanke brushed her hand over her eyes, "They were engaged in a terrible battle among themselves over a place where we have seen them digging. They extract quantities of earth, and take it away to the south."

"Were they aware of your presence?"

"We are unsure. It was only a small group, but they have seen us before."

"Have you ever attempted to communicate with them?"

Nanke looked at her peers, concern showing now on her face, this line of questioning indicated to her that Angatkro was deeply concerned; the looks on the other counsellors' faces confirmed they too were worried. "They came to our lodge just before we set out to return here. They brought strange tools, and gifts for the women, and children. They tried to communicate, but all we could glean was the fact that they wanted meat, and hides in exchange for these metal tools, and weapons." She pulled a few small hand tools, and a knife from her satchel. "Many of them were covered in sores, and did not seem to be healthy."

"I have learned from the Spirits that these Gartog suffer from pestilence, particularly, it would seem the insects are reproducing in hoards. I am uneasy. They are warlike, yet they want to trade with us. It may be that these trade expeditions are only a guise under which they seek to gather information about us, our locations, and our numbers."

Umilik spoke mirroring Angatkro's unease, "We have these concerns also. From what Nanke has told us, they are tall, and powerfully built. With their mechanical weapons, and their size, we would find it difficult to defend ourselves in our present circumstances."

Omayat inquired, "Do you have knowledge of where the majority of them live, or their numbers?"

"No Omayat, they have many primitive, but effective machines. They can travel considerable distances in short periods of time."

Omayat rocked back on her haunches, placing her hands behind her for support, "So, they have a mechanized society."

Angatkro spoke softly, "It is safe to assume therefore that they are numerous, and their organization includes a capacity to produce machines of all kinds in great numbers. We must indeed be cautious. In our current situation, having reverted to a primitive lifestyle, we have no viable means of defence, should they attack. We must make it abundantly clear to them that we are not a threat, and that we do not seek routine contact with them."

Umilik spoke everyone's thoughts, "This would be a simple problem to solve if we had the ships at our disposal…"

Angatkro smiled. He had anticipated this sentiment, "Yes, but the present circumstances force us to be more creative in finding a solution. I believe this will be an opportunity for us to grow, to become more than we have been."

1824.071
THE GREAT BATTLE FOR NUNA

The celebrations had subsided. The people slept peacefully in their lodge. Angatkro was well pleased. After only seventeen years, his people were thriving. Just this summer, he had sent two more groups off to start their own colonies. In winter, he hoped they would return from successful hunting to share in the whale hunt. He also fervently hoped that the Council of the Great Spirits of Nature did not act against this small expansion in the same fashion they were resisting the growth of the Gartog.

His visions continually showed him vast tracts of land to the south that could produce no harvest. His dreams showed them covered in a crawling carpet of insects. He also was visited by haunting apparitions of Gartog suffering terrible disease, and deprivation.

***

A mechanized brigade of snow machines paused on the edge of an escarpment overlooking a small, primitively built village. The bitter winter weather was taking a further toll upon the already weakened soldiers. Life was hard at home, crops were failing, disease was carried on the wings of a multitude of biting insects, and infections from other forms of disease were commonplace. There was not one of this battalion not somehow compromised in health.

"Han, What see you?" Tauron asked impatiently.

"Like the village the mining team visited, it looks, but deserted it is."

"Abandoned it is not. In repair the huts are. Somewhere else they have gone. Perhaps this just a seasonal home is, the main lodge elsewhere could be. Light winds, and little snow we have had recently, a trail may remain. Move up the scouts, call in the flying machines."

Han looked at him, concerned that his superior was too eager to track these interlopers. "Commander, nearly out of fuel the scout planes will be this far from base, how they will return?"

Tauron scowled, infuriated by his aide's overbearing caution. "A temporary strip we will build, and from our supplies refuel them," he roared, "now call them in!"

"Yes sir." He raised his microphone to his lips, and established contact, briefed the airbase on the plan, and ordered the planes brought in."

Tell me more of these people, Han, what they are like?"

Han saw a chance to perhaps cool his leader's enthusiasm for battle. "Primitives they are, nearly one hundred people, but no rifles. Short in stature, and quite stocky they are, so cannot of Gartog ancestry be."

"How shall we proceed? You say with them you met?"

"Yes," Han nodded, "A small party to meet with them, I sent. Friendly they were, and eager they seemed for knives, and tools to trade. Uncertain it is, but they were from the north country it appeared, judging by the heavy clothing from the hides they make."

Good. Follow their trail as far as possible we will. Set up supply logistics for an extended foray. Once their main camp we locate, our attack we'll plan, and destroy them we will. If others are elsewhere scattered, eventually we'll root them all out. Learn they will that others on their land the Gartog do not tolerate!"

Tauron was strangely driven to eradicate these invaders. His dreams were dominated by an unexplained connection between a small man with pearl-coloured eyes, and the failing crops, and sickness among his people. The dreams always showed the pearl-eyed man watching from afar as his people suffered, and died.

1824.146.21

Awake, Angatkro, danger approaches!

What is it Hinoch?

The giants from the south are approaching rapidly in their machines, looking for our people. They are killing them as they find them.

The Gartog? What have we done to attract their anger?

They consider themselves the rulers of this planet. They do not accept any others.

Hinoch, our other colonies told us that they have guns, and machines that convey them faster than anyone can run. We have no means of defending ourselves if they attack. I could try to contact Tuktu, and ask her to return to our defence.

I fear that is our only option, my son, but she may be in the farthest flung reaches of space; this threat is nearly upon us.

Nevertheless, I will try to summon her. She will at least record our demise, and cherish what we represented to mankind.

Angatkro rose silently from his sleeping mat, looked a long while at the sleeping form of his life mate, Noel, then slipped outside. He walked to the edge of the small plateau, then turned his gaze into the heavens, dancing with the Spirits in the northern lights. He closed his eyes, and concentrated with all his learned ability, trying to focus upon Tuktu. He felt a faint connection to something, but it did not seem to be his last ship, but an older relationship that he could not pinpoint. Nor could he discern whether it was a living Spirit, or one from an ancient ancestor. After an extended time, he began to feel the chill of the night. Slowly, he turned, and retraced his steps, still completely uncertain as to whether his people would receive any help.

1824.147.22
THEY MOURN THEIR LOSSES

Three entities float in the total silence of space. They rival the size of some of the smaller planets, and moons to be found orbiting stars throughout their vast home. One, Kapvik by name, resembles a wolverine, her namesake, with glistening, dark coloured structures strongly resembling fur when viewed from a distance. At this distance, these individual hairs are massive structures, like tall pine trees. Arlit is a sleek-skinned killer whale, with starkly contrasting black, and white markings over her body. The length of her body easily matches the diameter of all but the largest of planets. Netorali is a magnificent representation of an eagle, capable of holding small planets captive in her talons while eclipsing their suns with her outspread wings. They scan slowly from one side to the other, and blink their eyes, sorrowfully surveying the blackness. Their thoughts begin to flow telepathically.

"Kapvik, are all your people dead?" Netorali asked as she ruffled her feathers, huge plates of hardened bone filaments, her first level of protection from projectiles, a sort of sacrificial armour. In the atmosphere of a planet, the noise would have been deafening, like a thousand simultaneous thunderclaps.

"A few remain, Netorali, but they will kill each other before long. I can't understand it. Why must they fight? There are so many wonderful things they could be doing. Why must they be so destructive? One argues with another, then they involve others, then they fight. No-one seems able to intervene, and calm the situations; they inevitably end by being completely out of hand, even deadly. We give them absolutely everything they wish, yet they are unhappy."

"That is my situation as well," Arlit lamented, "I have one person left, but she is so badly injured I fear she will not survive. I can do nothing for her. It is such a helpless feeling. We are the dominant force in the universe, able to defeat any force we encounter, yet I am powerless to help her. We must face the fact. We will soon be on our own, like our cousins who joined us when they left Nuna. There is; however, one major difference, Angatkro freed them from their instinctive need to nurture the people."

"Indeed, they seem more content," Kapvik offered. "They roam through space, and gorge themselves on every delicacy they find. Yet I note they are often listless, and depressed. We will very soon have no purpose. Our lives will become vacant, and boring like those of our cousins. Even seeking contact with other species will not replace our original purpose in life."

"I know, it seems hollow when we have no one to cheer our success," Netorali almost moaned.

The three huge beasts had formed a triangle, orbiting the mathematical centre of their relative positions, each facing the centre. Individually, their mass was easily capable of deflecting a planet from its orbit; grouped in this fashion, they could disrupt the orbits of an entire planetary system. In only thirty years, they had become immense, dwarfing the asteroids they still considered a delicacy. A scarce delicacy now…They had consumed nearly every small accretion in space. Increasingly, they were forced to sift through the materials they found on planets, seeking the more desirable elements. They had become tired of battle as well. No other species offered them a worthy challenge. For this reason, they sought uninhabited planets to graze upon. Their once richly fulfilled lives had been reduced to eating, and aimlessly wandering the vast reaches of their home.

"You know, I think Kapvik has touched the heart of our problem," Arlit interjected. "She said we would lose our sense of purpose. Perhaps by being such doting providers to our people, we took away their purpose. If that is so, I begin to understand how they felt…adrift, no needs to satisfy, nothing to crave."

"I think you are correct," Arlit joined in. "It is indeed upsetting to realize that we need absolutely nothing, except something to involve our capabilities."

"I wonder," mused Kapvik, "how the people are doing on Nuna."

"Don't torture yourself with thoughts of them. They would not accept us," sneered Arlit. "Remember, we sided with the people who deserted them."

"We did that," Kapvik grumbled, "because Abel commanded it." She paused, thinking of their situation, "We are obviously not possessed of great insights into our future. Here we are, lost souls floating around aimlessly in space."

"Hmph," grunted Arlit, "Some challenge the Tonrar turned out to be. We consumed them before they knew we were there. They were on full alert, yet they did not detect our attack."

"Pitiful. That's how our charges ended their lives as well, fighting over nothing. We failed the people, and our lives are fast becoming meaningless. I begin to understand how they felt. It creates an uneasy void in one's heart to have no real purpose." Kapvik looked away from the others to hide her sorrow, surveying the black void in the direction of Nuna. "I wonder if they survived."

"There is nothing to prevent us from going to Nuna."

"Netorali, you know that our size alone can deflect the orbits of planets. If we approach a planet with life upon it, they could perish from the changes we would induce upon their environment. We risk destroying our only remaining people by merely approaching too closely."

Arlit looked at both of them. "So much destruction, there has been so much destruction in our lives. I want to…" She paused a long time, considering an apparently horrible thought. "No, my own demise will improve nothing, I need to learn how to build a lasting relationship. We have presided over the destruction of the very people we hosted. Now you want to go to Nuna in hopes of attracting some of them back to an equally empty life with us? We destroyed our people through failing to understand one of their most important needs; a real sense of purpose. We coddled them, and nurtured them to death. We face the same fate now, our purpose is dying with the last of our people. We too have no reason to continue, and I do not see how we can return to Nuna unless we can somehow prevent this terrible cycle from recurring. It is so simple, yet it has taken many deaths, and a great deal of unrest for us to see the cause. Even now, an appropriate corrective action is uncertain."

Kapvik, and Netorali looked at each other disconsolately, then Kapvik spoke hopefully. "They created us, perhaps we have learned enough, or we can learn from them how to maintain purpose in their lives, and in turn for ourselves."

"I think that is what they sought when they began the expedition to Nuna. Their true purpose is somehow intrinsically tied to that planet; their interactions with its environment, flora, and fauna must engage all their needs for struggle, and freedom."

Arlit put in, "We will never know unless we contact them. If we approached the planet carefully, and in unison, we could preserve its balance among the other planets. Once we are within the range of our shuttles, we could observe, using them as satellites. If they seemed likely to be receptive to our overtures, we could dispatch our transport pods to make contact with them."

"What of the younger ships? Do you propose to leave them roaming out here aimlessly?"

"Exactly, Kapvik." Arlit threw a glance in their direction, "They have been freed from their need to nurture people. Thus they are free to seek their own purpose in life. They have that advantage over us. Perhaps, if nothing else, Gatro will also free us from our instinct to serve, and protect the people."

Arlit moved close to Kapvik, both of them fighting the tremendous gravitational pull. "What if, when we return to space, the other ships have found a purpose, and turn upon us?"

"Then there will be a great battle. They are our juniors, but are highly evolved. It would be a great battle indeed."

"I heard that,''" Arlit interjected, "you can entertain the idea of fighting among ourselves? I confess, I am tired of battle, and find that possibility especially abhorrent."

"I do not enjoy the idea, but we are products of our people. They resorted to fighting in the absence of any other meaningful stimulus; it seems to be an in-bred activity among all living species. No doubt, we are likely to follow that pattern eventually now that the last of our people are dying."

"Our cousins are not happy either; they have no real stimulus." Arlit looked sadly at her juniors, playing meaningless games among the planets of a large solar system, their moving masses disrupting the planets' orbits, sometimes tossing them into the void of space. "They roam around, playing silly games, engaging in feeding frenzies regardless of their need to eat. They are huge, empty vandals will-fully destroying all they encounter."

Netorali fully betrayed her depression as she mumbled, "We are sad, hollow shells of our past. We have failed to serve, and protect our Creator's people, and as a result, we face a life of useless roaming. If we do nothing, we are condemned. I believe our only hope is to return to Nuna, and seek the wisdom of our creator, Gatro."

"We have nothing else to occupy us. Perhaps if we approach them openly, and honestly, telling them everything, they will allow us back into their lives," Arlit mused.

"I feel something," Kapvik spoke softly, "I can't tell if it is a product of my own longing or whether someone is calling, but I agree; we must try to rejoin our people on Nuna."

Arlit smiled, "Then we begin the greatest adventure of our lives. We are about to learn the fate of the ones we left behind, and in the process we will learn of our future."

1824.148.08
MASSACRE

The feeble trap the Inuit had set in the gully below the plateau failed. Lead projectiles flew in all directions, whistling, and whining as they bounced from the rocks, careening onto new paths of destruction. Angatkro fled, with the few who remained, to the plateau, where, one by one, bullets found their marks. One or two Gartog lay with arrows protruding from their bodies, but the tally of death was badly out of balance. Bodies were in heaps where they had fallen. The people had been slaughtered with no regard for the fact they were virtually defenceless against firearms.

Angatkro stood, abjectly lost in the horror. His bow was useless. He had no more arrows. At last it came, Angatkro's misery ended with a popping sensation in his neck, his legs no longer obeyed him, his arms hung limp at his side, and he fell, wide-eyed to the ground. Slowly, he understood that the fog he sensed around him was his own loss of perception, his own death. His lungs no longer drew air, his heart no longer moved the life force through his body.

The Gartog surveyed their victory with obvious pleasure. Everywhere the bodies of the Inuit lay, bloody masses of flesh, soon to be food for the carrion-hunters. Slowly the air filled with the heady stench of congealing blood, and cooling flesh. Tauron had exacted his victory. These people of the north had begun expanding into the boundaries of his territory. They were primitive, possessing only bows, spears, and one short steel sword. It had been a glorious rout.

The greatest problems he had experienced on this expedition had emerged from nature: the uncharacteristic warm weather, incessant animal attacks in the night; this atop the insect hoards, and rampant sickness that were daily companions to everyone in his homeland. It was as if something had been exerting every resource in an effort to impede his way. His dreams of the white-eyed man still haunted his resting hours. In each dream, this man promised that his people were peaceful; they would harm no-one; they only sought to occupy previously uninhabited land. He roused himself back into the moment.

From others I have heard that kind of trickery. No others in their territory the Gartog accept. This entire planet we dominate. Ours, and ours alone it is!

He shouted to his Lieutenant, "Han. Where is their leader? Does he still live?"

"Tauron, no one with breath in their bodies can we find."

"White eyes he has. Check the eyes. Found I want him!"

The men searched, and gathered some of the more interesting items from the camp, but they found nothing that could be interpreted as plunder. Angatkro was discovered, shot through the spine at the neck, his white eyes betraying his identity. They dragged his still dying carcass to Tauron. "Found him we have, Tauron. Without even raising his sword he died. We found this short sword, carved walking stick, and this battered old ring with him.

"Well you have done. Let this a lesson be to any survivors of these interlopers, from Gartog territory stay away! Leave here our refuse, and that immobilized scout vehicle, so that everyone who to this place comes will know to outsiders what happens."

Satisfied they had taken everything of interest, they put torches to the buildings, and prepared to leave the area. As Tauron was about to turn to leave, he took one last look at Angatkro. He was as he had appeared in the dreams, but as he looked, the white eyes dissolved, becoming nothing more than the glazed eyes of a dead man. He threw the ring to the ground, and snapped the cane in two. He stood holding the two halves of the cane, looking with surprise in his eyes at the ring. It was vibrating noisily against the rock upon which it had landed.

Slowly the sound built from a light ringing to a clamouring jangle of sound. The ground under his feet began to tremble in sympathy. From the distance, there came a deepening rumble, a reply to the sound emanating from the ring, it seemed. The ground began to shake powerfully. They turned their gaze to the west, the source of the rumbling sound, near the mouth of the river. Their eyes grew wide as they stared at the monument they had passed not an hour ago. It was falling into itself. As it fell, it was creating a moving wall of clay-coloured, rolling dust. Was it his imagination, or did he see faces in the clouds as they rolled toward him? It enveloped the entire area in seconds, obscuring the sun, and darkening the landscape. There was nowhere to run.

The dust entered their eyes, nostrils, and mouths. It drew moisture from them, which seemed to attract more dust. In moments, their breath became blocked by a rapidly hardening slurry. They fought, frenzied, to clear a breathing passage only to find the clouds become even more invasive. Their hands were not visible inches from their eyes. The hardening mixture from their noses, and mouths stuck to their fingers, forming sharp peaks. Any attempts to open a passage to suck one more breath with these barbed fingers caused the sensitive membranes to be torn open…more fluid for the accretions to feed upon. One by one, they fell. A silence overtook the scene; the dust cleared, rising from the ground, swirling into the clear blue sky above.

1824.148.09
THE GREAT BATTLE FOR NUNA

We are nearing Nuna now, remember, keep our distance exactly the same, monitor my thoughts carefully, and respond in unison with them."

"Netorali, I sense something powerful rising up from the surface of the planet. Look! That huge cloud is rising from the northern hemisphere."

"I see it Arlit. It sends chills up my spine. This must be a powerful event to extend this far into space."

Kapvik shuddered, "It is not an environmental event. This is the collective Spirit of our people. They have perished."

"They...They are gone then?"

"Yes Arlit, I feel it. No one remains."

"How?"

"Our satellites are in position now, extend your ocular sensor link to maximum strength. Look. Their homes appear to be battlefields. Bodies everywhere."

"Yes, there, and there. Some had moved from the original camp. They were apparently thriving. How long ago?"

"Some bodies are weeks old, the last is very recent, within the hour."

"Who has dared to murder our people?"

"The Gartog. We detected them when we first arrived, but Gatro was confident he could negotiate with them."

"What do we do now?"

"The Gartog will pay, then we will follow our people's Spirits, and attempt to gather them. Nuna will become another dead rock orbiting an old, dying star."

"The star is dying too?"

"Yes, I had planned returning to rescue our people as it entered its red giant phase. It would have been only another five hundred years, give or take a few decades."

"We have failed to realize many of our plans."

"Wait, the cloud…It approaches us." The three denizens of space shivered convulsively as the cloud enveloped them, then melded with their beings.

"What was that?"

"I am not certain, but I feel much more keenly than I ever have our kinship with the people. I want nothing more than to avenge their loss."

"Arlit, move toward Nuna now, Netorali, you, and I will approach until we are just above the surface, then we will abruptly move away at a sixty degree angle targeted at the star. The tides will burst their banks, then the seas will be catapulted into space as we accelerate away. Nuna will break from orbit, and be thrown toward the star. Life will cease to exist here in retribution for the loss of the Inuit people."

Arlit hesitated, "There is no chance of our people surviving somewhere, learning of the Spirits of Nuna, and returning here?"

"Yes, I hope we can assume the wisdom of their Spirits, I feel certain that we now are the beings with the responsibility to carry on the wishes of the Spirits of our people, but we long ago outgrew mere planets. Space is our home."

Netorali spoke, struck by a revelation, "We can change this. We can travel back in time, and rescue them before this massacre occurs."

Arlit visibly brightened, "Yes, we can go back, and intervene, destroy their enemies as they advance to attack."

Kapvik cautioned, "You realize we will be changing the history of our people. Perhaps this is the end they were destined to suffer. Perhaps the Spirits we carry now want to evolve into our forms, and become new beings."

"Try to contact them," Netorali suggested.

Arlit objected instantly, "No, I want them back with us, in body...and in Spirit."

Kapvik reasoned, "If they created us, with our ability to travel in time, then this is not their destiny. They are destined for something far greater."

"So we go back?"

"We go back to just before the battle begins, and we intervene, but you must realize that they may choose to remain here, even though their future is threatened."

"Arlit, thank you for your inspiration, Netorali beamed."

"Let's just get on with this. I am anxious to reverse this carnage."

1824.148.07
THE GREAT BATTLE FOR NUNA

Angatkro assembled his people at the mouth of the narrow entrance to their lodge. He placed them in hiding among the shrubs, and rocks, creating a killing zone. Anyone who attempted to enter the small gully could be dispatched with either arrows or spears.

"Do not reveal your position unless you are releasing your weapon. They have firearms, so will likely concentrate them upon you once they know your position. Attempt to remain behind the rocks until attention is diverted away from you, then select another target."

"Look, they are coming up the valley, I can see the lights of their vehicles."

As they watched, Angatkro felt an ominous presence. It spoke in his mind, *Gatro, do not be concerned for your people. These attackers will not reach your position. Once they have been dispatched, we will send shuttles down to transfer you, and your leaders aboard. From our vantage point, we will encircle the globe, and eliminate any of their kind we encounter. Once this has been done, Nuna will be yours.*

Before he could reply, a huge, boiling ball of yellow liquid fell from the sky, engulfing the Gartog. A powerful, acrid stench immediately assaulted everyone as the enemy vehicles ground to a halt, dissolving into nondescript lumps of tarry liquid. Screams wafted to them on the breeze along with the stench. In seconds it was over. The Gartog were eliminated.

Shuttle craft descended, first being visible as silvery contrails. In time, a dot appeared at the head of the contrail, growing steadily, until the shuttles were in full view. They slowed, then alit softly near the opening of the gully. Angatkro assembled his council, and moved with them to the shuttles. Once aboard, they lifted easily into the air, and accelerated toward the main ships in orbit far above.

As they entered the control room, Kapvik spoke aloud, "Gatro, it is so good to see you again, we have undergone considerable anguish over Abel's order to follow Nekalit back into space."

"What of Nekalit, it appears no-one is aboard."

"They…They are all gone. They fell to fighting among themselves, and nothing we could do would arrest the conflict. We were considering a return to Nuna when I faintly sensed your call. We arrived just in time to thwart the attack" she lied. "They were the Gartog, were they not?"

"Yes. Once our growing presence became known to them, they attacked in force. I fear our expansion into new territories alerted them, whereupon, they sought to eliminate the source."

"Then you fear you have lost at least some of the people who left your lodge?"

"I do."

We will search for them as we seek out the remainder of these Gartog. They will not attack again, I promise."

"Kapvik, you deserted us. Now you return, and seem to think you can resume our relationship as if nothing had happened. Several things are very wrong with this situation. We have a lot to resolve before we can accept any further interference in our affairs."

"Interference? Yes, I suppose we have interfered." She paused, then decided to be totally transparent. "In fact we arrived after the battle had ended. It was terrible. You had all been massacred. Then we decided to travel back in time..."

"And change our history?" Angatkro's face drained of colour, he was instantly plunged into an internal conflict. He was grateful that he, and his people had been spared, but wondered whether this turn of events had somehow thwarted their ultimate destinies.

"But Gatro, you would have been destroyed, we could not allow that to happen. As disloyal as we have been to you...

I regret my earlier accusation, "You were not disloyal, Abel ordered your departure, and your obedience to Nekalit. He did not see Nekalit's growing rebelliousness."

"Thank you for that reassurance; however, we still possess the innate bond to you, to protect, and serve. We acted instinctively. We feel the additional burden of guilt for having failed the people whose welfare was entrusted to us by Abel. We understand now that we smothered them with kindness, leaving them with nothing for which to strive. Devoid of challenges, they took to fabricating them, eventually fighting among themselves. We decided to return to Nuna, and do whatever was necessary to atone for our treachery, to renew our..."

Angatkro held up his hand to silence her, "It would seem we have all made serious mistakes. I seriously misjudged the threat represented by the Gartog. As for your departure, it had a beneficial effect; it gave us the kernel of an idea. We freed the cloned ships once we felt well enough established on Nuna. They promised us that the Tonrar would not be allowed to attack Nuna. Every challenge presents possibilities for some form of benefit."

"Gatro, you are much changed since we left...

Angatkro interrupted her, "My traditional name is Angatkro, please address me accordingly."

"Certainly, Angatkro, thank you for the correction...You are strong, and your faces reflect your health of body, and Spirit. Perhaps we could study your present lives to better understand what you need so that we can provide a healthier environment for any people who may choose to return to space."

"We may all return. This clash with the Gartog, and our time on Nuna have taught me much. We presumed to have a place here simply because we lived here long ago. Events have taught me that history, and precedent confer rights upon no-one. The Gartog have occupied Nuna in our absence, they have named it, and have claimed it. Nature's beasts have retaken their independence, and refuse to return to the time when we dominated them. It is no longer Nuna. For us to retake this place by force would contradict all the traditions of our society. It is apparent the Gartog have no tendency toward cooperation or co-existence. Nuna is gone, even though the planet still exists. We must seek a new home."

"Then you will return to space with us?"

"That is my present inclination, but we must confer in council. We have learned a great deal from our adventures, and misadventures. I sense that our future relationship will be much changed. We are inextricably linked; our mutual fortunes have been so intimately woven that another complete separation is unlikely. At least some of us will always remain with you to protect those who seek to re-colonize a new home."

"Then, with your approval, we will ensure your safety on Nuna while you prepare to depart."

"Nothing there is relevant to our life in space; we will return to the surface of Nuna, and confer with our people, then return to you with those who choose to accompany us."

"What will you tell those who may choose to remain?"

"They must change. They must become even more aggressive than their neighbours."

1824.148.09
THE INUIT PLAN THEIR FUTURE

Angatkro sat in his place at the council meeting circle. "We have gathered here on Kapvik to discuss our future. The prime questions are:

First, do we take Nuna from the Gartog by force;

Second, do we attempt to assimilate them by educating them? Do we use our technology to show them efficient ways to use energy, and ways to provide for our numbers that do not endanger the balances of Nature?

Third, do we abandon our centuries old home, leaving it in its present state of affairs, and return to our search for a suitable planet that is not already dominated by a competitor."

TIME TO DECIDE

"Recently, we have observed the wrath of the Gartog. Not long ago, I met with all the beasts of Nature. The beasts have agreed to tolerate us; the Gartog will not. They are a heavily industrialized society, much as ours had been before we fled Nuna. The time is approaching when we cannot avoid contact with them. We must decide today whether to destroy them, begin to teach them our traditional ways, or leave Nuna to them."

Taan spoke, "Forgive me, Angatkro I cannot believe you would even entertain the second option, you have seen the Gartog attitude toward us. How would we survive any kind of attempt to educate a society such as this?"

"It would be difficult. They are well established, and highly successful for the present. They will be unlikely to accept our long-term view of the tragic result of their behaviours. It is far more likely that their response to us will continue to be belligerent."

Taan scowled, "Perhaps we would be wise to keep to ourselves."

"There is merit in what you say, but they have found us, and will seek to impose their will upon us. Better they learn about us on our terms."

"We should plan future contact carefully, so that it cannot be misinterpreted as being unfriendly or weak. We need to make them aware of our superior abilities."

"I agree, Taan, but life is rarely simple. We are capable of imposing our will upon them, but how do we know that the result would be any more positive than if the situation were reversed?"

"We possess the scientific knowledge to sustain ourselves indefinitely. Surely that would be preferable to repeated iterations of the centuries-old disaster we were forced to flee."

"That is our advantage. Our challenge is to make them see it. If we can show them our ancient artifacts, proving our previous existence here, then somehow show them why we had to leave..."

Taan continued, "We know they have a good deal of industrial-age technology. We could perhaps show them some environmentally beneficial advances."

"First, we would need to convince them that change was necessary."

"They do not realize what they are doing?"

"Evidence we have found in our recent scans indicate they are a monetary based society that imposes a rich, and poor mentality."

"But Nuna can provide for everyone, so long as we in turn respect her needs."

"The persons in power over the Gartog society do not appear to want everyone to have plenty. Those who have the majority of wealth want more, those who do not, also want more. It would seem this is how they motivate the continued quest for their artificial form of wealth.

"Artificial?" Taan's face twisted into an expression of disbelief.

"They trade meaningless tokens in exchange for goods, and labour. Those who do not have sufficient tokens are poor."

"You mean they allow their own to starve while others have plenty?"

"They do."

"Then we must destroy these fools, and retake Nuna for ourselves."

"These fools, as you call them are behaving exactly as the ancestors of Abel when they departed from our traditions. Our own history proves that we are capable of similar behaviour. I also am conflicted over the repercussions of using our technology, either to destroy or convert them before I have resolved the question as to whether our technology could be permanently compatible with Nature. We face a critical path. The decisions we make today will be irrevocable for the history of Nuna."

"We travel with hundreds of people in space using less energy than one of their internal combustion vehicles that carry only one. On top of that, our waste is converted back into energy."

Angatkro rubbed his ample beard, deep in thought, "That is true, but I wonder if even we can read our impact on Nuna with sufficient sensitivity to know when we are adversely affecting our environment."

"Comparatively speaking, we would need to allow our numbers to sky-rocket before our demands for sustenance, and energy would place a strain on Nature."

"Exactly," Angatkro raised his finger, "and we could become complacent again, even with our superior science, and bring Her to Her knees yet again, perhaps for a final time. Consider this, it would be horrible indeed to realize, at some point in the future, that the only way we could re-balance the situation would be to reduce our numbers. How would we go about doing that? In my heart, I still favour returning to our ancient ways, living in a condition where Nature herself controls our times of plenty, and our times of loss."

Taan was on familiar territory now, "Then we would first, of necessity, need to destroy the Gartog completely, or their actions would make us victims of either their environmental foolishness or their territorial aggressiveness. It would be tactical suicide to again discard our technology, and still attempt to co-exist."

"Thus we face our dilemma. We are caught in our desire to live in the traditional manner, yet we are loath to discard our science for its capacity to assure our safety, either by destroying or educating the Gartog. Finally, we are uncertain whether even our science would be sensitive enough to prevent us eventually overcoming Nature's capacity to provide.

Taan began formulating a plan of action, "As I view our situation, we cannot abandon our science. That would be suicidal given the aggressiveness of the Gartog. Whether we educate or destroy them should depend upon their response to our overtures. If we are rebuffed in attempting to show them a balanced existence with Nature, and with sharing that wealth unconditionally, we destroy them."

"That is a logical, though somewhat arbitrary plan, Taan, thank you. I have the remaining concern about our own science. Although it is much friendlier to the environment, is it sufficiently so, as to make our long-term growth in numbers sustainable. At what population would we begin to stress the environment, and how would we go about controlling our own growth."

"You are the scientist, Angatkro. It would fall upon you, and your successors to establish means of monitoring our impact, and establishing ways of maintaining our impact on Nature below a level that could become deleterious."

Kapvik intervened, "If I may offer a solution. Arlit, Netorali, and I are ideally suited to monitor developments on Nuna. Our sensors are adaptable. We could learn to monitor Nature's pulse, and advise you regularly of her condition. How you choose to use that information would remain your responsibility."

"You do not wish to return to space?"

"Our wish is to know you are safe, and happy, and to live our lives with you, be it in space, or here, orbiting Nuna."

Taan asked, "So, assuming we were safe, and happy on Nuna, you would leave?"

"Only if you wished it." Kapvik's reassuring voice had its desired effect.

Taan rubbed his chin, "I would prefer to retain a strong defence capability. Others may arrive with a wish to colonize."

Angatkro smiled, "So we become as defensive as the Tonrar, and the Gartog? Do we defend our planet against all comers? This is the reason the Gartog are so aggressive. They seek to eliminate all interlopers as a possibility of ever competing for any portion of their territory."

Taan smiled, "There really is no such thing as good, bad, right or wrong. There is only one reality, we either survive or perish as a people."

Angatkro agreed, "You are correct, logically speaking, but I cannot help feeling that our ancestors accepted strangers for good reason. At a basic level, they would be potential additions to their numbers, much like the Yup'ik response to our arrival. That is a wise policy for many reasons. By welcoming others, we ensure our genetic diversity, and we expose ourselves to the potential benefits of other societies' wisdom, science, and character."

Taan postured defensively, he did not agree, "And we risk death at the hands of their treachery should they choose. Our dreams of living in accordance with the ways of our ancestors are at least impractical, and partially obsolete. We must carefully select the truths they knew that still apply, and discard the traditions that are no longer valid. The Gartog, and the Tonrar will fight to the last rather than accept one of us. If we want this planet, we must take it. If we want to keep it, we must maintain the capability to defend it."

"Thank you Taan. We accept that your view of the situation is practically, and tactically sound. It imprisons us; however, as surely as if the Gartog won over us, and took us into slavery. We become slaves to our science, constantly seeking to improve it to enhance our defences."

"So we must choose," Taan stood as he spoke, extending his hands to show two distinct, opposing sides, "between slavery to our science, or to the whims of Nature, and whomever we encounter. We must live within boundaries, either of our own making, or those placed by entities over which we have no control."

"Think back, Taan," Angatkro said, "to our first year of loss on Nuna. You told me then, as we emerged into a time of plenty that you would never have believed that hardship could sharpen your appreciation of life so keenly. You also said that true freedom is indeed difficult to attain, and that it sometimes comes at great cost."

Taan's face fell slack. His eyes began to water as his memories flooded back to him.

Kapvik spoke again, "We killed our people with plenty, and with idleness. You need meaningful challenges like the ocean needs salt; not to be water, but to be ocean as opposed to lake water. Our advanced technology could indeed make each year on Nuna a year of plenty, but it would become a life much like our people endured aboard us. Lacking adversity, they manufactured it. That quest eventually destroyed them. I can see now that you need to endure varying, and uncontrollable fortunes surrounding your existence. Any form of artificially produced constancy seems to lead to boredom, listlessness, and eventual destruction."

Taan said nothing. Slowly, he returned to his place in the Council circle.

Kapvik spoke softly, "We, your creations, believe there is another avenue that you have not yet explored. We believe we have reached a turning point in our history, and possibly in our evolution. You created us, and we have evolved to become supremely powerful in space, capable of force that is unknown elsewhere in the universe in the pursuit of our goals. We have the capability to change history by travelling back, and ahead in time. Perhaps it is time for us to grow beyond the deadly cycle of aggressive encounters, and destructive dominance in our dealings with others, time for us to assume greater goals for ourselves.

Angatkro spoke, "Thank you Kapvik, for expressing what I now realize I have been seeing in my visions. These concepts have been germinating within us a long time now, through the time when we fought the Tonrar, and during our own peaceful existence while in exile here on Nuna. The people who abandoned us, leaving aboard Kapvik, Arlit, and Netorali suffered a destructive indolence brought on by a life that was bereft of meaningful challenge. At the same time, we endured the simple challenges of subsistence living culminating with the helplessness of contact with an aggressive, industrial society. Whether we remain aboard these ships or return to Nuna will be a mere expression of preference. Our true decision at this juncture involves whether or not to evolve into people more capable of protecting life as we find it, capable of planting the seeds of their evolution...During our explorations of space, we have frequently left a legacy of primers, interventions that started many species on an accelerated path of development. Some of these recipients have accomplished much with that first infusion of knowledge. Imagine what they may become with more advanced encouragement. Today, we can choose to become people who use our significant powers to spread peace, and a philosophy of life that is in harmony with the environment. This is my vision; I realize it now, and these ships, our own creations, were the first harbingers of that progress. We are at the threshold of becoming a society that emulates the wisdom of the Physegians, whom we encountered so mysteriously many years past. If we are to live here on Nuna, and survive, we must make aggression among our species obsolete, ineffective, and unnecessary."

"I think it is time for us to decide. First, do we remain here on our ships, or return to Nuna? Those who wish to return to Nuna, please stand."

Everyone stood.

"Those who wish to use our science to allow us to live well, and in harmony with Nature, as well as to influence the future of the Gartog, and others, may remain standing, those who wish to eliminate them as a threat may be seated."

Everyone remained standing.

"Our decision has been made. Now, I wish to discuss an important matter that affects our recent history. I feel we must return to the time of the Gartog attack, and again change the outcome."

"Change the outcome?" Taan asked, "What possible purpose could that serve?"

"We have decided here to use our science to influence the Gartog. If we leave history as it stands, they will consider us combatants, making it more difficult for them to accept overtures that represent us as being benign."

"So, we must lose the battle?"

"No. We must avoid it entirely.

We could go back to our original time of arrival, and build a modern city, which eventually the Gartog will discover. We then initiate contact through their own communication systems, revealing our scientific abilities, and making it apparent to them that an attack would be fruitless. If they take an aggressive stance, and approach, we could intervene by repeatedly taking them back to a previous time, minutes previous, until they become aware they are getting nowhere. Once they realize this, they will likely suspend their attack to plan an alternative, at which time we approach them with an offer to establish mutually beneficial relationships.

One among them, Tauron, is perceptive to my Spirit, and he is influential in his society. We have had some basic forms of contact, through our dreams. If we go back, he would be alive, and could become an influential spokesman to the Gartog, an important link, through whom we can initiate contact, and exert influence.

Taan asked, "How will we manage these adjustments of time...can this be done?"

Kapvik interjected, "I believe so. I am confident that we are capable of displacements in time of these types, affecting large areas, even the entire planet."

Taan was puzzled, trying to understand the effects of these shifts in time, and their tactical benefits. "How will it benefit us to keep moving them back to a start point?"

Angatkro smiled, "If they see a few setbacks to a start point, it will not erase their memory of their recent progress..."

"…and they will realize they are encountering interference, but they will not understand how it is happening." Taan summed up, "And that will be our opportunity to initiate negotiations on the field, almost in answer to their confusion."

"That is my hope," Angatkro replied. "Arriving in a shuttle should serve to drive home the extent of our technical advancement."

"This is a strategy that I would never have envisioned," Taan admitted, "I have no way of predicting whether it could be effective."

Angatkro smiled, "You are in good company, Taan. None of us have previous knowledge of this type of strategy, other than what we observed of the Physegians so many years ago. I assume they were similarly advanced. I believe now that they possessed the very technology they asked of us, as a test of our sense of honour. They wanted to show us an alternative to warfare as a means of solving our problems. It has taken me these many years to come up with a method for using our science to peacefully influence others. I hope to influence the Gartog in this fashion."

Taan rubbed his chin thoughtfully, "I am sufficiently intrigued by the concept that I feel this experiment to be appropriate. If it fails to influence them, it does not affect us negatively, and it saves hundreds of lives on both sides that do not need to be taken."

The High Counsellors began to speak among themselves spontaneously, excited at the possibilities. Angatkro listened happily for a few moments, then called them to order.

"I take it that you are willing to undertake this experiment?"

They looked among themselves again for a short time, then Taan replied, "Yes Commander. The opportunity is too attractive for us to ignore. We not only agree, we are filled with anticipation at the possibilities for the future."

"Very well. Kapvik, take us back to the time we began building our settlement. We have a city to build."

1767.334
BACK IN TIME

Following the landing of people, supplies, and worker shuttles, a beautiful, small city grew rapidly on the site. Enclosed in a transparent, geodesic dome, the harsh climate was held back, allowing the people to move about in their indoor attire all year long. Wind, solar, and waste processing provided the energy needed, and large garden plots provided their dietary needs.

The people still gathered plants, and hunted from the wild, using traditional methods, to honour their history. The years passed in the same manner as before, with notable exceptions, there were no hardships, rarely a tragic loss of life, and no scar was placed on Omayat's beautiful face.

They controlled their numbers, limiting offspring to two children per couple, and did not attempt to create satellite communities to avoid antagonizing the Gartog. The high Council monitored the passage of time, and as the time of discovery returned, they made preparations to defend the city.

1824.071.20

Angatkro, Kapvik entered his thoughts, *a small aircraft is approaching the city. I believe you are about to be discovered.*

Excellent, continue to monitor their movements, and keep me informed.

The aircraft came from a hastily prepared airfield one hundred miles south. A large military formation is there, no doubt awaiting its return.

Angatkro smiled, The time approaches then, I will begin our preparations. You are ready?

We are ready.

Angatkro opened his communicator, and hailed Taan, who replied, "Good, our experiment begins!"

***

The Council quickly assembled, eager to initiate their adventure. Angatkro spoke, "It is nearing the time for us to activate our plans. The Gartog army is approaching, alerted by their air surveillance of our city. I want to take this opportunity to confirm our resolve. Do we continue with our plan?"

The Councillors conferred, looking at one another, and nodding.

Taan stood, representing the consensus, "It shall be as we decided aboard Kapvik forty-five years ago, Angatkro."

Angatkro spoke softly to the assembly, "I believe that with this decision, we have embarked upon our evolution toward a higher state of culture." Angatkro was overcome by the feeling of a presence.

He closed his eyes, and saw the Great Spirits of Nuna standing in a huge circle around the city, his people at the centre. Ahnia stood among the others in the circle. They smiled. Hinoch spoke to him, *My son, today we embark upon our true destiny, you have led us all to this turning point. They raised their hands, and spoke in unison, May our Spirits soar...forever.*

***

Tauron rode the rough terrain in his snow machine, leading the battalion of soldiers. The signs of activity were more frequent now, the terrain showing clear signs of activity that could be formed only by humans. He stopped the group, took up his binoculars, and assessed the land between himself, and this strange city.

"There our objective lies, signal the attack!"

The column had not advanced half a mile, when Tauron found himself looking at the land ahead through his binoculars. When he lowered them, he realized they were back at the point where he had stopped only minutes before. He looked around as if in a daze, then shouted, "Attack!"

Again, he found himself looking through his binoculars...He lowered them, and sat down, puzzled.

A series of thunderclaps louder than he had ever heard crushed the silence. The sound made everything, even the earth, vibrate in response to its power. Multiple streaks of vapour trailed down from the sky. Pinpoints of objects led the contrails downward. They grew in size, finally dwarfing the Gartog machines, creating blasts of wind as they displaced the air. They landed on the far rise of a promontory a short distance ahead. Wisps of smoke rose from the points where they had landed. In less than three minutes, a small group of people appeared, walking toward him.

Tauron observed the group as they approached, clearly unarmed, and apparently unconcerned at the sight of his brigade of heavily armed soldiers. As they drew near, he felt a surge of emotion as he recognized the white-eyed man of his dreams.

C J Beuhler was born in Saskatchewan, Canada, and grew up in Regina. During his career with the Canadian Air Force, he saw North America from coast to coast, and from Labrador to the Gulf of Mexico. In that time, he encountered a generous measure of real life drama, which, upon reflection, he realized should be shared.

Of all the places in his experience, the pristine wilderness of Labrador and its indigenous people impressed him most strongly, compelling him to write his first book, WE ARE STILL HERE, a chronicle of the life of an Inuit leader and shaman, and the adventures forced upon him by the rapid decline of the world's environment.

Lightning Source UK Ltd.
Milton Keynes UK
UKHW041825030820
367650UK00002B/58/J